For Brenda

Silent Night

December 24th, 1987, Christmas Eve in downtown Winnipeg—a nondescript prairie city remarkable only for its location in the dead center of the North American continent. Midnight is approaching and the stores are closed, the streets deserted. Portage Avenue, bustling with last-minute shoppers a few hours ago, is a ghostly carnival midway strung with colored lights whose festive glow is reflected from darkened shop fronts and office building windows. All is calm; all is bright. Except on the third floor of one of these deserted buildings where a shadowy figure crouches in front of an ancient vault in a Dickensian office, poised like a cat. He seems to be listening for something. Sleigh bells on the roof? Surely no mortal would be haunting the halls of the Grain Farmers Building on this holiest of nights. But Failik Finkelman is a cautious man. His legendary patience and meticulous attention to detail have earned him a reputation as something of a genius in his profession.

Of course, Fritz "The Cat" Finkelman doesn't look any more like a genius than he does a thief. If you passed him on the street, carrying his worn leather satchel, you might take him for a country doctor - if you noticed him at all. Medium height, wiry build, frizzy black hair, slightly hooked nose, no visible scars or birthmarks - there is nothing to set the legendary safecracker apart from the middle class multitude. Except his chosen profession – and he seems to be having doubts about that.

"I'm too old for this business," he mutters, as pain from arthritic knees radiates up his legs to the base of his spine. It's been a long time since he's pulled his last job - and will be even longer before he pulls his next one. Like never, he thinks, squinting at the glass-paneled door adorned with the words "Samuel J. Wolfson, Barrister & Solicitor." *Apart from the faded gilt lettering Fritz sees nothing but the dim glow of the hallway light. Satisfied that his less-than-reliable hearing has*

i

deceived him, once again, he rises with a groan to let the blood flow back into his legs. When the tingling subsides he re-crouches in front of the vault door and resumes his manipulation of the dial. That was the beauty of stealing from a fellow "gonif "—you didn't have to worry about fingerprints.

After another eternity Fritz pauses, pulls a handkerchief from his back pocket and wipes the sweat from his forehead, eyes and palms. Why did they keep the buildings in this country like steam baths? He pulled his sleeve back and pressed the button on his wristwatch to illuminate the face. Klutz! He should have had this cracker box open half an hour ago. Could he be losing his touch?

Yielding to an impulse Fritz reaches into his bag and fishes around for the solution of last resort. But when he feels the wax paper in which the plastic explosive is wrapped his hand recoils. What was he thinking? He withdraws his hand, closes the bag, takes a deep breath and resumes his manipulation. Suddenly the tension evaporates from the his lined face. He removes his fingers from the dial, takes out his handkerchief, wipes the sweat from his palm, grasps the vault handle, takes a deep breath...and pulls down. The handle yields with a reassuring thunk. The old thief rises with a groan and the trace of a smile. Fritz "The Cat" hasn't lost his touch.

Inside the vault Fritz works the beam of an extremely large flashlight over rows of ledgers and file folders. It falls on what looks like a strongbox half-hidden in a corner. As Fritz hurriedly pulls the battered metal box from its hiding place a few files fall to the floor. He shuffles them back into numerical order before replacing them. It's essential to leave things exactly as he found them. He can trust Wolfson not to report the burglary but a secretary might not be so discrete. The blond airhead who opened the mail might not even know about her boss's shvartze gelt. "Black money" – the Yiddish expression for under-the-table cash lost something in translation. You'd think a lawyer could figure out a more sophisticated way to avoid paying income tax, not to mention a more secure location for his retirement fund. The old shyster had probably gotten this piggy bank for his bar mitzvah.

Fritz has the cheap strong box open in seconds. He trains his flashlight on a stack of orange bills bound with a wide elastic band. Hundreds. Fritz sighs with relief. He makes a cursory count, divides the bills in four roughly equal stacks and distributes them into his breast and pants pockets. The sixty thousand barely makes a bulge in his pinstripe suit. If Fritz is seen emerging from the building, even at this hour of the night, he won't draw a second glance. He returns the empty box to its hiding place and shines his flashlight around the interior of the vault to make sure nothing is out of place. The beam falls of on a file folder lying at Fritz's feet. "Klutz," he mutters and stoops to pick it up.

Then freezes.

No, it can't be.

But it is.

Fritz hurriedly replaces the file folder and stands there, with baited breath, listening to the hum and groan of the elevator rising relentlessly. There's no reason to panic. It's probably just some caretaker or maintenance man and the odds are twelve to one against his stopping at the third floor.

But he does.

The doors clank open. Footsteps echo down the marble corridor. Fritz's heart begins to throb so violently it's obliterating the sound of the footsteps. No, they've stopped. Fritz leans forward and peers through the darkness to the outer office door. He sees a shadowy figure on the frosted glass. Unbelievable, on the first night of Chanukah! Was nothing sacred to that money grubbing... No, Fritz can't afford to indulge in recrimination. He has to come up with a plan. Maybe he should brazen it out. As long as the old shyster got to keep his ill-gotten loot he'd probably be prepared to laugh the whole thing off.

That makes one of us, Fritz thinks, bitterly. No, he wasn't going to hand over his "retirement fund" to an even bigger thief. Fritz Finkelman wasn't prepared to spend his "golden years" sleeping in roach motels and eating in soup kitchens with drunken Indians and other lowlife goyim.

Keys jingle on the other side of the door.

Fritz makes a conscious effort to breathe slowly and deeply. What was he afraid of? It wasn't an S.S. officer out there, just an old shylock who can't get his keys in his own office door. Since his wife died Wolfson was known to take the occasional drink. If he was on the way home from a Chanukah party, possibly at his daughter's, he was probably shikker as a goy. Fritz almost laughs. What is he worried about? All he has to do is wait until Wolfson gets the door open and make a run for it. With the element of a surprise working for him he'd be down the stairs before Wolfson knew what hit him. And once he was on the street he'd be home free.

The lock clicks. Fritz leans forward, his eyes fixed on the doorknob. He notices a pool of light at his feet. Klutz! He switches off the flashlight. It's a good thing this is his last job--he's too old for this business. The doorknob turns. Fritz shifts his weight to the balls of his feet and involuntarily tightens his grip on the heavy metal flashlight. There is a prickly sensation in his solar plexus that's not entirely unpleasant. His blood is singing. Every nerve is alive. Slowly, the door opens...

When rookie detective Angus Duncan arrived at the third floor of the Grainfarmers Building on Christmas morning Sam "Shylock" Wolfson was as cold as the marble floor on which he was lying. From the position of the body, at the head of the staircase, and a brief study of the crime scene it wasn't difficult to reconstruct the sequence of events. The victim had obviously caught the perpetrator in the act of burglarizing his safe and a struggle had ensued. Wolfson was no spring chicken but he knew the value of a dollar and managed to hang onto the fleeing thief like a pit bull until he was beaten off with some type of "blunt instrument". Hopefully the deceased's fingernails would furnish the DNA that would lead to the arrest and conviction of the perpetrator. But Fritz "The Cat" Finkelman had already been tripped up by a more solid piece of physical evidence – a leather bag lying at the entrance to vault, its contents scattered over the floor.

Part One
Rolling Thunder

1

Good morning, Crosstalk."

"That last caller, the one who was talking about the poor mistreated Indians."

"Yes…"

"She owes me five bucks."

"How's that?"

"That's what I paid for my breakfast, she made me throw it up."

Nothing like a little tasteful humor to get the morning off to a rousing start.

I punched in another line. "You're on the air, go ahead…"

"I'm waiting to speak to Val."

"That's my name."

"But I hear someone else…oh for goodness sakes, that's terrible!"

"Turn down your radio, please."

"What?"

"We have a three second delay; turn down your radio please."

"Oh. Sure. Just a sec…"

Well, it was a living. Six years in the wasteland of commercial radio, where I'd done everything from write my own scripts to brew my own coffee, now six months in the promised land of bureaucratic broadcasting, where I couldn't wipe my butt without an army of paper pushers instructing me on the proper procedure. *Val Virgo, King of the Open Line*! (Okay, The Great Pretender.) Why would a cat who'd been calling his own shots on the town's number one morning show agree to become just another cog in the Dominion Broadcasting Corporation meat grinder? Well, stupidity might have had something to do with it. Of course there are thousands of other reasons—and

1

they all have a picture of the Queen. You can call what I was making in private radio a lot of things—waves, an ass of myself—but "a fortune" isn't one of them. Winnipeg may be the heart of the continent but it's not the media hub of the country. The DBC isn't the only game in town but it's the only one that doesn't pay off in Monopoly money. When "The Peoples Network" called me up from the farm I figured I'd be batting in the majors. And here I am, in the middle of season, shagging fungos in a broom closet.

Actually, a sound studio is a pretty congenial place to spend your working life—if your name happens to be "Neil Armstrong". Once I enter this hermetically sealed capsule, connected to the planet earth by an electronic umbilicus, my world consists of four walls, two chairs, a table, a mike, clock— did I forget anything? Oh yeah, there's a window but it's not for looking out, it's for looking *in*. My producer, Patricia St. John Hogg, kept her jaundiced peepers trained on her lab rat and a nail-bitten finger hovering above the panic button until the craft was safely back on the DBC launching pad. The "Girl Wonder" acted like I something she had stepped in and couldn't scrape off. And the feeling was mutual.

But maybe I should start at the beginning - wherever the hell that is. That's the trouble with life, it has no hard edges. You try to paint a picture of the past and the colors bleed together. If there's a recording angel working this gig he's doing a hell of a mix on the master—when I replay it in my head I can't separate the melody line from the rhythm section, even though I was on lead guitar. But I guess half a dozen mixed metaphors (or similes or whatever the bloody things are) should be enough of a running start, even for a novice at this scribbling game, so I'll just hold my nose and take the plunge.

The story of Val Virgo's rise and fall in the world of talk radio begins and ends during the "Season to be Jolly"—which has always been the low point of my year. This should come as no shock when you consider how many times I've spent Santa's big night watching a colorized rerun of *It's A Wonderful Life* in a musty motel room or belting out *Rudolf The Red-Nosed Reindeer* to a handful of red-nosed strangers. Even as a kid Christmas bummed me out. For one thing I'm of the Hebrew persuasion, which put me on the outside looking in, for another I grew up in Winnipeg, which put me on the inside looking out. *I'm Dreaming of a White Christmas* doesn't warm the cockles of the old ticker when you've been shoveling snow since Halloween. The only dream I had, sitting in my overheated bedroom, looking out the frosted windowpane, while strumming my Gibson Hummingbird, was to fly south. Which is exactly what I did as soon as I'd mastered the requisite number of chords to fake my way past a less than discriminating honky tonk audience. Unfortunately the climate in Music City, USA, was no more hospitable for an urban shit kicker with a Canadian accent than "Nashville North" so Muddy Rivers packed up his hurtin' songs and rode out on the same Greyhound he'd rode in on. Unfortunately the media hadn't been alerted and the prodigal picker did not get a ticker tape parade. Winterpeg was too busy planning Fritz "The Cat" Finkelman's going away bash.

I don't suppose many of you out there in Radio land remember Winnipeg's most famous murder trial. Let's face it, justice fans, once the media circus left town I had a little trouble remembering it myself. And I had ringside seat. The big event took place in Queens Bench Courtroom "A", the showpiece of the old Manitoba Law Courts Building, and as we waited for the star of the show to make his entrance the cavernous courtroom was jammed to the marble walls and abuzz with speculation. The local news hounds had painted such a vivid word-picture of the "elusive gentleman thief" that I was expecting to see Canada's answer to Cary Grant in the prisoner's dock. And I wasn't the only one. After what seemed like an hour, but was probably ten minutes, a breathless hush fell over the room. Followed by a rumble of disappointment. "That's Fritz The Cat?" the guy beside me snorted. "The old gonif looks like a potato that's been sitting in the basement too long!"

My seatmate throughout the trial—a poolroom acquaintance whose color commentary kept me awake during the duller stretches of testimony—had a way with a metaphor. Or is it a simile? Whatever it is, it was right on the money. Since his arrest Finkelman had been cooling his heels in the Remand Center and the primitive conditions of the "Suicide of the Month Club" had obviously taken their toll. His complexion was pasty, his shoulders stooped, his cheeks hollow and his eyes had a haunted look with which I was only too familiar. As he sat slumped in the prisoner's dock, sandwiched between two beefy bailiffs, Failik Finkelman looked about as capable of murder as my sainted father, a fellow holocaust survivor.

Of course "felony murder" was murder only in the technical sense. It didn't require pre-meditation—or, as the hanging judge would make painfully clear in his address to the jury, any *meditation* at all. You cause the death of an innocent bystander while engaged in the commission of an "indictable

3

offense" (like, say, safecracking) you go down for the count. Game over. (Insert coin to continue.)

Poor old Fritz, if he was a broken man when he shuffled into the courtroom he was gefilte fish when he slunk down from the witness box. The articulate young Crown Attorney—a rising star in the AG's Department—had the manners of a gentleman and the instincts of a shark. If Fritz had bitten the bullet and thrown himself on the mercy of the court, rather than trying to feed the jury that bogus alibi (that he was forced to eat himself) the judge might have given him a break. When the old gonif pulled a life sentence he had no one to blame but himself.

At least that's what I told *myself* as I adjourned to my friendly neighborhood pub to wash the bad taste out of my mouth. A broken old Jew being led out of a courtroom in shackles was not a picture I was anxious to paste in my mental scrapbook. When my current gig was up I filed the distasteful incident in the dead letter section of the old memory bank and headed down the road to a new career, convinced that my first close encounter with the "Justice System" would be my last. Little did the prodigal talk jock realize that when the Season of Goodwill raised its maudlin head a few decades later The Ghost of Murder Past would be on the line.

2

Is that better?

"Much, do you have a question for my guest?"

"No, I'm calling about my garbage…"

"Could you call in tomorrow, sir, Inspector Duncan has taken time from a very busy schedule…"

"He's taken time? I should have been at work an hour ago."

"Okay, make it fast."

"The city hasn't picked up our garbage in two weeks, the dogs are dragging it all over the street."

"What day are you on the cycle?"

"Five."

"All right, leave your name and telephone number with my producer and I'll see what I can do."

"And what am I supposed to with all that garbage in the meantime?"

"Shove it up your ass," suggested a helpful voice over my headset. In public my politically correct producer wouldn't say "shit" if her mouth was full of it (rather than just her head) but in the privacy of her soundproof booth she gave vent to her true feelings. The Girl Wonder was convinced the only thing keeping Crosstalk from being the number one phone-in show in the city were all those inconsiderate people who kept phoning in with their half-baked opinions and half-assed problems.

As she fielded the latest "nuisance call" I punched in another line.

"Good morning, Crosstalk."

"Am I on the air?"

"Yes, do you have a question for our guest?"

"Can he hear me?"

5

Angus Duncan snapped to attention.

"Loud and clear, madam!"

The Girl Wonder, who had made short work of the garbage man, picked up her cue. "Tell him not to eat the bloody mike," she snarled into my ear.

I tossed my guest a back-off gesture and he tossed me a look that made my scrotum shrivel. Inspector Angus Duncan had the kind of eyes that said they never saw anything good—and no longer expected to. As we were waiting to go on the air the vibes that emanated from my guest's middle aged bulk were like those from a bull prior to the entry of the matador. With Christmas around the corner, and retirement on the horizon, the unsolved murder of a prominent citizen was the last thing the senior homicide man on Winnipeg's finest wanted to discuss over the public airwaves. But two weeks had passed since a package bomb had elevated Mr. Justice Robert Brown to the great courtroom in the sky and the natives were getting restless.

Not to mention the *natives*. Credit for the "execution" was claimed by an unheard of terrorist group that called itself the "North American Aboriginal Peoples Army of Liberation". *NAAPALM.* Clever, what? Inspector Duncan was not amused. Nor did his humor improve when a second bomb went off in the bag of mail carrier, Leon Coleman. The Daily Tabloid published another "communiqué" from NAAPALM—apologizing for the miscue—and the excrement really hit the fan. The muckrakers were foaming at the mouth and the talk show lines were sizzling. After decades of beating the "Quebec Separation Question" like a lame horse the rednecks were suddenly singing a new tune: *What Shall We Do With The Drunken Indian*? There was anger and recrimination, accusation and denial, fear and loathing—the only thing in short supply were suspects.

Throughout this feeding frenzy my producer showed admirable restraint. For which I was extremely grateful. Then, after every other news outlet in the city had bled the topic to death, Ms. St. John Hogg woke up and smelled the NAAPALM. "Maybe we can shed some fresh light on the subject," she said, and booked the man least likely to accomplish that objective, Inspector Angus "The Bull" Duncan, a guy who would stonewall his own grandmother—whom, I hoped, was not on the line.

"What is your question, ma'am?"

"I want to know what the police are doing to catch the maniacs mailing these bombs?"

Angus Duncan's eyes glazed over. Time to recite the speech he'd been practicing in front of the bathroom mirror. "There is no need for concern," he droned. "We are doing everything humanly possible to apprehend the perpetrators of these acts and bring them to justice." Having delivered this reassuring prologue my guest paused to collect his thoughts. At least I assumed that was his intention until I saw him settle back with a self-satisfied sigh and realized he had shot his bolt—and would probably need the rest of the time period to reload.

"Prime the pump," a voice shrieked in my ear. "Prime the bloody pump!"

Prime *this*, I though, adjusting my Joe Boxer's and removing my headset. First she forces this dud on me then deafens me with useless advice on how to ignite his damp fuse. "Perhaps you can brings us up to date on the investigation, Inspector."

"It's proceeding satisfactorily," he said, evenly.

"Are there any suspects?"

"There are suspects in every investigation."

"What about NAAPALM, do you think they may be behind the bombings?"

"Police officers don't indulge in speculation," my guest informed me. "We go where the evidence leads."

"What about those letters to The Tabloid?"

"What about them?"

"Aren't they evidence?"

He paused to consider the question. "Yes," he said. "They're evidence that the press will print anything that improves circulation, without bothering to verify its authenticity."

"Are you suggesting those letters are a hoax?"

"No—you are."

My pump priming wasn't exactly producing a gusher. Time to remove the kid gloves and get out the brass knuckles. Not my weapon of choice but the only one with which I could provoke a reaction from the zombies the Girl Wonder insisted on digging up for me. "Pardon my bluntness, Inspector, but don't you think the people who pay your salary are entitled to a little more than 'we're working on it'? After all, there have been two homicides in less than…"

"One homicide," the zombie said, rising from the grave.

He was right. Leon Coleman's mailbag had ended in a different postal zone but he was still around—sort of. As we spoke, the second NAAPALM victim was lying in the rehabilitation wing of the Health Sciences Center trying to regain the use of—anything.

"I stand corrected, Inspector, one homicide and one *attempted* homicide. But since we're playing the numbers game how many victims are necessary before the taxpayers of this city become entitled to a little information from the people who are hired to protect them?"

Duncan fixed me with those steel ball bearings he used for eyes. A flush was creeping up his bull neck like alcohol in a thermometer but his voice remained icily calm. "I'm sorry if the police haven't been as vocal on the subject of these bombings as you people in the news media, but perhaps that's because we have to do something other than talk about them."

"Pardon me, Inspector, I thought that's what you were here for. Look, I'm not asking you to compromise the investigation. Just be a little more specific. Does it look like the same party is responsible for both bombings?"

"It's possible."

"But is it probable, was it the same M.O.?"

"The same what?" Our hausfrau had gotten back into the act.

"Mr. Virgo is obviously a fan of detective fiction," Duncan said, shooting me a sneer. "M.O. is an abbreviation of modus operandi—a Latin phrase that refers to the manner in which a crime has been perpetrated."

"Who cares about that?" the caller said. "Surely the important thing is to find out who's committing these horrible crimes not how they're going about it?"

"That's true, madam, but in order to find the who we have to study the how and the why."

"What?"

Both men in Studio 14 laughed—except the one in the shiny pinstripe—who gritted his pearly whites and soldiered on. "What I am trying to explain is that if we hope to solve these bombings we have to study the whole picture. Crimes that appear random on the surface invariably have some underlying pattern. Even when dealing with a homicidal maniac there's always a motive as well as a method his madness. For instance, why was Judge Brown the first victim? Was it because of his work on the Aboriginal Justice Inquiry? Or

8

did the perpetrator, or perpetrators, have a more personal reason? In every investigation there are a thousand questions that have to be answered. They are like links in a chain that ultimately leads to the perpetrator or perpetrators. But there's no telling how long this chain will be, nor how many twists it will take, so we can't ignore any scrap of evidence, no matter how small, or discard any theory, not matter how unlikely, until a pattern emerges. And that, unfortunately, takes time…"

"Speaking of which," I said, eliciting an eye-rolling grimace of non-amusement from Neil Bannerman, my terminally bored technician, "ours is running on." I punched in another line. "You're on the air."

"Wal Wirgo?"

"That's my name," I said, smiling to myself. Wanda was my most loyal caller—one of the few listeners who had followed me from CHAT.

"I talk to you yesterday about home care," she said. "My mother din't get no home care."

There was a familiar squeal from the headphones lying around my neck. From the corner of my eye I saw my producer draw a scarlet claw across her throat. A characteristic gesture—that I characteristically ignored. "I told you to do something, did you do it?"

"I phone few places…"

"Who did you phone?"

"Larry Cobb. He tells me he got no bodies—what he means by bodies, he got nobody to send…"

"Who else did you phone?"

"Wait, I made list. Where is dat paper…" As Wanda trotted off in search of the elusive list there were a few seconds of dead air during which I could picture my producer turning a fetching shade of magenta as she vainly tried to attract my attention with a semaphore of "cut" signs. Just as the Girl Wonder was about to go into cardiac arrest the air became "live" again. "I got phone numbers," Wanda announced, triumphantly. "Nine, four, seven, two, tree, one, six. Tree, tree…"

"Did you phone the places I told you to phone?"

"I phone Care Service—they say can't do nothing about it. Up to my social vurker."

"And what does your social worker say?"

"He say he got no bodies—dat's the way he puts it."

"Well, if your social worker doesn't have anybody, Care Services has to provide somebody. You're going to have to phone back this morning and give them the name and phone number of your social worker…is it a he?"

"Yeah, Larry Cobb."

"Well, you tell them Mr. Cobb says he doesn't have any people available and Care Services will help you."

"Tank you."

"Don't mention it."

As I was about to punch in another line, Garth Grenfel lumbered into the studio with a few sheets of yellow paper clutched in his pudgy hand. I glanced at the clock. Old moon face was almost pointing heavenward, the sign that I could temporarily lay my burden down. As my faithless announcer hovered over me like the Good Year blimp, and my terminally bored technician cued up half a dozen DBC promos and public service announcements, I went into my break-spiel.

"My guest this morning is Inspector Angus Duncan of the Winnipeg homicide squad who has kindly consented to answer all your questions about the so-called NAAPALM bombings. Our number is 488 TALK. That's 488 8255. We'll be back after these messages."

Unfortunately I couldn't speak for the listening audience. By the time Garth had finished vocalizing the same news, sports and weather he had read twenty-two minutes ago (and would encore in another twenty-two minutes) even the most loyal Virgo fan (or DBC masochist) might indulge in a little dial spinning. Garth slipped into my chair and I left the studio to relieve myself. On my way back into the studio Ms. Hogg waved me into the control room so she could do likewise—on her favorite talk show host. "What the hell do you think you're doing in there, Virgo?"

It was a good question—one I'd asked myself many times. Talking on the telephone isn't the kind of profession a guy would want to brag about—or even admit. "Just doing my job, Patsy."

"Patricia," the Girl Wonder said, pointedly. My freckle-faced producer insisted on the use her full name to keep the lines of authority clear. The only thing that irked her more than my shortening her first name—and pronouncing he last name the way it looked, rather than "engine" with an s in front of it—was my refusal to play Charlie McCarthy to her Edgar Bergen. I gave her a boyish smile. "A rose by any other name…"

"Very funny," she said, blushing to the roots of her carrot-colored hair. Actually, she wasn't that hard on the eyes—it was the nerves she beat the hell out of. She was like a yappy terrier bitch protecting her ass from every hound that wandered onto her territory. "What's the idea of ignoring my cut sign?" she snarled.

I looked at her innocently. "You gave me a cut sign?"

"As if you didn't see it! The next time you take off those headphones, Virgo, will be your last. If you can't curb your ego long enough to take a little direction, hotshot, there are plenty of people around here who would be glad to take your place."

And the leading candidate, she indicated, directing her gaze through the glass at The Voice that Walks like a Man, *is sitting in your chair as we speak.* Garth Grenfel, DBC lifer, had raised such a stink on being passed over in favor of an "outsider" that he caused the guy who hired me—former Program Director, Morgan Riley—to beat a hasty retreat back to the world of "private" journalism from whence he had recently come. Fortunately, old Lard Tonsils was going into his coda which gave me an excuse to make a strategic withdrawal. "I'd love to continue this productive discussion, Patricia, but the salt mines are calling…"

As I retook possession of my still-warm chair the homicide dick on the other side of the mike eyed me, suspiciously. Having witnessed the little scene in the control room Inspector Duncan was probably wondering if his services might not be required before the morning was over. Not wanting to add to his discomfort I put on my headset, suspended my boat-rocking, and let him roll out the platitudes to his beefy heart's content. As the show crawled toward its dreary conclusion the non-listening audience was equally discreet. Those who hadn't switched to the opposition during Grenfell's somniferous spiel had obviously nodded off. As we limped toward the finishing line I had a little trouble keeping my own eyes open.

"Time for one last call. Good morning, Crosstalk."

(Silence)

"You're on the air, go ahead…"

(Silence)

Just what I needed to complete my morning, a breather! One of those strong silent types who stroll up to the plate and can't get the bat off his or her shoulder. Well, this wheezing beauty was entitled to one more strike. "We're off the air in two minutes," I said, tossing up a nice soft one, "so take your best shot."

He came in from deep left field and sent a screamer back at the mound.

"You're next, you two-faced bugger!"

3

Nice try, but no cigar. The space jockey who launched that misguided missile didn't get clearance from ground control and his mission was aborted by the fastest finger in the west. The only ones who caught his act were the stunned quartet in studio 14, and, thanks to the miracle of modern technology, we were treated to encore, after encore, after encore… "You're sure none of you recognize that voice?" Angus Duncan asked, as Neil Bannerman rewound the tape for the tenth time.

"Positive," my pissed-off producer said, speaking for the group. The first time the Inspector asked the sixty-four thousand dollar question I thought I detected a slight hesitation on her part, and a fleeting glance at Bans, before she answered in the negative. But her denials had become firmer and more impatient with each repetition.

"Actually he sounded a little like Tom Waits," I opined.

Duncan was taken aback. "Who?"

"Tom Waits is a country singer," the girl wonder said grimly. "Mr. Virgo is trying to be funny," she added, hitting a bit closer to the mark.

Duncan heaved a resigned sigh. "Well, I guess there's no point beating a dead horse." With a grunt he hoisted a dead buffalo onto his back. "What time are you finished here, Virgo?"

"He's finished now," the girl wonder volunteered.

I don't know what I would have done without her—but was more than willing to give it the old college try. "I usually leave about three p.m., Inspector, why?"

"I'd like you to come down to my office for a chat. After forensic has had a chance to listen to that tape." Duncan put a battered gray fedora onto his balding dome and turned to Bans at the editing machine. "Can you put it in some kind of box for me?"

The girl wonder turned pale. "You want to take the tape of this morning's show with you?"

Duncan turned and looked at her. "Will that be a problem?"

A Problem? Getting the Bureaucratic Broadcasting Corporation to deviate from its time honored routine? Hell no, he merely had to wait "half a second" while she raced upstairs to cover her ass with the Director of Current Affairs; who would stroll down the hall to cover his ass with the Station Manager; who would make a long-distance call to Toronto to cover his posterior with someone who would pass the buck a little further up the line until it stopped, somewhere in the vicinity of the Prime Minister's office, long enough for an army of lawyers to draft a ninety page release form, to be signed in triplicate—preferably in blood—while Neil Bannerman made two or three dozen back-up copies for the DBC archives. "Well, I hope you're happy," the girl wonder glowered, when the studio door had finally hissed shut on Angus the Bull's backside.

"It was kind of an exciting show wasn't it?" I gave her a winning smile.

She was not won over. "It was a bloody fiasco! If you think I'm going to put up with this kind of circus every morning, Virgo..."

"If you two lovers will excuse me," Neil Bannerman interjected, from his seat at the console, "I'll let you continue this discussion without me." Having announced his plan of action the DBC's senior technician rode his chair across the floor to the editing machine, lifted a tape from the spindle, labeled it, placed it in a blue cardboard box, drained his coffee cup, crushed it in his nicotine-stained fingers, hook-shot it into the waste basket, plucked a pack of Export Plain from his shirt pocket, shook out a fresh "coffin nail", lit it from the one that was hanging from his pockmarked face, ground the spent butt under the heel of his cowboy boot, took a deep satisfying drag, launched a flotilla of smoke rings and sauntered out the door.

Throughout this familiar ritual the girl wonder was rocking on her heels like someone dying to relieve herself. And as soon as Bans was out of earshot she proceeded to do so, on her favorite target.

"Okay, Virgo, I'm through arguing with you. Just tell me one thing, are you or are you not prepared to conduct yourself in a professional manner?"

"What seems to be the problem, Patricia?"

"You're the bloody problem. It's that smart ass attitude of yours that invites this kind of nonsense."

"By nonsense I take it you are referring to the only spark of life that lit up this morning's slumber fest. A wake-up call that, thanks to your itchy trigger finger, our faithful listeners didn't get to share."

"Yeah right. I'm sure you were just dying to have your *faithful listeners* hear some drunk call you a two-faced bugger."

I smiled, modestly. "A rose by any other name…"

"That's exactly the kind of thing I'm talking about," she exploded. "It's impossible to have a serious discussion with you! You insist on turning everything into a joke. It may come as a shock to you, Virgo, but some of us around here take our jobs seriously."

I heaved a resigned sigh. "Yes, boss, I'm just clown. But I happen to be a clown with more of a track record in open-line radio than all the rest of the bozos in this building put together. You want me to behave in professional manner, Patricia? Then stop treating me like someone who's never seen the inside of a sound studio. Instead of trying to pass me off as some kind of political pundit or "investigative reporter" let me do the things I know how to do. It you let me choose a few of my own guests and topics I might even be able to pump some life into to this lame turkey you call a talk show. As you may recall, my dear, I was number one in this time slot for five years running."

"Ratings aren't everything," the girl wonder informed me, haughtily.

"No, but they're *something*. It's a bit difficult hosting a phone-in show when there's nobody phoning in. It may come as a shock to you, Patricia, but the housewives of Winnipeg aren't lying awake nights worrying about the political situation in Darfur."

"Well, maybe it's time they started."

"And maybe it's time you stopped treating the people who pay your salary like naughty children who refuse to take their medicine. The idea of an open line show is to give callers a chance to air the stuff that *they* care about."

"Like some cleaning lady who can't find her welfare worker's phone number I suppose?"

"Otherwise known as the listening audience."

"Otherwise known as *your* listening audience. It's time you realized you are no longer the star of country music radio, Stompin' Tom. The Corporation has a mandate to produce thought-provoking programming, not cater to the lowest common denominator."

I shook my head and heaved a resigned sigh. "Man, you DBC lifers take the cake. You've been choking on private radio's dust for so long you can't see the trees for the forest. You're constantly bitching about public apathy yet the minute you get a show that begins to attract a bit of an audience you can't wait to sabotage it."

My producer reddened. "Nobody's trying to sabotage anything, I'm just trying to give the show a little more..." she searched for the right word "... polish."

I didn't know whether to laugh or cry. "Patricia, an open line show isn't *supposed* to be polished, it's supposed to be spontaneous—like life. The only thing that makes this soap opera an adventure instead of a long, drawn-out death sentence is that you never know what's going to happen next?"

The Girl Wonder drew herself up to her full height and looked me right in the...Adam's apple. "Virgo, I'm *producing* this so-called soap opera; if I don't know what's going to happen next I'm not doing my job."

It was my turn to explode. "*Your* job? I'm the one whose ass is on the line in there," I pointed at the empty seat on the other side of the soundproof glass. "What about *my* job?"

"Well," my producer said, icily, "what about it?"

It was a conversation-stopper if I'd ever heard one. As a freelance "troublemaker"—with a verbal commitment from a long-gone Program Director—El Virgo had as much future at the Dominion Broadcasting Corporation as a brassiere salesman in a hippie colony. "Well, now that you've brought up the subject," I said, evenly, "whatever became of my contract?"

The Girl Wonder suddenly discovered a script that required her immediate attention. "It's coming," she muttered into its dog-eared pages.

So is Christmas, I thought, as I headed out the door. *And Jew boys don't hang up their stockings.*

One of the joys of living on the Canadian prairie, as opposed to Southern California, is that we get all four seasons up here—occasionally in the same week. Due to unseasonable spring-like weather I'd left my long johns in the drawer that morning and now, as I slid behind the wheel of my trusty Valiant, after scraping a layer of frost from the windshield, I almost froze my butt on the plastic seat cover. I inserted my key, pumped the gas pedal a few times, offered up brief prayed, and cranked the ignition. The old girl coughed twice and shuddered into action. I expelled my breath and punched her into reverse. She moved six inches and conked out. I cranked the ignition again. My trusty companion whined like my ex and claimed to have a headache. I gave her a few seconds to think it over, then made another pitch. She whimpered once and fell silent. On the third try she clucked her tongue at me. I heaved a sigh, popped the hood latch and went out to take a look—and saw just what I expected to see: an engine block and a bunch of wires.

"Battery trouble?"

I looked up and my heart leapt. The "goy wonder" had ridden to the rescue. The mechanical problem that Neil Bannerman couldn't solve—with an elastic band and a paper clip—had yet to come along. But we couldn't have him getting overconfident. "Lucky guess," I said.

Bans gave me a brown-toothed grin. "Hold on," he said, spinning on the heel of his cowboy boots, "I'll get my jumpers."

With an enthusiasm never displayed within the confines of the control room Bans jogged across the parking lot, jumped into his '96 Firebird, roared back across the lot and, in matter of seconds, had goaded his muscle car into imparting the kiss of life to my comatose senior citizen. "How can you drive a piece of shit like this?" the car doctor wondered, as he detached the cables.

"Piece of shit?" I said, indignantly. "The '73 Valiant is one of the most reliable machines ever to roll out of Detroit."

"So was the model A," Bans observed, peering at the laboring engine. "And it looks like you've got the original battery in this shit box."

"You think I should have it recharged?"

"I think you should have it *replaced*." Bans slammed the hood shut. "Did you plug her in?"

"I don't have a plug."

Bans looked at me, oddly. Then he noticed where I was parked. "What the fuck are you doing in the visitor's section?"

I shrugged. "Apparently, the Corporation has a rule about not assigning parking stalls to freelancers."

"Who the fuck told you that?" Bans hawked up an oyster of phlegm from his smoke-ravaged lungs and expelled it onto the frozen tarmac. "You don't have to put up with that kind of shit, why don't you talk to Patricia?"

I smiled. "Who do you think told me about the rule?"

Neil Bannerman did not return my smile. He was not about to denigrate a DBC bedfellow to an "outsider"—lest he upset the whole feather bed. "Well you better do something about that battery," he said, turning on the heel of cowboy boot. "If you can't get the fucker to turn over this early in the season what are you going to do when winter really hits?" he added, stowing the cables in his trunk.

"No problem," I said. "Pop's going to come out ever few hours and warm her up for me." I was referring to the DBC's non-security guard, a friendly old guy who sat at a table beside the switchboard guarding the inner sanctum of "The People's Network" from the unwashed masses. It was such a boring sinecure that even going outside in forty below weather to keep a semi-stranger's battery from freezing was a welcome change of pace.

Bans looked at me, incredulously. "Why in the fuck would he do that?"

"Hell man, I'm a star."

"Yeah right, how much you paying him?"

"I'll give him a bottle at Christmas."

The president of local 234 was not impressed with my generous wage package. "And for that you expect him to freeze his nuts off all fucking winter?"

"I don't expect anything. It was *his* idea. He wouldn't take no for an answer."

Why did I feel guilty? I wasn't exploiting the old guy, just giving him a chance to feel useful. Bans knew as well as I that so-called "security" job was a joke. Another DBC make-work project for unemployed paper pushers. In theory no one got past the front desk without signing Pop's "day sheet" but since no one was required to produce ID the mad bomber could have waltzed in simply by claiming to be an employee. "Val Virgo" was one of the few names Pop could actually match with a face. For some reason the old boy—who would have been a dead ringer for Santa if his blue uniform had been a red suit—had taken a liking to me. He and Bans were the only ones in the building who didn't treat me like I was HIV positive. "Look, Bans, the old guy wants to do me a favor. I couldn't insult him by offering him money."

Bans gave me a look that said "try insulting me like that" so I fished out my wad, peeled off a twenty and held it out. "Here."

He looked at the bill as if it was covered with shit. "What the fuck is that for?"

"Boosting my battery."

He looked at me and hawked up another oyster from his polluted lungs. For a second I thought he was going to spit it in my face but he turned and chose another target. Then he gave me a shit-eating grin. "Okay, I get the point." He got into his muscle car, gunned the idling engine, and rolled down the window. "But how will you feel if one of these frosty Fridays, when it hits forty fucking below, you come out here and find that your fucking battery isn't the only thing that's fucking dead."

I laughed out loud. "All right, you've made *your* point. I'll pick up a new Diehard after work tomorrow." Famous last words.

4

By the time I got to the Public Safety Building a light snow had begun to fall. Public safety! Why didn't they call it the "Motherhood Building" and stop beating around the bush? When The Peg was still "a good place to bring up children" we had a Central Police Station that was like something out of the dark ages; now that there were teenage hookers on every corner and gang bangers on every block the "Murder Capital of Canada" has a white limestone sepulcher with a reassuring name. We're living in the age of the ubiquitous euphemism, language fans; the grimmer the reality the more innocuous the label.

Only the smell hasn't changed, I thought, as walked through the glass doors. Someone told me the urine-like odor that permeates every penal institution—from jailhouse to schoolhouse to zoo—is disinfectant but I don't buy it. Unless they make a disinfectant called Misery. The garishly lit lobby was deserted except for a fresh-faced cop who was passing the time of day with a toothless old codger lounging in an orange plastic chair in front of a glass-topped coffee table. I moved to the elevator and pushed the 'up' button. A few seconds later the young cop came over and pushed it again. Give a guy a badge and gun… As we awaited the arrival of the car I decided to break the awkward silence by priming myself for my confrontation with Angus "The Bull" by engaging in a little cop talk. "Your friend seems right at home," I said, amiably.

Little boy blue looked at me blankly.

I nodded at the old geezer who was now thumbing through a discarded copy of the Daily Tabloid.

The young cop chuckled. "Oh yeah, Pop's one of our best customers."

I was shocked. I knew the financial situation of the senior citizenry wasn't exactly bright but the old guy looked so harmless. "Shoplifting?" I ventured.

The cop laughed. "No, entertainment. If it weren't for Pop and his cronies we'd be playing to empty houses on the third floor." He was referring to the Provincial Judges Court, where the late Judge Brown had presided.

"Well, the price is right," I said. As the elevator doors closed behind us I thought of another "Pop" who sat around all day twiddling his pen. Maybe we should recruit juries solely from the ranks of the senior citizenry; they have a lifetime of experience to bring to their deliberations and nothing but time on their hands. People with families to support will crawl over broken glass to get out of jury duty so why not give the job to someone who would not only welcome the opportunity to do something useful but who could use the income? The young cop didn't think much of my plan to reduce the geriatric welfare rolls. "Income?" he said, with a snort. "Do you have any idea how much jurors get paid?"

"Eighteen dollars a day."

My new friend looked at me, quizzically. "It's low but not *that* low. I don't know where you got your figures, sir, but you're ten years behind the times."

He was wrong—it was closer to twenty.

The door said: *Detective Division, Central Registry, Walk In*—so I did. Business must have been brisk, the only guy who wasn't on the street, detecting, was a grizzled veteran doing a two-finger tango on a vintage Smith-Corona. He had a bloodshot face and a juicy mole on the side of his pitted nose with a road map of purple capillaries running through it. I could have plotted the route to Lima, Peru, waiting for him to acknowledge my presence. "Is Inspector Duncan in?" I finally ventured, when my throat clearing failed to elicit a response.

"Busy," the warthog muttered and rattled the carriage back to go.

"I believe he's expecting me."

Pickle puss looked up with a glare that said *who in hell are you?* so I played my ace.

He was not impressed but did pick up the interoffice phone. "Sorry to bother you, inspector, but there's a gentleman out here by the name of Fargo…"

"Virgo," I interjected.

The old dick shot me a glance that said *why didn't you say so in the first place?* Then said, aloud, "Correction, it's Virgo." He listened, nodded, cradled the receiver and turned back to his manuscript. "Third door on the right, mister Virgo." I hadn't taken more than a few steps when the penny finally dropped. "Say, you're not Virgo from the Morning Line?" He was referring to my former show—the one that actually had an audience.

I turned and smiled, modestly. "Guilty."

The old cop's lined face lit up. "Well, it's a small world," he chortled. "My wife never used to miss your show." He opened his drawer and began rummaging around. "Do you mind giving me your autograph for her? She'll get real kick out of it." He found a note pad and held it out.

I pulled out my Parker Jotter. "What's her name?"

"Charlene."

To Charlene. Thanks for the memory. I scrawled my pseudonym across the bottom of the page and handed the pad back. The old cop read the message and grinned like a schoolboy. I resumed my journey to the "bullpen" feeling ten feet tall. "By the way, Virgo," my new fan called after me, "what are you doing these days?"

Suddenly I felt the same height as I did five minutes before—four foot, three. "Pissing into the wind," I said over my shoulder. And on Duncan's door.

"It's open," he called from inside. When I walked in he didn't look up. "Close the door and sit down," he said to the sheet of paper in front of him. I sat down and waited for him to finish reading. Page after page after page—now that I was on his turf we'd would play by *his* rules. Sitting there, waiting for the other shoe to drop, I suddenly realized why so many felons were convicted out of their own mouths. Another five minutes and I would have confessed to the assassination of John Kennedy.

The minute I stepped inside the cop shop I'd felt guilty.

Of what?

Good question—maybe of being a member of the human (rat) race—the only species that locked its fellow creatures in cages. Now Duncan was writing. I craned my neck and strained my eyes but couldn't read his handwriting upside down. I'd have had trouble with it right side up. It was as legible as Japanese calligraphy. And almost as elegant. Could the soul of an artist be buried under all that bulk? Angus Duncan wasn't as thick as he looked. He had good head on his shoulders. Too bad he didn't have it on a neck...

"Do you have any enemies, Virgo?"

"Besides you?"

Someday I was going to learn to not to put my mouth in motion until my brain was in gear. But Angus The Bull's hide must been inured to the slings and arrows of outrageous smart mouths because he didn't flinch. Just heaved a world-weary sigh and re-pocketed his fountain pen. "Save the snappy patter for the housewives, Virgo, it's been a long day."

"So why make it longer?"

"Which means?"

"Inspector, do you really think this is the first disgruntled crank who's threatened to blow me off the air?"

It was a rhetorical question but Duncan seemed to be having trouble with it. After a thoughtful pause he said, "Ever get anything in writing?"

"Does a Polar bear piss in the snow?"

Rhetorical questions were obviously not Angus Duncan's strength. After wrestling this one to a draw he slipped something out of a file folder and pushed it across the desk. It was a sheet of paper enclosed in transparent plastic. "Ever get anything like this?"

I gave it cursory glance and pushed it back. "Sorry, the stuff I get is usually in crayon."

"Read it," Duncan said.

"I did. A long time ago."

"Refresh your memory."

I didn't want to refresh it; I wanted to cleanse it. Not only of the stench of NAAPALM but of every group of self-appointed messiahs who were going to save the world through indiscriminate murder. But Duncan had made an offer I couldn't refuse so I made a show rereading the manifesto that had been published in The Daily Tabloid the morning after judge Brown had been elevated to that great Appeal Court in the sky:

Citizens of Manitoba,

Judge Robert Brown has been executed for crimes that have gone unpunished for centuries. This is the first blow struck by the North American Aboriginal People's Army of Liberation of Manitoba against the forces of white oppression. But it will not be the last. We will continue to defend our people against the genocidal policies of a racist government who, under the guise of benevolent paternalism, blah, blah, blah…

Read it? I could have written it! It was the same paint-by-numbers rhetoric used by the FLQ, the PLO, the IRA, and every "army" of misfits that had floated to the top of the "Revolutionary" alphabet soup. "No, I've never gotten anything like this," I said, handing it back. "Have you been able to trace it?"

"How do you suggest I go about doing that?"

I looked at him, suspiciously—was it some kind of trick question? "Well, correct me if I'm wrong, but doesn't every typeface have unique characteristics—like a fingerprint?"

"Very good, Sherlock. Unfortunately, even if I had an army of uniforms to round up every printer in the city, it wouldn't do me any good because the typeface—or *font* as we say nowadays—on this piece of evidence," he waved it in my face, "wasn't determined by the hardware by which it was printed but the software loaded into the computer on which it was composed. And a computer program does *not* have unique physical characteristics."

I smiled, lamely. "Never thought of that."

"Well maybe you *will* think of it," Duncan said, getting slightly red in the neck, "the next time you feel like mouthing off over the public airwaves about brain dead law enforcement officers sitting on their hands while the taxpayers are getting murdered in their beds."

As I snuck a glance at his leathery mitts it occurred to me that they were well suited to the purpose of sitting on. They were as thick as the cushion under his behind—and probably as well broken-in. "I'm just doing my job, inspector."

"Which is to tell me how to do mine?"

"I'm sorry if you got that impression, Inspector, but…"

"…*I don't make the news, I just report it.* Spare me the speech, Virgo; I can recite it by heart. News people make the news all right," he snatched up the NAAPALM manifesto, "every time you print something like this. These cockroaches wouldn't bother to come out of the woodwork if they didn't know there was an army of you media types ready to turn them into instant celebrities? There's a new screwball organizations springing up every week and you garbage collectors give them all the free publicity they can use." He slammed the note back into the file folder, rose, walked to the window and stared at the street as if trying to spot the cockroaches who were crawling out of the cracks in the sidewalk looking for a little publicity.

"You don't believe in a free press?" I said to his back.

He spun around and fixed me with the death ray. "Free for *who*? If Jesus Christ came back he'd have to hire a press agent. But every time Charlie Manson breaks wind every media vulture in the country—no, the continent— is ready to fly down to San Quentin with a television crew. Tell me, Virgo, if the press is so free why doesn't it ever report any *good* news?"

It was a good question. For which I didn't have a good answer. I'd fallen into the role of Devil's advocate more from habit than conviction. So, for lack of any better rejoinder, I gave him a winning smile.

He was not won over. "You find this amusing?"

I shook my head. "I'm just happy."

"About what?"

"About just being here for a friendly chat; if this is the way you treat potential victims I'd hate to be a suspect."

Duncan didn't blink but his bull neck went a little pinker. He snorted, went back to his desk, sat down and picked up the file. After shuffling papers for a few seconds he said, without looking up, "Does the name John Lonechild mean anything to you?"

"Yes".

He looked up, expectantly.

"It means the nut who wrote that bogus manifesto wants us to think he's an Indian."

The spark in Duncan's eyes went out. "You don't think he is?"

"Do you?"

Duncan's face clouded over. "We're not on the radio now, Virgo, I'll ask the questions if you don't mind. What's your show's position on the aboriginal situation?"

"The subject has never been discussed."

"Well, what's your personal opinion? Do you think the original Canadians are drunken welfare bums or noble savages who've been corrupted by the white man?"

I laughed. "Are those the only choices I get?"

"Take as many you like, I just want to know how do you feel about your aboriginal brothers."

"Would I want one to marry my sister, you mean?"

He nodded. "Something like that?"

It was a good question. For which I didn't have a politically correct answer.

"Frankly, I haven't given it much thought."

"So give it some."

I did. It didn't help. How could I tell this no-neck gentile the only hypothetical stranger to whom I would entrust my nonexistent sister was a member of my own tribe? "So you *do* think there's a terrorist group behind these bombings?"

"Let's just say I'm not as eager to dismiss the possibility as you are to dismiss that threat," Duncan said, following me onto the dance floor.

I was getting antsy. Since I didn't intend to devote more than a meter's worth of time to this fool's errand I had parked on the street and I was in danger of having to pay a parking fine. "The reason I'm willing to dismiss that bogus threat is that I know who's behind it."

I'd always assumed 'his jaw dropped' was just a figure of speech—now I knew better. Duncan's jaw almost bounced off the floor. "You what?"

My asshole closed like a clenched fist. The words were out of my mouth before I had a chance to stop them. Nevertheless I made a frantic grab for the barn door. "Well, I don't actually *know*," I said, with a chuckle, "it's just an educated guess. No, more of a…hunch. If I told you who I had in mind you'd think I was paranoid."

"Never mind what I think," Duncan snarled, "just spit out the name."

I smiled, apologetically. "I'd prefer not to."

Duncan leveled the death ray. "Your preferences have nothing to do with it, Virgo, if you have information concerning a crime you are bound by law to disclose it."

My mouth went dry. "A crime?" I croaked.

"Uttering threats is an indictable offence."

It hadn't occurred to me that the perpetrator of that tasteless prank had committed a criminal offense. And now that I knew I was determined to keep my mouth shut. If Duncan thought that icy glare was going to make me rat out my buddies he obviously didn't know he was dealing with a "stand up" guy. Who happened to be sitting down. "Pat Hogg," I muttered.

Duncan's jaw dropped—further. "You think your *producer* is responsible for that call?"

I shrugged. "I told you you'd think I was crazy."

But he didn't—a little neurotic, maybe, but not completely bonkers. I could tell from the bemused look on his beefy mug that he was recalling the soundless fury of the Girl Wonder's wrath as he watched her chew me out in the control room. He was obviously thinking that even a paranoid talk jock can have real enemies. "But she was sitting right in front of us when the call came in," he said, more to himself than me.

"She could have set it up ahead of time. Any one of her DBC cronies would be glad to do the honors. They all hate my guts."

For the first time in our brief acquaintance I thought I detected the shadow of a smile break the plain of Angus Duncan's stone face. "Any special reason? Or just on general principles?"

"On broadcasting principles. I'm not a member of the DBC club; I'm a contract freelancer. I actually have to earn my salary to collect it."

Duncan gave me a thoughtful nod. "So you think that call was some kind of practical joke?"

"Very practical. If my beloved colleagues can put the fear of God into the carpetbagger maybe he'll fold his tent and steal away. Look, Inspector, if some screwball organization really *did* have me on their hit list why would they warn me ahead of time? There's only one reason I can think of, to get some of that free publicity you were talking about. But you don't get much publicity from a commercial that doesn't go over the air. Anyone who had ever listened to Crosstalk would know that we have a tape delay and that a call like that would be cut off in the control room."

"By your producer?"

"Exactly. Patricia could cut the call off and still achieve her purpose because I was the only person who was supposed to hear it."

"What about me? She knew that I couldn't help hearing it. Do you think your beloved colleagues, as you call them, would send *me* on a wild goose chase just to put the fear of God into *you*?"

"You can't make an omelet without breaking a few eggs," I said with a shrug.

Duncan chewed on it for a few seconds but was having trouble swallowing it. "If you're such a thorn in her side why wouldn't she just get the DBC to fire you?"

"She doesn't have that kind of clout. Besides the DBC doesn't believe in firing people. They just make it so impossible for the square pegs to do their jobs that you quit of your own accord. Which is what happened to the guy who hired me, Morgan Riley."

Duncan frowned. "Isn't he the editor of The Tabloid?"

"He is *now*."

I could tell from his dark expression that Angus Duncan was not Morgan's biggest fan. The Tabloid had not only published the inflammatory (and probably bogus) NAAPALM manifestos before turning them over to the police but had gotten on Duncan's case and stayed aboard. "What happened?" he said.

A quick glance at the old digital told me my parking meter was about to expire. But I didn't have any choice so I told him the whole sad story. It seemed to cheer him up. He leaned back in his chair, made a bridge with his fingers—across which a railway train could have chugged—favored me with one of his rare Mona Lisa smiles and observed, "So you're not too happy in your work, Virgo?"

I shrugged. "It'll do until something better comes along."

"Such as?"

I gave it some thought.

"Death…"

5

Darkness had fallen and the light snow had escalated to an embryo blizzard. What a country. A few months of endless summer, when the sun never seemed to set, followed by an eternity of frigid darkness. Still, the prairie winter is not without its charm. As I crunched up to the old Valiant a carillon was piping a computerized carol over the rooftops, there was the smell of wood smoke in the air and the snowflakes sparkled like tinsel in the blue-white aura of the streetlights. It was quite heartwarming—in a gloomy kind of way. The mood of tranquility evaporated when I brushed the snow from my windshield to find a parking ticket wedged under the wiper. "This isn't my day," I muttered, trying to pry it loose. It was frozen to the windshield. I struggled with it, fruitlessly, then gave it a yank and it finally came loose—along with the wiper blade. My day? This wasn't my decade!

I opened the passenger door, tossed the blade onto the seat and headed back to the PSB to pay my fine. Thanks to "Ticketgate" I couldn't even ask Angus Duncan to tear up the bloody thing. Ironically, the ticket fixing scandal that forced the resignation of Chief Judge Gerald Styles may have led to the untimely demise of his successor, the late Judge Robert Brown. "Honest Bob" was appointed because of his reputation for unshakable integrity and shortly after his appointment presided at what became known as the "Drunken Indian Inquest".

The inquiry into the death of Billy Joe Parker, a teenage native, was a page one story in The Daily Tabloid for weeks. According to the statement of constable M.D. Ross, he was attempting to apprehend the deceased "pursuant to The Intoxicated Persons Detention Act" when B.J. grabbed Ross's service revolver out of its holster and in the ensuing struggle it "accidentally discharged". Three times. That was Ross's story and he was sticking to it. You might think the "investigating officer" who took the statement would view it as a slight improvement on the truth but where a fellow officer's career is at stake even cynical veterans like our friend Angus Duncan have been known to buy a little swamp land. Within twenty-four hours of the incident, and without interviewing a single civilian witness, he handed his boss a six page handwritten report in which he found that all the cops involved in the shoot, from the one who pulled the trigger to the ones who stood around, comparing notes, while young B.J. bled to death on the sidewalk, had acted in "a competent and professional manner".

The Chief gave Duncan's report the thoughtful consideration it deserved—a brief glance and an approving grunt—and promptly filed it under the carpet. Where it would have stayed if the Tabloid's muckraker-in-residence (a pseudonymous columnist known as "Renegade") hadn't pulled the rug out from under his feet. How could a teenage kid with a blood alcohol level in the comatose range, Renegade wondered, editorially, knock a two hundred pound cop on his keester and steal his gun? Was the officer really that "unstable"? And did his fellow officers really refer to him as "Mad Dog" Ross?

The Chief didn't dignify these impertinent questions with a response; just hunkered behind the blue wall and waited for the media storm to blow itself out. But as the parade of trained seals took the stand, and barked on cue, Morgan Riley's watchdog continued to ask leading questions. Why had Ross waited a full two minutes after the shooting to radio for assistance? Why had he re-holstered his weapon before turning it over to the "attending officers"; and why had they "passed it from hand to hand like a donation plate" before turning it over to Duncan? With the notable exception of Chief Taylor and Deputy Chief Duncan everyone in town was dying to hear the answers. The Tabloid was walking off the newsstands; they couldn't print enough copies. The other local rags jumped on the bandwagon and by the day M.D. "Mad Dog" Ross was due to testify the hearing room was so jammed with news hounds and spectators there was hardly room for the lawyers.

They could all have stayed in bed. When they called Ross's name the lawyer for the Police union stood up. "I ask the court to excuse the witness from testifying on the grounds of mental incapacity," he said. The previous night his client had checked himself into the psychiatric ward of the Health Sciences Center.

A police psychiatrist was called to the stand. Yes, Mad Dog had indeed gone over the edge; he was suffering from post- traumatic depression syndrome "aggravated by alcohol"; his mind wandered and his thoughts rambled; he would laugh one minute and cry the next—even if they wheeled the deranged police officer into court it was doubtful he could give "coherent" testimony.

Judge Brown was less than overjoyed at the news. Was there any chance "the witness" would recover in foreseeable future? Oh sure, the good doctor replied, the prognosis was quite favorable; as soon as the hearing was "behind him" Mad Dog would be as right as rain. It wasn't the shooting that had sent him over the edge ("actually, he's handling that quite well") it was the prospect of having to testify in open court that gave him the screaming meemies.

Honest Bob Brown was on the horns of a dilemma. He didn't want to force Ross to eat his gun but without his testimony the inquest was a sham. The fledgling jurist took five minutes to ponder the matter and then made a Solomon like decision. The witness would not be excused from testifying but neither would he be subjected to "rigorous cross examination". He reminded the lawyers for the deceased's family, and the Indian Band, who had no legal status at the hearing, that he had allowed them to question witnesses as a "courtesy". If they abused the privilege they would lose it.

After the great buildup the testimony was letdown. Ross's shrink pumped him full of tranquilizers and he testified like an automaton. He couldn't remember his own name without "referring to my notes". When pressed for a "spontaneous response" he would cast a helpless look at the bench and Judge Brown would tell the lawyers to "move on". Everyone treated Mad Dog like a live bomb. His potentially "traumatic" ordeal turned out to be a walk in the park.

Honest Bob's findings were a model of impartiality—they made everyone equally unhappy. He tore a strip from Ross and his buddies but stopped short of holding them responsible for B.J. Parker's untimely demise. Verdict: "death by misadventure". But "to clear the air" Judge Brown recommended that the Provincial Government convene a commission of inquiry to "investigate the relationship between the aboriginal people and the justice system." This recommendation brought Chief Taylor out from behind his blue wall of silence. Why should the taxpayers be burdened with another make-work project for overpaid lawyers? Judge Brown's implication that there was the slightest taint of racism among Winnipeg's finest was as ludicrous, as was his suggestion that Inspector Angus Duncan, that paragon of professionalism, was anything less than diligent in his investigation. The death of this "unfortunate aboriginal lad" had been thoroughly aired in a court of law. Case closed.

Renegade chose to disagree. The inquest had raised more question than it answered. Ross's testimony had been a joke. As was his supposed illness. The Tabloid stuck like dog shit to the constabulary shoe. The Chief kept applying whitewash but the stink wouldn't go away. The Premier licked his finger, saw which way the political wind was blowing, and appointed his old NDP crony, "Honest Bob" Brown, a one-man Commission to investigate…whatever the hell he felt like. Chief Taylor was not amused. He dashed off a personal letter of protest to the Premier. As a former Minister of Northern and Indian Affairs Judge Brown couldn't possibly conduct an impartial inquiry. Next day the "confidential" letter was published in the Tabloid. The Premier was not amused. Nor were the leaders of the aboriginal community, who dashed off an open letter to the Tabloid. Brown should stay; the Chief should go. Renegade didn't play favorites; he thought they should both go.

They both stayed.

During the televised sittings of the Native Justice Inquiry the daytime soaps must have plunged in the ratings. The "Brown Commission" was Manitoba's answer to the O.J. Simpson trial. Honest Bob's handpicked staff had a little more success than Angus Duncan in digging up civilian witnesses and they painted a much darker picture than the boys in blue. Two young native witnesses swore they saw Ross running down the street with his gun drawn. Another swore she heard the words "freeze you little fucker" just before the fatal shots. Yet another claimed to overhear one of Ross's buddies say—as they waited for the ambulance to arrive—"if you're lucky, he dies."

On the day Ross was due to testify half the working population in the city probably called in sick. I know I did. The atmosphere in the hearing room was so charged you could feel it emanating from the TV. Judge Brown walked in and sat down. A hush descended. Ross's lawyer stood up. Mad Dog was no longer represented by the Union lawyer but had hired his own high priced mouthpiece. So how would his client answer these new charges? "Your honor," the lawyer said, "I request that my client be excused from testifying on the grounds of ill health."

You could feel the air go out of the balloon. Mad Dog had checked himself back into the heartbreak hotel.

The committee chairman was not amused. Nor did his humor improve as Ross's lawyer paraded a fresh batch of trained shrinks, who all jumped through familiar hoops. Honest Bob was not impressed—he'd seen the show before. It was no more Mr. Nice Judge—not only would Ross be compelled to testify he'd be subject to the same rigorous cross examination as any other witness. If his shrink didn't think he could handle the stress she could increase his dose of happy pills before he took the stand. Ross didn't wait for his doctor; he prescribed his own medication—half a bottle—washed down with a mickey of Golden Wedding.

Constable Ross's suicide sent a shock wave through the city and a wave of indignation through the police department. The Chief called a press conference and laid "the death of this courageous young officer" on the doorstep of the "Native Justice Inquiry". The Chairman of the "Brown Commission", who had suspended the hearings for ten days, would shortly find a more tangible item on his doorstep. Ordinarily he would have sent the package back, unopened, but there was no return address so he unwrapped it. And found a gift from an anonymous admirer—a novelty lamp. He plugged it in and turned it on. And the rest, as they say, is history.

I reemerged from the Public Safety Building, a poorer but wiser man, and stopped in my tracks. Some guy was looking into the passenger window of the Valiant. I couldn't see his face—just the "Winnipeg Jets" logo on the back of his hockey jacket—so I approached with caution.

"Can I help you?"

He turned and my heart went into overdrive. This cat made Geronimo look like a pacifist. His eyes were bloodshot, his lower lip was swollen, his nose looked like someone had stepped on it and his hockey jacket was open to the navel, revealing what looked like knife scar on his bronze ribcage. I was about to go into cardiac arrest when he broke into a toothless grin.

"Can you spare any change? For a cuppa coffee?"

The "coffee" to which he referred was served by the glass, not the cup, and "spare change" wouldn't cover the tab so I crossed his palm with a loonie. He gazed at the large coin in silence, swaying slightly on his feet. Was he overwhelmed by my generosity or too bleary-eyed to recognize Canada's new designer currency? "Keep the change," I said, snapping him out of his reverie.

He gave me another toothless grin. "Tanks brudder."

As I watched my aboriginal brother stagger back into the night, leaving a wake of beer fumes on the frosty air, I thought of Angus Duncan's hypothetical question. No, Angus, I *wouldn't* want him to marry my sister. But then I wouldn't want you as a brother-in-law either. Did that make me a closet bigot? Or just a realistic Jewboy with five thousand years on deposit in the racial memory bank? Sure, I knew the aboriginal people weren't all drunken welfare bums and that "goyim" weren't all drunken wife beaters but I wouldn't bet my sister's life on it. In the absence of a track record you have to rely on the history of the breed.

I brushed the snow from my windows, got behind the wheel, inserted the key, pumped the gas pedal a few times and cranked the ignition. The motor started on the fourth crank. I uncrossed my fingers and flipped on the defroster. The windshield immediately clouded over. What a country. As I sat there waiting for the motor to warm up, my fingers numb, my teeth chattering, I thought of my red brother wandering around, half-naked. Was it simply alcohol that inured him to thousand shocks to which my pale flesh was heir or did genes have something to do with it?

Before the answer revealed itself the blower had melted a porthole in the frosted windshield and the old girl wasn't beginning to purr so I punched her into "drive" and goosed the gas pedal. The engine raced, the wheels spun on the icy tarmac and the car didn't move. I eased up on the gas pedal and inched away for the curb. What a country. "Maybe we *should* give it back to them", I thought, as I crawled down the icy street, my nose pressed to the windshield, in the direction of the steel and concrete bunker I laughingly called "home".

6

***Welcome to LOUIS** RIEL TOWERS.* Who was the public relations genius that came up with that gem, I wondered as I pulled into the underground garage, the Manitoba Metis is History Rewriting Committee? A century ago the half-mad half-breed was strung up for treason and now they were selling him like a laundry detergent. *Tell me, Mr. Riel, what does your wife use to get the bloodstains out of your buckskins?*

Why the new Batoche Detergent, with the miracle ingredient, Gatling Gun Powder.

Listen to Louis, folks, for a snow-white wash, ask for Batoche!

Maybe the marketing of "traitors" was an idea whose time had come. Why keep recycling those shopworn patriots when there was an untapped gold mine of turncoats just waiting to be mined? *The Benedict Arnold Hilton!* Has a novel ring, what? Novelty is the lifeblood of fashion and fashion sells. Innocence, once lost, can never be regained but "guilt" is always negotiable.

As I rode the elevator to the fourteenth floor The Otis Symphonette was piping in the usually narcotic but I thought I detected a hint of tension in the car. Was that surly black dude in the combat jacket looking at me funny? And what about that inscrutable chick who looked like an oriental Barbie, all the right parts but in miniature? And that green haired Goth with the death's head tattoo and more body piercings than St. Sebastian? It suddenly occurred to me that I knew none of my fellow tenants, any one of whom might be the mad bomber. The seeds of paranoia sewn by Inspector Shreck were beginning to germinate.

I could hear the phone ringing on the other side of the door. If I hurried, I could intercept the call before my answering machine kicked in. I didn't hurry. Sufficient unto the morning were the calls thereof. While my electronic watchdog took care of the intruder I switched on the hall light, reset the dead bolt, dropped my junk mail and pressed the rewind button. My roommate, who was curled up on the chesterfield, opened one green eye and watched me hang up my jacket. Then he yawned, stretched, sprang to the floor and ambled over. "What's the idea of leaving me cooped up in this shitty pad all day?" he complained, rubbing against my leg.

"Don't tell me your troubles, I've got troubles of my own." I picked up my mail and headed for the kitchen—and almost took a header over my shaggy roommate. "For Christ sake, Nuisance!" I shoved him aside with my foot, dropped the mail on the kitchen table, opened the cupboard, took down a can of Luxury Seafood Dinner—the only brand the fussy bugger will eat—scooped a dollop of the evil-smelling concoction into his Tender Vittles dish and set it on the floor. He ambled over, gave it a sniff, then followed me back to the cupboard. I took down a bottle of scotch, poured myself a few fingers and added some tap water. Nuisance leapt onto the edge of the sink, squeezed past my elbow, and stuck his nose in the glass. I elbowed him aside, picked up *his* glass (he refuses to drink from a dish) filled it with water and set it in front of him. He eyed it, suspiciously. Then, after gauging the depth with his nose, began to lap.

I followed his example—except for the nose bit. The scotch exploded warmly in my empty stomach and spread through my capillaries like ink through blotting paper. I began to mellow out. I took another pull, freshened the drink, replaced the bottle and sat down at the kitchen table to confront my junk mail.

Duncan had cautioned me about suspiciously thick envelopes but there was only one bulky enough to cause concern and I didn't think Shell Oil was out to get me. By anything other than the credit card, that is. Their latest offering included a number of essential motoring items, including a combination AM/FM Radio TV Cassette- Recorder $439.95, plus shipping and handling and a Digital Still/Video Camera $779.99, accessories extra. Apparently, the only thing you couldn't get from your friendly neighborhood service station are repairs to your automobile. Not that mine needed any; a new battery would suffice.

My MasterCard statement had arrived. I'd have to draw some gelt on my Visa and pay it. When my Visa bill came I would reverse the process. I used to keep three balls in the air but now that I was a highly paid bureaucrat I only had to borrow from Peter to pay Paul. But Mary wouldn't take no for an answer—she kept sending me "Dear Val" letters:

Virgo, how could you leave home without me?

Something brushed my pant leg.

I looked down.

My roommate looked up and meowed.

"Bugger off, Nuisance." I wasn't playing headwaiter to dumb animal— if he was hungry he could eat. I dumped my mail into the wastebasket, popped what was left of last night's pizza into the microwave and moved to the answering machine. Nuisance followed me, meowing, pathetically, but I didn't weaken. They say a watched kettle never boils but who ever heard of an unwatched cat that wouldn't eat. I pushed the replay button. Then lost *my* appetite:

Virgo, Patricia. Give me a call; (beep) Me again. Call me as soon as you get home, I have something important to discuss with you; (beep) What the hell are doing, telling him the story of your life? (beep) All right hotshot, I know you're probably standing there, listening to this, so you'd better pick up the phone, because if I have to come down there...

I pushed the rewind/erase button with an empty feeling in the pit of my stomach—and not just because it was empty. I'd made some Olympic blunders in my forty-two years on the planet but the gold medal performance was moving into the same building as my producer. I was tempted to let Ms. St. John Hogg stew in her own rancid juices but if I didn't call her back she'd make my life miserable the next morning. Well, more miserable. I refilled my glass, took a long pull, sat down on the couch and punched in her number. Nuisance sat at my feet and looked up at me like that RCA Victor mutt as my (task) mistress greeted me in her usual cordial manner.

"Well it's about time; where in the hell were you?"

"You know perfectly well where I was."

"He certainly kept you long enough. So, how did it go—did he check out that number?"

"He didn't have a copy of the Fantasy Land Telephone Directory. For Christ sake, Patricia, do you *really* think that fruitcake gave you his right name and telephone number? I've told you a hundred times that call sheet is about as useful as..."

"Okay, let's not get into all that again, just get your ass up here, I have something to discuss with you."

"Give me a break, I haven't even eaten since..."

"So I'll pop a pizza into the microwave."

"I'm already zapping my own junk food, thanks; what's so important it can't wait until morning?"

There was a pregnant silence. "I have an idea about that call."

My heart skipped a beat. Confession time? "What about it?"

"I think we can get some mileage out of it."

My heart resumed its former rhythm. "What are you talking about? Nobody even heard it."

"No, but we still have the tape."

"Well I hope you don't intend to play it? Angus Duncan would love that!"

"We don't have to play it, if Garth listens to it a few times I'm sure he can imitate that voice. We can do a re-creation. You know, like Unsolved Mysteries. Of course we'll have to get the go ahead from Brad, and he may want to check with Toronto, but I thought I'd run it by you before I went upstairs. So, what do you think?"

The biggest unsolved mystery was how my producer had managed to survived in the world of broadcasting for a whole six months. Whatever marginal news value that bogus call had, went up in smoke the instant my producer cut it off at the pass. To re-create a dramatized version, several days later, would be the lowest form of yellow journalism. "Whatever happened to your scruples about people calling me nasty names over the public airwaves, Patricia?"

"No problem, we can edit the *bugger*."

"You've already accomplished that little trick, my dear—you blowed that sucker up *real* good!"

"I'm talking about the word, as if you didn't know."

I knew only too well. It was a familiar DBC story: choke on a gnat and swallow an elephant. "Patricia," I said, "aren't you the person who is always telling me we shouldn't stoop to cheap sensationalism?"

"And aren't you the one who's always saying we should try to liven up the show?"

"Running my butt up a flagpole so every nutcase in the city can use it for target practice isn't exactly what I had in mind. Why don't I just take a

swan dive from the roof of the building? That's sure to attract an audience."
From the silence that greeted this suggestion my producer could have been
considering it. But I knew she was just sulking. She cherished this hair brained
idea like an only child. Unless I agreed to march to the spastic beat of her toy
drum she was prepared to keep me on the phone all night. Nuisance rubbed
against my leg and yawned. I decided to follow his lead. "Look, Patricia,
maybe this isn't such a bad idea (yawn) but I'm too bushed to make any kind
of rational decision. (Yawn.) Why don't I sleep on it and..."

"Don't you dare hang up that phone, Virgo! I know your tricks. First
thing tomorrow morning you'll sneak out of the building, with that mangy
cat of yours in a shopping bag, and won't show up at the studio until it's too
late..."

For your kisses, I crooned to myself, and gave her a taste of her own
medicine. "Virgo" must have been numero uno on her speed dial because
the phone chirped within seconds. But it was too late—I'd unleashed
my electronic pit bull. "Eat that, bitch," I snarled, as he throttled the
intruder.

"Meow," someone replied.

I looked down. "Not you, stupid, you're a Tom." Well, a *Bruce* anyway.
I still felt guilty about that little betrayal but what choice did I have? It's not
like I went out and bought a cat just for the joy of mutilating it. One day,
when I was on the road, an orange fur ball showed up on our doorstep and
my ex insisted on feeding it. "Take him to the vet for his shots," she said,
the minute I got back off the road. The vet suggested that I also have him
"fixed". I knew the cat was "used" but didn't know it was broken. "When they
mature," the vet elaborated, "they have a tendency to spray."

I had no idea what he was talking about.

"They do it to establish their territory," the would-be emasculator
explained.

"Do what?" I inquired.

"Spray," he repeated.

I decided to take a pass on the surgery. But within a few weeks I discovered
"piss all over the house" was the phrase Doctor Euphemism couldn't bring
himself to utter. So I was forced to take our adopted son back to the butcher
shop so the problem could be "fixed"—a sin against nature for which I was
finally paying; what I'd done to my innocent roommate the Girl Wonder was

now doing to her lab rat—with a dull knife.

"All right Nuisance, come on."

I walked into the kitchen, with the fussy bugger padding after me, and stopped at his dish. He gave his dinner a cursory sniff then, with a sidelong glance to make sure I was still standing there, began to munch. And purr. Every cat is entitled to make a little noise when he's groovin' but Nuisance abused the privilege. If he didn't put muffler on that thing he was going to alert the authorities to the fact that I was living with an illegal alien. If the Girl Wonder hadn't already done me that little favor.

I called my fresh-faced producer the "Girl Wonder" because you had to wonder if she was a girl. When it came to broadcasting Patricia St. John Hogg had the instincts of a lemming. Her penchant for bandwagons was exceeded only by her knack of choosing the ones that were going rapidly downhill—then shoving my sorry butt onto the tailgate as they were circling the toilet bowl. She had pulled a lot of weird shit since taking over the show a few months ago but this latest move took the prize. Was she miffed because I hadn't taken her little prank seriously? Or had she finally lost her balance on the fence she straddled and fallen all the way into the Twilight Zone? Who knew what went on in that kitty litter between her ears? And who cared?

I tiptoed away from my purring roommate to silence my own growling stomach. Yeah, it tasted like "delivery" all right! My dinner had the consistency of soggy cardboard but not quite as much flavor. I should have saved the box and dumped the contents in the garbage. I remedied the error, refreshed my wine glass, put on a CD and moved into the living room.

As Waylon Jennings sang the story of my life—*Old Five and Dimers*—I stood at the panoramic window admiring the view. The old hometown was blanketed in a sheath of multicolored lights that twinkled up at me like sequins on a black velvet gown. Peg o' my Heart was all decked out in her holiday threads; a flat-chested country chick trying to pass herself off as a sophisticated lady. Winnipeg was all dressed up with no place to go. It wasn't a city; it was a railway crossing. Disillusioned farmers and unemployed Indians poured in from one end, disgruntled business and professional types poured out to the other. Ontario had iron ore; Saskatchewan had potash; Alberta had oil; British Columbia had timber but the "Keystone Province" had only one natural resource to export—talent.

Which is why I was back here for good. The prodigal picker was chained to his homely home on the prairie like a henpecked husband and what did he have to show for it? A stack of unpublished songs gathering dust in the closet; a wallet full of credit cards; a job that was getting harder to go to every day…Angus Duncan was right; news biz was even phonier than show biz—and a lot less nourishing. The same junk food for thought that's served up in the morning paper is digested on the ten o'clock news, regurgitated in weekly news magazines, re-masticated on the talk shows, etc., ad nauseam. The public's appetite for its own shit is insatiable. And Valentine Virgo was shoveling along with the best of them. I drained my glass and went to soak away my regrets.

As I sat on the edge of the tub, eyes closed, letting the steam caress my naked body—and the drumming of the water drown out the sound of the girl wonder's voice—Nuisance wandered in, purring noisily. He leapt onto the vanity and started to lap up the water I'd left for him in the toothbrush glass. Watching him trap the stale water against the side of the plastic tumbler with his sandpaper tongue it suddenly occurred to me that it was *easier* for a cat to drink from a glass than a bowl. Nuisance wasn't being contrary just doing what came naturally. So why wouldn't he eat his dinner unless I stood there watching him? Having satisfied his thirst (if not my curiosity) my practical cat stretched, cleaned his whiskers, jumped onto the toilet seat and settled himself on my bath towel. I took him by the scruff of the neck and tossed him out. He immediately began to scratch at the door. I ignored him. Guilt or no guilt I wasn't putting up with cat hairs on my bath towel. I turned off the tap and lowered myself into the tub. As soon as I hit the water the cares of the day begin to dissolve. I leaned back and closed my eyes. Heaven! I could hear the "plop" of the water droplets as they formed on the end of the faucet and dropped into the tub and feel the bass-heavy thrum of The Waylors right through the floor:

Where does it go?
The Good Lord only knows.
It seems like it was just the other day...

Where did it go? Time? Life? Liberty? The Saturday Evening Post…once I'd had a future full of money, love and dreams; now I wasn't even a honky tonk hero. Just an old crock, sitting on the dock of the bay, watching his life ooze away like molasses in December. Nuisance had stopped scratching at the door. He was probably curled up on top of the television set. Well, as long as he kept his hairy paws off the remote control. My cat spent most of his life in the fetal position and I was following his example. I began to drift and dream.

Part Two
Blood on the Tracks

Fritz Finkelman was *having a bad night. He hadn't had very many good nights in the last fifty years. When he was liberated from Auschwitz, at the age of fourteen, he had thought the nightmare was over. They had just begun. Scarcely a week went by when he didn't wake up in the middle of night, in a cold sweat, his heart pounding. Ironically, when he was living the nightmare, his dreams, when he had them, were pleasant. He'd find himself back home, sitting down to a sumptuous Sabbath meal. He'd stuff his face with gefilte fish, chicken soup with matzo balls, roast goose, potato kugel, dill pickles...and wake up with a gnawing in the pit of his stomach and frantically feel around for the half crust of bread he had saved from the night before. He was the youngest "heffling" in the block but the only one with the discipline to husband his meager supply of food so he would have something in his stomach, beside black coffee, when he went to work in the morning.*

Since coming to Canada he had never gone to bed on an empty stomach but seldom had a pleasant dream. He was always a young boy, marching down a country road, in the middle of winter, with men twice his age. No, not men, scarecrows. Walking corpses. Failik thought no hell could be lower than a slave labor camp but he was wrong. Even a slave laborer gets to rest at the end of the day. He sleeps indoors, not on the icy ground, by the side of a country road. The camps were a vacation resort compared to the "death march". Mile after mile, day after day, week after week, putting one foot in front of the other, fighting off the temptation to just lay down, close your eyes and welcome the bullet in the head that will put you out of your...

That's when Fritz would wake up, in a cold sweat, and heave a sigh of relief to find himself an old man in a shabby room rather than a helpless young boy. Except when he found himself in a prison cell. Stony Mountain was a different kind of hell than Auschwitz. In a penitentiary it's not starvation and exhaustion with which you have to cope but boredom. The days are soul-destroying and the nights are torture. Tossing on a narrow bunk in a cell that smells of formaldehyde, your head a few inches from an open toilet, the light from a bare bulb shining through your closed eyelids, your ears assaulted by the clang of steel doors, the rattle of locks, the creak of shoes patrolling up and down the corridor, the muttering, swearing, groaning, sobbing of fellow inmates—it was like trying to sleep in the ante chamber of hell. You have too much time to think.

Throughout his life Failik Finkelman's agile mind had been occupied with plans, schemes, projects—that was his survival technique. Not in the camps, where he had been too physically and mentally drained to think of anything but his next crust of bread, but in the "Golden Land" where you had to be equally ruthless with those who were out to destroy you. As he lay in his furnished room, unable to sleep, Fritz forced himself to plan for the future, just as he had done for all those years in his prison cell. It was the only way he could keep his mind from dredged up the past, like muck from a swamp.

7

I'm driving to Stony Mountain to visit my father. Perched on a small rise just outside of town, the ancient penitentiary broods over the prairie landscape like a giant bird of prey. I park my car and head for the entrance. The stone walls envelope me like wings. The steel door clangs shut behind me. The black-robed warden glowers down from his perch. His face is vaguely familiar. Empty your pockets. The voice of authority! I empty them. Take the book in your right hand. Do I solemnly swear… As I hand the bible back I see the gold lettering on the cover and my heart sinks. I've sworn an oath on the New Testament. My father will turn over in his grave. And then I remember…

He shuffles into the visitor's area flanked by two S.S. guards. There's a mossy growth of white stubble on his sunken face and his complexion is as gray as his prison uniform, which has stripes, like pajamas. My heart sinks lower.

"Forgive me, Pop, I had no choice!"

He looks right through me. The guards begin to drag him away, like a dog, by a leather collar. They're wearing black uniforms and peaked officer's caps with a death's head insignia. My father is going to the gas chamber. And it's my fault. His last words to me, as they drag him away, stab me in the heart. "Judge not, lest you be judged."

I'm cleansing my sins in the Jordan. The river is crystal clear and as warm as a bath. No, it's not the Jordan; it's the Dead Sea. I'm floating just below the surface, suspended like an astronaut in space. But there's pressure on my chest, and the sting of chlorine in my nostrils. I hear a voice. It's the lifeguard. Time to come out of the pool. I try to swim to the surface but my limbs are paralyzed. I'm seized by panic. I can't hold my breath much longer. My lungs are bursting. I gather my strength and make a supreme effort…

My eyes popped open. I was lying in bed and a semi-familiar face was frowning down at me.

47

"Virgo, do you know who I am?"

What the hell was Angus Duncan doing in my bedroom? I didn't have the strength to ask. I felt weak as a kitten and my head was splitting. And who was that guy beside him; the one in the suit that didn't come off the rack at Goodwill Industries?

"You're in the Health Sciences Center, Mr. Virgo. You've had a little… accident."

Accident? What kind of accident? I opened my mouth but the words wouldn't come.

Angus Duncan supplied the answer. "You almost drowned in your bathtub."

The loonie dropped. I must have fallen asleep in the tub. But why would a homicide cop…It hit me like a freight train. They were talking about a *deliberate* accident. I tried to sit up.

Not the wisest move.

"Are you experiencing much discomfort," the Health Scientist asked, as I sank back with a moan.

Discomfort? Hell no, doc, just garden variety pain. I looked at him, helplessly.

"Can't you speak?"

I tried to shake my head.

Another bright move!

"Just relax," the healer said, his calming hand on my chest. He removed a pen light from his breast pocket and shone it into my eyes. "Hmm" he said, scientifically.

"Do you think he's up to answering a few questions?"

The doctor looked at Duncan as if he was the one who'd been hit on the head. "He's suffering from a concussion, Inspector. He can't talk."

Angus the Bull grabbed the straw by the horns. "But he can still think." He looked at me. "If I ask you a few questions, Virgo, do you feel up to writing down the answers?"

"I think the questions better wait until morning," Dr. Feelgood said, re-pocketing his penlight. He turned and gave his patient a reassuring smile. "After a good night's sleep Mr. Virgo will feel much stronger, and will probably have recovered his voice."

For once, I was on Angus Duncan's side—I didn't want sleep; I wanted answers. But the faces looking down at me were beginning to swim. I was slipping back into the therapy pool. I fought to keep my eye open but the undertow was too strong. I sank back and let the healing waters wash over me.

8

The doctor's prognosis was on the money—when I woke up my voice was back. And so was Inspector Duncan, who also seemed to be a new man. He didn't barge into my room but lingered in the hall and greeted me with a reassuring grimace. "Well Virgo, I guess the practical joke got out of hand."

I feigned indignation. "Insult to injury? Shame on you, Inspector. But don't just stand out there, come in and make yourself homely. Or did nature beat you too it?"

Duncan had used up his daily allotment of smiles. He approached my bed like he was walked walking across a minefield. Having made it safely across, he took off his hat, unbuttoned his coat and perched his butt on the visitor's chair, like a cat on picket fence—a very *large* cat.

"So, how are you feeling this morning?"

"Much better."

"You look better," he lied.

My mirror had been more candid. "For a giant panda."

He smiled, uncomfortably. "So, I guess you're wondering how you ended up in here?"

Duncan had finally gotten the hang of rhetorical questions—he didn't wait for an answer but proceeded with a tentative explanation. According to the kitchen clock, the shit hit the fan at precisely 7:10 p.m.—which raised an obvious question.

"About seven," I said, answering it. "At least that's when I closed the door."

Duncan shook his head. "Somebody up there, must like you, Virgo."

"But not you, right?"

Duncan heaved a weary sigh. "Would it be too much of a strain to lay off

50

the wisecracks until we get this thing sorted out?"

"Sorry, Inspector, it's a conditioned reflex. Do you know where the explosive was located?"

"Somewhere on the east wall of the living room. What did you have on that wall, any kind of electronic equipment?"

"All kinds: Stereo, TV..."

"That's it," Duncan said, lighting up, "the television set. If the detonator was hooked up to on/off switch you'd be directly in the line of fire when you turned the set on."

"But I wasn't, I was in the bathroom."

He frowned. "Maybe it was a delayed fuse."

"What would be the point? Besides, I didn't watch television last night."

"Are you sure?"

"Positive, I was listening to a CD."

The frown evaporated. "Then it must have been hooked up to the CD player."

"So why didn't it go off until I was in the bathtub?"

Duncan's face clouded over. Why was I putting these roadblocks in his way? He continued to question me about the layout of my apartment and grew increasingly impatient with my unhelpful answers. After we had gone around the block for the sixth or seventh time the penny suddenly dropped.

"Nuisance!"

Duncan's neck turned scarlet. "Look, Virgo, I know you've had a pretty traumatic..."

"No, you don't understand, Inspector; Nuisance is my cat. The bomb *was* hooked up to the television set and he was the one who triggered it!"

Duncan looked at me as if my concussion was a little more serious than the doctor claimed. "You think your *cat* turned on your television set?"

"It wouldn't be the first time. He lies on top of the set, because that's the warmest place in the apartment, and occasionally plays with the remote control."

Duncan smiled, grimly. "I was wrong, Virgo, somebody down *here* likes you."

"*Liked* me." I heaved a resigned sigh. "Poor old Nuisance."

Duncan felt my pain. "Well, he's got eight lives left." Then, with a slightly slyer smile, "Of course there's no way of knowing if this was his first...kick at the cat." I smiled in spite of myself. Old Angus was pretty swift for a cop—and Godzilla is pretty nimble for two-ton lizard. Having had his moment of mirth Duncan shifted back into serious mode. "Okay, now that we know *where* the device was let's see if we can figure out how long it was there. When was the last time you watched television, Virgo?"

"The previous night, around ten."

"Are you sure? You couldn't have turned it on for a few minutes before you left for work, to catch the news?"

I shook my head. "Even if I were so inclined, I don't have time." I spared him the image of me taking Nuisance out for his morning stroll and dump.

"So they must have planted the device between the time you left for work—when would that be?"

"About five-fifteen."

"So that narrows the time down to...wait a minute." He had been struck by an inspiration. "Virgo, remember when you asked why a publicity-seeking nut would make a call he knew wouldn't go over the air?" I nodded and Duncan explained his theory. What if the call wasn't directed at me but at *him*? Whoever made that death threat would know that even if I didn't take it seriously my "guest" couldn't laugh it off—and was bound to keep me tied up long enough for him to redecorate the interior of my apartment without fear of interruption.

"I suppose it's possible," I said. "But how would he get into my apartment? When I got home the dead bolt was still engaged."

"Are you sure?"

"Positive, I couldn't get the door open in time to answer the phone."

"It was ringing?"

No, Angus, I always answer the phone before it rings—it saves time. "Yes."

Duncan took out a small black recorder from his jacket pocket and fixed me with those steel ball bearings he used for eyes. "Alright, Virgo, let's start at the beginning, tell me everything you did last night, from the time you got home until you went into the bathroom. And don't leave anything out, even if you don't think it's significant." He clicked the record button and laid the recorder on the night table. "Okay, go ahead."

I cast my mind back and tried to recall the sequence of events, exactly as they occurred. When I got to the point where I was replaying my telephone messages Duncan flagged me down. "How many were there?"

I shrugged. "About half a dozen."

"Do you remember who they were from?"

"My producer."

"Who else?"

"That's it."

He frowned. "You said there were half a dozen callers."

"I said there were half a dozen messages."

"*All* from your producer?"

I smiled. "Ms. St. John Hogg isn't the most patient person in the world."

"But she knew you were going straight from the DBC to the Public Safety Building. Surely she knew that you'd be at my office for at least an hour or two."

"Like I say, Ms. St. John Hogg isn't the most…"

"Alright I get the picture, what did she want?"

"She had an idea for the show. She wanted me to come up and discuss it."

He looked at me, oddly. "Up?"

When I told the old bloodhound that my producer occupied the apartment directly above mine his nose began to twitch. "Your relationship with Ms. Hogg," he said, with studied casualness, "is it strictly…professional?"

"It is now."

His ears perked up. "There was a time when it wasn't?"

I should have left sleeping bloodhounds lie. "You're barking up the wrong tree, Inspector. Ms. Hogg and I had a one-night stand that we would both rather forget about. She may not be president of the Val Virgo fan club but she is not a homicidal maniac. Besides how could she plant a bomb in my apartment without leaving the studio?"

Duncan couldn't refute the logistics but wasn't quite ready to give up the "hell hath no fury" theory. "I don't suppose she has a key to your apartment?"

"You don't suppose right."

"Is there anyone else you might have given one to? A relative, friend…"

"No."

"Don't be so quick to dismiss the possibility," Duncan said, with slight irritation. "This is too important to just gloss over. *Think* before you answer."

"It doesn't take much thought; I've only been living in that apartment for a few months and there are only two keys—one in a desk drawer in my apartment and the other on my key ring."

"Where is your key ring now?"

I smiled. "You tell me."

Duncan grunted. "I guess the first thing you'll have to do when you get out of the hospital is contact your insurance agent."

"What's an insurance agent?"

Duncan looked at me incredulously. "The contents of your apartment weren't insured?"

I didn't say anything. Unlike Angus Duncan I don't answer rhetorical questions.

"Well, it's only money," he said, philosophically. He switched off the tape recorder. "Have you given any thought to where you're going to live?"

I shook my head. "Not really."

"Well, when you do decide," he said, putting on his gray fedora, "don't broadcast it."

A lump rose in my throat. "You think these bastards would go after the same target *twice*?"

"Frankly, no," Duncan said, buttoning his overcoat. "But it's better to be safe than sorry." Too late, I was sorry already. And the roach motel the good inspector suggested as a place to "keep a low profile" did nothing to uplift my spirits. "Don't look so glum," he commiserated, "it's only temporary."

"Yeah, right," I said, as he headed for the door.

Like life...

9

No sooner had Angus Duncan gone through the door than Florence Nightingale materialized with a "pain pill" and a glass of apple juice. I passed on the former, knocked off the latter and placed another order. The nurse was happy to oblige. Was there anything else "we" wanted? A TV set, a back rub, a little champagne and caviar? After all, it wasn't every day they had a "celebrity" on the ward.

"No, just a radio."

"I guess we're anxious to listen to our show," the nurse bubbled, as she bounced back into the room.

I gave her my best celebrity smile. "Anxious isn't the word." Try *apprehensive*. I couldn't wait to see how The Girl Wonder was going to stoop to the occasion. The lady in white bounced out the door and I inserted the Mickey Mouse earphones and tried to find 990 on the dial—which isn't as easy as it sounds. The "People's Network" spends so much of its zillion dollar budget for the care and feeding of paper-pushers there's not much left over for minor niceties like upgrading the signal to the point where anyone beyond the range of three blocks can actually tune it in. When I finally managed to accomplish this miracle I heard Garth Grenfell's oily tones break through a blanket of static with a sanitized version of the local news. A "fire of unknown origin" had destroyed an apartment at the Louis Riel Towers and one male resident was slightly injured. The tenant's name was being withheld "pending notification of (non-existent) relatives". When Garth wound up the bowdlerized news and announced the last segment of Crosstalk, the host's absence was attributed to the old reliable...

"...special assignment. But in his place we have a real treat for our twenty-six million listeners. So here she is folks, direct from an extended engagement in the control room, that charming, incurable romantic, Patricia St. John Hogg!"

"Taa, taaa!" The Girl Wonder's nasal soprano trumpeted into my incredulous ear. In considering every conceivable possibility the one that never occurred to me was that General Hogg would my throw *herself* into the breach, let alone provide her own fanfare!

"Aw gee, Patricia," her aide-de-camp simpered, "I'm sure glad you could come to our party."

"Me too, Garth, I love being invited to parties."

Say what?

"And, as a romantic, I'm sure you agree with me that birthdays are special occasions..."

So are funerals.

"I do, I do! I put on my silver bracelet, see..."

"Yes..."

"...and lined my eyes..."

"Um hum..."

"...and brought along my very best..."

"And what, dare I say, are you going to prepare for this morning's repast?"

"...menu. Well this is a dish...actually, I haven't thought up a fancy title (girlish giggle) but I'm open to offers."

I switched off the radio. It was too painful to listen to those two clowns sink what was left of my show. They had torpedoed the best program manager in the business because he hadn't given Grenfel a chance to compete for my job and now Tweedle Dum and Tweedle Dumber had a chance to strut their stuff what do they come up with? I still wasn't sure so I switched the radio back on and heard what sounded like static, but turned out to be frying fat.

"...it doesn't have to be crab," the Girl Wonder shouted over the hiss, "lobster bits will do. By the way Garth, there's a new imitation crab on the market that's just..."

"It's Japanese isn't it?"

"...fabulous. I don't know, but it looks just like..."

"How much of that—some people would say that looks like margarine..."

"...crab meat. No, never! This is..."

"..real butter, of course! And you've got about…"

"..an eighth of a cup here. Of course this is a fat free frying pan because we're so health conscious at the…"

"I think I'll just steal…"

"…DBC. See how quickly these shrimps are going from that sickly gray color…"

"…a little of this."

"…to a lovely, rosy…"

"Mmmm, this is great!"

"…plumpness. Do you really think so?"

"I do! I do! I just wish the listeners could smell this, Patricia!"

We can! We can! I switched off the radio again. Only to switch it back on, thirty seconds later. It was like trying to walk past a traffic accident without looking; an impossible exercise of self-control even when it *wasn't* your vehicle being dismantled by the "Jaws of Death". I turned off the radio for the last time and went to empty my bladder.

It hurt a bit to pee but at least there was no blood in my urine. Just in my mind. I was dying to find out what The Girl Wonder thought she was playing at but *The Julia Childish Show* had another half hour to run so I took a stroll down the hall to the visitor's area, where there was no radio, and picked up a superannuated *Time* magazine. The minutes dragged by. Finally, I looked at the clock and the farce was over. Time to report to my parole officer.

"Current Affairs.."

"Hi Patricia."

There was a moment of dead silence. "Val?"

"Got it in one."

"I don't believe it! How are you?"

"Oh, not too…"

"I'm sorry I haven't been down to see you yet, sweetie, but it's been absolute chaos around here this morning. Did you listen to the show?"

"Off and on."

"So what do you think, didn't Garth do an incredible job?"

"Yeah." *That's the word for it.* "What's with this birthday party business?"

"Oh, just something I came up with off the top." She laughed, modestly. "Did you know Crosstalk is six months old today?"

"No I didn't." *Time flies when you're having fun.* "Look Patricia, the reason

I'm calling..."

"Hold it a sec..." The line fell silent, followed by muffled banging and scraping. My producer came back on, sounding slightly out of breath. "Okay, go ahead."

"Where did you go?"

"Nowhere, I've just hooked up the tape machine."

"What the hell for?"

"I don't know, maybe I'll use it on tomorrow's show. Edited of course. People will want to know how you're doing."

"I thought I was supposed to be on 'special assignment'."

"Didn't you read the paper?"

Just the obits, to see if my name was there. "Not yet, why?"

"Your friend Riley couldn't pass up a scoop. Are *you* the one who told him about that call?"

"What makes you think he knows about it?"

"That Renegade creep—you know, the one who writes those long-winded editorials about police incompetence—mentioned it in his column."

"Well he didn't get it from me, I haven't spoken to Morgan in months. By the way, you'd better shut off that tape recorder; Duncan wants me to keep a low profile."

Silence. "You're not coming back to host the show?"

"Not right away, no."

My producer bore up amazingly well under this devastating blow. "Gee that's too bad, but I guess he knows best. Well, take care of yourself, Val..."

"Hold it! Don't you want to know where I'll be staying—in case you have to get in touch with me?"

"Oh. Sure. Let me get a pen." (Banging and scraping.) "Okay, shoot."

"I'll be staying at...say, have you turned off that tape recorder yet?"

"What? Oh. No, just a sec." (Banging and scraping.) "Okay, go ahead."

"The New Moon Motel."

"New Moon. Fine."

"You know where it is?"

"Sure, it's that dump on Market and Main where all the hookers hang out."

"That's the dump. But keep it to yourself. If you have to call me, ask for mister Miller."

"Who's he, the manager?"

"No, I'm registering under my real name, Isadore Miller."

"Got it: New Moon, ask for Miller. Well, it's been nice shmoozing with you…Izzy." She giggled. "And don't worry about the show, Garth and I will hold the fort."

"Who's going to produce?"

"I will. But I've recruited Lloyd to screen the calls and help out in the control room."

My spirits sank another notch. Lloyd Cringley was the station's designated rally killer. A veteran "team player" with three insignificant weaknesses—hitting, running and catching.

"No kidding," I muttered, "how's his cooking?"

"What?"

"I'll call you in a few days to see what's cooking."

"Oh. Sure. Keep in touch."

Because you'll be in touch—just not with me..

10

My conversation with The Girl Wonder had its usual uplifting effect. When the nurse brought me breakfast I felt like a condemned man eating his last meal—crow under glass. How the hell did Morgan Riley find out about that call? Silly question. He was a former Director of "Grapevine Central". Morgan probably had more spies on his staff that the C.I.A.

"Hello, Val."

I looked up and laughed out loud. Speak of the devil. "Morgan Riley," I said, rising to greet my second—and what would turn out to be my last—visitor. "Well, you're a sight for sore eyes." And I had the eyes to prove it. I hadn't seen the treacherous little weasel since he'd left me holding the bag at the DBC but he hadn't changed. He was still wearing the same rumpled Harris Tweed, droopy ginger mustache and hangdog expression. Morgan Riley always looked like he'd just lost his best friend—and I didn't qualify on either count. But if the editor of *The Daily Tabloid* was willing to take time from his busy schedule to visit me in my hour of need maybe I had misjudged him. "So," I said, pumping his limp paw, "what brings you down here?"

"My job."

I gave him back his hand. "What took you so long, Morgue? If you had come last night you could have gotten some dandy shots of me in a coma."

"I *was* here last night, they wouldn't let me see you."

I laughed out loud. "You're a fucking vulture, you know that?" My journalistic mentor smiled, sadly. Which is the only way the lugubrious little muckraker ever smiled. "Don't look so pleased with yourself, it wasn't a compliment."

He shrugged his narrow shoulders. "Vultures are pretty useful."

"Yeah, they keep the jungle clean. But I wouldn't want one as a pet." I was feeling a bit lightheaded so I sat down on the edge of the bed. "Since when did you start doing your own leg work?"

Morgan sat down in the chair across from me. "Since someone tried to kill my friend."

"Don't flatter yourself."

"Former colleague, then." He withdrew a small green notebook from his baggy coat pocket and held it up. "Do you want to tell me about it?"

"Why, so you can sell a few more papers?"

"It's what I do for a living, Val."

"Well *breathing* is what I do for a living, Morgan, so you'll pardon me if I don't jump at your generous offer to plaster my name, address and phone number in the 'Assassins Wanted' section of that snot rag you edit."

Morgan was stung to the quick. "You think I'd publish something that would put your life in danger?"

I shouldn't have been so hard on Angus Duncan; those rhetorical questions could be a bitch. "Well just what is it you expect me to reveal to your forty million readers?"

He shrugged his narrow shoulders, withdrew a ballpoint from his inside jacket pocket, crossed his pigeon legs and opened his notebook. "How about starting with that call to your show."

"What call is that?" The old news hound didn't reply, just sat, pen poised, a mournful look in his basset hound eyes. The silence yawned like the Grand Canyon. I was the first to blink. "Okay, who told you about it?"

"You know I can't reveal my sources, Val."

"Well, *excuuuuse* me. I wouldn't want you to violate your journalistic integrity. What's the life of an insignificant human being compared to the sanctity of that fish wrap of yours?"

Morgan looked genuinely hurt. "You act as if I was responsible for your ending up," he waved his arm around, "in here."

In a way he was. If Morgan hadn't gotten the ball rolling by giving me my first radio gig I'd still be a low profile singer/songwriter not a semi-famous talk jock. Not that my fairy godfather had to drag me into limelight kicking and screaming. When "Muddy Rivers" landed the graveyard shift on the city's number one country music station he thought he'd died and gone to hillbilly heaven. Spinning discs from midnight to dawn left the evenings free to play the odd pub gig and the days free to pen the (very) odd tune. Then, one frosty February 14th, old man Fate delivers this comic Valentine; the kind that blows up in your face. Just as I'm signing off, Morgan's voice comes over my headset with an urgent request. Stan "The Morning Man" Kozak hasn't shown up, would I mind filling in? I'm about as anxious to host a talk show as I am to audition for the Royal Winnipeg Ballet but it's an offer I can't refuse. And the stars are favorable: *You'll feel romantic, Virgo, not only because of this special day but because of letters, calls and cards that assure you of love. As your personal horizons expand, judgment and intuition are on target.* My friendly convenience store astrologer had never lied to me before—more than once a day—so I grabbed the nearest pseudonym for cover and took the plunge, expecting to lay the kind of egg that would make Hiroshima seem like a silent fart. But my laid-back don't-give-a-shit style must have been a refreshing change from the hyperthyroid case I was filling in for because the housewives seemed to dig my act. Even my laconic producer was impressed. "I don't know what you're doing in there," he tells me during a station break, "but keep it up; Stan's fallen off the wagon, you're going to have to fill in all week." Stan The Man never managed to climb back onto the wagon, the "week" turned into a month, the month into a year, the year into a career and the nightlife, which, in retrospect, doesn't seem like such a bad life, was no longer my life.

"Look I'll make a deal with you, Morgan, I'll spill my guts if you tell me everything *you* know about NAAPALM."

"Sounds fair."

Not any more it didn't. If the shifty horse trader was ready to lay his cards on the table he was probably holding a dead hand. But it was too late to close the barn door so I bit the bullet and let him pump the well dry (to mix a few metaphors).

"Okay, your turn, what do you know about NAAPALM?"

Morgan retracted his poison pen and closed his notebook. "It's jellied gasoline used to clear away ground cover in jungle warfare. The U.S. military employed it extensively in Vietnam."

"Very amusing, professor. Now if you're finished your lecture on military history can we get down to local warfare? What do you know about the North American Aboriginal Peoples Army of Liberation of Manitoba?"

"Just what I've read in the papers."

I waited for the punch line.

He kept me waiting.

I looked at him, incredulously. "Are you serious?"

"I haven't been able to dig up a single person who even heard of NAAPALM until judge Brown was killed. It's probably a figment of someone's diseased imagination."

"Yeah, *yours*," I spat. "For Christ sake Morgan, if you don't even know if this so-called terrorist army exists how could you publish their bogus communiqués?"

"It's news."

"Really? And I thought it might be propaganda!"

"Could be," he said, evenly. "But why would an aboriginal organization want to eliminate the best friend they ever had. A more likely scenario is that some skinhead figured he could kill two birds with one stone; put a halt the Native Justice Commission and lay the blame on the native people. *See, you try to help these savages and this is the thanks you get.*"

"So you figured you'd help this sicko out?"

"I'm not helping anybody; I'm just reporting the news. Look, Val, even if those communiqués *are* a red herring, or a sick joke, or whatever, they could still have been written by the person responsible for these bombings."

"And who do you think this joker might be?"

He shrugged. "Who knows? Some disgruntled failure who thinks he's got a score to settle."

"With me and a guy I didn't even know?"

Morgan smiled, sadly. "Don't take it personally, you're just a symbol."

"Of what—apathy? You know me, Morgan, I've never read an editorial page in anger. Or in any other state of mind. What could I possibly have in common with the late Judge Brown?"

"Celebrity. The higher the profile the more tempting the target. Val Virgo and "Honest Bob" Brown are pretty big fish for our little pond. Two North End boys who made good."

Good what, I wondered, as Morgan packed his notebook slouched out the door, *bomb fodder?* I moved to the window and looked out at the run down area in which the hospital was situated. It had begun to snow and the flakes were running down the window like tears. Why me? I wasn't an activist; I was an entertainer. Live and let live, that was my motto. Unfortunately, someone wasn't too happy with that arrangement. But whom could I have so gravely offended? On the others side of the parking lot I could see the gray silhouette of Rehabilitation Center, where my fellow survivor, the mutilated mail carrier, was holed up. What was I whining about? A paid vacation from a job I could barely stomach? A few aches and pains? I was the luckiest man on the face of the earth. According to all reports Leon Coleman was a basket case. And he had just been an "innocent bystander". I should pay the poor bastard a visit when the warden gave me my walking papers. We could trade war stories. In sign language...

Next day the warden gave me my walking papers. Ah, freedom, it was great to be alive, upright and breathing air that didn't smell like Javex. The DBC had neglected to send a limousine—an oversight, no doubt—but the sun was shining, the air was crisp and there was fresh blanket of snow on the ground so I decided to return to the scene of the crime on the old heel and toe. Not that I had much choice. It was so long since I'd used mass transit that I wouldn't have known where to catch a bus, let alone which one to take. I could have called a cab but why squander my diminished resources on avoidable luxuries?

That must have been the philosophy of my landlord who had belatedly hired a minimum wage peon as a security guard. Unlike the DBC's geriatric guardian of the inner sanctum this teenage iron-pumper demanded "some I.D." Since I was deficient in that department, albeit due to circumstances beyond my control, he refused to let me up to my pad. Celebrity indeed! After several frustrating minutes of fruitless explanation I finally succeeded in talking him into calling the building manager, an oily sycophant who fell all over himself apologizing, not only for the "misunderstanding" about my identity but the "inconvenience" of almost being blown to hell. The management had authorized him to upgrade me to a more "desirable" unit at no increase in rent. When I said thanks, but no thanks, the color drained from his flabby face. But when I made it clear that I had no intention of launching a billion dollar lawsuit against the international conglomerate that signed his paycheck—that I'd simply made other arrangements—and the poor guy looked so relieved I thought he was going to kiss me. Instead he offered to pay for a van to move what was left of my furniture and belongings.

"Thanks, but I think my car is big enough for the job," I said. I was wrong; a shopping bag would have been big enough. What the mad bomber hadn't managed to destroy, the fire department had taken care of. The prodigal deejay would be traveling light—for a change. I stowed my gear in the back seat of my faithful companion and unplugged the block heater. The old girl roared into action without a whimper of protest. Shit box, indeed! With a minor transplant my vintage chariot would outlive Neil Bannerman's muscle-bound gas guzzler. As I headed across town to my new digs I felt like a man reborn. I thought of punching in a little traveling music but decided my mobile sound system should remain in hibernation until I could afford a new battery. This unseasonable weather could evaporate as suddenly as my personal possessions—and my former life.

The New Moon Motel (a.k.a. Hooker Hilton) was on the corner of Market and Main, a stone's throw from the Public Safety Building. Which was, no doubt, why Duncan had recommended it. The "luxury" room he had booked hadn't been made up yet from the last customer so I stowed my gear with the desk clerk and hit the street to fill the sock and underwear gap from the few surviving wholesale/retail outlets in what had once been "the garment district". In the 50s Winnipeg's thriving rag trade was shredded by the Asian Tigers and the area West of Main Street, bounded by Portage Avenue on the South and the Canadian Pacific Railway on the North, became a ghost town of boarded-up buildings inhabited by mice and decorated by pigeon dropping. Then, in the 90s, the baby boomer descendants of the sweatshop owners were infected by the nostalgia bug and "Old Market Square" rose from the ashes. Since I had nothing but time on my hands, and had never given the transformation more than a passing glance, I picked up a pair of shades at the local Shoppers Drug Mart and took a leisurely stroll around the terminally quaint Turn-of-the-Century village of sand-blasted buildings, fake-Parisian bistros and the odd Disco.

It was almost noon when I got back from my sightseeing tour but my room still wasn't ready (they usually rented them by the hour) so I picked up a *Tabloid* from the lobby dispenser and ducked into the beverage room. It was like stepping into a time machine. Twenty years since I'd played this zoo and nothing had changed. I took a table near the back wall and ordered a Sleeman's (draft) and a double order of perogies. "Don't forget the fried onions," I said, as the waiter lumbered off. I opened the paper but couldn't read it. I removed my shades but it was still too dark to read anything but the headline. VIRGO THIRD BOMBING VICTIM!

Tell me something I don't know, Morgan. I stashed the paper and looked around. Déjà vu all over again. Those low-rent hookers and high-capacity elbow-benders could have been the same zombies I'd been ignored by in my callow youth. Sitting there in the semi-dark, staring into space, day after day, year after year, preserved in alcohol like the pickled eggs on the bar. I felt a twinge of the same apprehension as when I'd first stepped onto the stage—actually it was just a space they had cleared for dancing—and looked out at those stony brown faces. I felt like General Custer. But after playing a few gigs I discovered those ugly customers were no rougher than any other pub crowd. Red, white, yellow, black or beige—dedicated drinkers don't bother looking up from their brew, let alone throw beer bottles, when "entertainment nightly" hits a clinker. Not that I was entirely ignored. When Muddy Rivers switched on his amp everyone sat up and took notice—it was the signal to talk a little louder.

The waiter arrived with my beer. The perogies were "coming". So was Christmas. I handed him a five spot and he folded it lengthwise, slipped it between two thick fingers—beside the other bills that were radiating from his ham fist like a Japanese fan—and clicked out my change from the metal dispenser dangling from his beer belly. I tossed a quarter onto his tray, he waddled off, and I raised my beer to my thirsty lips. But I didn't get to drink it.

"Excuse me."

I looked up to see a buck-toothed blond staring down her long thin nose. She looked like a "professional"; not a hooker but a member of a less reputable profession, a social worker maybe. She was wearing a suede suit, a beaded headband and a pissed-off expression. "Those men are bothering me," she said, nodding at two bleary-eyed patrons on the other side of the room.

I clucked my tongue. "Some people have no manners," I said sympathetically, and took a swig of my beer.

"Is that all you're going to do? Just sit there and drink beer?"

I looked at her. "What do you expect me to do?"

"Your job."

"Which is?"

She hesitated. "Aren't you the...bouncer?"

It was the best laugh I'd had since someone had tried to blow my ass to kingdom come. "I hate to disappoint you lady but you're talking to a card-carrying pacifist."

"Yes, I can see that," she said, with a derisive snort.

Suddenly, the penny dropped. "I know you won't believe this," I said, with a sheepish smile, "but I walked into a door."

I was right; she didn't believe it—but still considered my unsavory company preferable to the alternative.

"Do you mind if I share your table?"

"Be my guest." I rose and pulled out a chair.

She misconstrued courtesy for enthusiasm. "Don't get the wrong idea, I just don't want those two hassling me."

"Hey, I'm a happily married man."

"Where have I heard that before?" she said, putting her attaché case on one chair and her well-clad butt on another. The waiter arrived with my two orders of perogies—each on a separate Styrofoam plate with a paper thimble of sour cream. No fried onions were in sight. As he placed them in front of me I turned to my uninvited guest. "What are you having?"

"I'll order for myself, thanks." While she wrestled with the problem the waiter stared into space with an expression that indicated he was about to die of boredom, if emphysema didn't get him first. "I'll have a glass of ginger ale," his customer finally decided. "And a plate of those," she added, with a furtive glance at my perogies.

"With fried onions," I said, as the waiter moved off.

"No," my companion cried after him, "I don't want..."

"Don't worry," I said, cutting her off, "he won't bring any. Besides they're not for you. They're for me. These are for you." I pushed one of my orders at her.

She gave me a scathing look. "Look, Mr. ahhh.."

"Miller," I said. "Isadore Miller—but you can call me Izzy."

"How do you do, Izzy, I'm Elizabeth Borden." She didn't invite me to call her Lizzie. "You're not a lawyer are you, Izzy?"

I laughed. "Well, that's a step up from bouncer but no, I'm not a lawyer. What made you think I was."

She hesitated. "Well, in spite of those bruises on your face, you don't look like the kind of person who ordinarily spends his lunch hour in a place like this."

"A person like you, you mean?"

She didn't return my smile. "I didn't come here to eat lunch, I'm looking for a client."

"I take it he's an Indian?"

"Yes, he's a member of the First Nations. Most of my clients are. Do you know that half the prison population in this province is aboriginal?"

"No kidding," I said, as if it was a closely guarded secret.

"Unbelievable isn't it? A white-collar criminal steals millions and gets a slap on the wrist and some native kid steals a package of cigarettes and is treated like public enemy number one. No vocational training, no conjugal visits—the penal system in this country is barbaric. When I think of the primitive conditions up at Stony Mountain it makes me ill!" She did look a trifle feverish. "Can you imagine what a bright young man with all sorts of untapped potential must feel like sitting in a six by nine foot room watching the best years of his life go down the drain?"

"I think so."

"I doubt it," Lizzie lawyer said with a contemptuous look. Then she seemed to have second thoughts. "You've never done time have you, Izzy?"

I shook my head. "Not in the penitentiary."

"Then you can't possibly know what it's like."

"Look, I know Stony Mountain isn't exactly the Holiday Inn but let's face it, Liz, there aren't too many candidates for the Nobel Peace Prize up there."

"That's a typical white, middle-class attitude. If you square Johns would visit a few penitentiaries you'd see that most of your so-called criminals are no different than anyone else. More people are killed in car accidents than in prisons. Statistically, you're safer on the inside than you are on the street."

"Especially this street," I said with a smile.

She opened her mouth but didn't have time to put me in my place. The waiter had arrived with her ginger ale. "Sixty five cents," he said, placing it in front of her. I reached for the money that was lying on the table but Lizzie Lawyer shot me a dirty look so I let the sleeping bills lie. She opened her bag, removed a change purse, counted out the exact change, and handed it to the waiter. His face betrayed no sign of disappointment. Beer waiters at the New Moon did not expect to retire on their gratuities. At least not until the night shift, when the patrons were too bleary eyed to distinguish a toonie from a loonie. Ginger ale drinkers, on any shift, were a dead loss. Fortunately you only got one every decade or so. He slipped the coins into his apron and moved off.

My luncheon companion took a sip of her drink and resumed her lecture. "Take this boy I'm looking for. He didn't show up for his trial because he couldn't get a ride into town from the reservation. So the judge revokes his bail, issues a bench warrant and if I don't get to my client before the cops he'll end up in the PSB lock-up waiting for a new trial date, which won't be for another six months. And that's more time than he'd get if he were found guilty. So he'll probably cop a plea even though he has a perfectly good defense." She took another sip of ginger ale and continued, with renewed energy. "And we wonder why the aboriginal community is on the war path!"

"Speaking of which..."What do you know about this NAAPALM outfit, Liz?"

She looked at me and smirked. "Only that it doesn't exist. Whoever's behind these bombings is as white as you are."

"What makes you say that?"

"Experience. I'm not saying my clients are angels but when they commit a crime of violence it's invariably a crime of passion; a spontaneous explosion of rage born of frustration and triggered by alcohol. Cold-blooded murder is just not in the aboriginal nature. Besides, Judge Brown was hardly an *enemy* of the aboriginal community."

"Was he a good judge?"

Lizzie lawyer shrugged. "He wasn't on the bench long enough to find out," she said, eyeing the plate of perogies.

"Go ahead, they're just getting cold."

She picked one up, gingerly, dipped it into the sour cream and bit into it. "Mmmm, these are pretty good."

"They're even better with fried onions," I said. "Of course, onions for lunch might not be such a good idea for someone in your profession."

"You still didn't tell me what your profession is," she said, licking sour cream from her fingers.

No, but I've bought enough time to invent one. "I work for DBC Radio, I'm a producer." Taking my cue from Mark Twain, who said no one had a good enough memory to be a successful liar, I skated as close to the edge of truth as possible.

And Lizzie Borden seemed delighted with my choice. "Then you must know Val Virgo!"

"We've met," I wheezed, over the chunk of perogie that was lodged in my throat.

Lizzie Lawyer clutched my sleeve in a death grip. "Do you think you could introduce me? I have a great guest for his show!"

"Well, I don't know him that well..."

"Speak of the devil," my new fan said, cutting me off. She released my sleeve, looked across the room and waved. "Reg, over here!"

I followed her gaze to a surly looking dude with long black braids who looked vaguely familiar. When he caught sight of my luncheon companion his surly expression got more so. Nevertheless, he headed toward our table and by the time he arrived I knew where I had seen him before. "We were just talking about you," Liz Borden said and proceeded to introduce us. "Reg Johnson, Izzy Miller."

"We've met," he said, crushing my hand in his bear paw. "How's it going Muddy, long time no see."

Liz Borden looked at me, strangely.

"Muddy Rivers is a stage name," I said. "I played this toilet a couple of centuries ago. And Dakota Slim here was my sideman. Of course he was carrying a few less kilos in those days. And I'm talking below the neck. Who's your hair stylist, Tonto, think she can squeeze me in for a blow dry?"

Liz Borden glared at me. "Braids are traditional among the native people. It's not a question of style, they have religious significance."

"No kidding, and I always thought old Slim here was the village atheist."

Lizzie Borden looked like she was about to reach for a hatchet. "Look here Mr. Miller—or Rivers—or whatever your name..."

"Give it a rest, Liz, he's just yanking your chain." Reg shot me a *see what we poor Indians have to put up with* look and lowered his ass into a chair. "So what brings you to this neck of the woods, Goldberg? You on some kind of nostalgia trip? Or just slumming?"

"He's getting background for a radio show," Liz Borden said, leaping aboard a wishful conclusion. "That's why I called you over, Reg, Izzy works for the DBC. He knows Val Virgo!"

My old sideman looked at me with new respect. "No kidding. Just how *well* do you know Virgo, Goldstein?"

"Berg. I don't really know him, I've just seen him around the building."

"Still," Liz Borden said to her protégé, "I'm sure once you explain the wonderful work we're doing he'll agree to have you on the show." She turned back to me, her eyes shining. "Reg is the executive director of the Core Area Initiative Outreach Project."

"No kidding."

"Never heard of it have you?" Reg said, evenly.

I smiled, lamely. "Well, it's been a long time since..."

"Don't bother to apologize," Liz Borden broke in. "Nobody knows about the work we do and nobody cares. That's why we need the publicity being on Virgo's show would give us."

"Just what *do* you do?" I said, turning to her.

"Liaise."

"I beg your pardon?"

"Liaise. We're a liaison group between the native ex-cons and the straight world. We help them upgrade their skills, find jobs and generally adjust to society. We think of ourselves as bridge builders."

"Sounds like a worthy cause," I said, doing my best to look sincere. "But I don't think it's Virgo's cup of tea. Besides, his new show doesn't have much of an audience."

"Yeah, it's pretty lame," Reg said. "I don't think I want to be interviewed by this Virgo character. He sounds like an asshole." Liz Borden's face fell. "Still," her pet Indian said, throwing her a bone, "I'm prepared to meet the guy." He surveyed me with his pouchy black eyes. "Think you can set something up, Epstein?"

"*Gold*stein. Why don't we discuss it over a brew? What kind of ale you quaffing these days, hoss?"

"Ginger."

Well, it wasn't just his appearance that had changed. My old sideman used to *spill* more than I drank—and had the battle scars to show for it. Not only the broken nose but the circular red welts on his forearm that were a result of a parlor game Reg and his native buddies used to play to see who'd buy the next round. They would each hold a burning cigarette a fraction of an inch from each other's bare arm and the first to yank his arm away was the loser. Reg drank a lot of free beer in those days. And the more he drank the meaner he got. Sober, he was a student of philosophy who would quote St. Thomas Aquinas. Drunk, he was a "Geronimo."

"Reg is a recovering alcoholic," Liz Borden informed me, happily. Reg looked at her like a mosquito he was dying to swat but she didn't notice—her attention had flitted off the other side of the room. "Excuse me, I think I see my client." We sat there watching her scurry across the room, collar a good-looking, bronze-skinned kid and start reading him the riot act. It didn't seem to have the desired effect. He didn't hang his head or shuffle his feet but looked her in the eye with a cocky sneer. Lizzie Lawyer was the one who looked flustered. From the girlish flush on her cheek I got the impression she was rather enamored of her handsome young client.

"Alright Virgo, the axe lady's out of earshot, you can drop the act."

I flashed my old sideman a guilty smile. "So you're on to me?"

"I may be dumb, hoss, but I'm not deaf. I could recognize that thing you call a voice with cotton in my ears. Which, frankly, is the way it sounds best. I don't know how you bluffed your way into the DBC but you should have quit while you were ahead. You were never much of a picker, hoss, but you've got a way with words and you know a good tune when you steal it."

"I see you've been following my career."

"When I was in P.A there wasn't much else to do."

I didn't have to ask what he was doing in Prince Albert, Saskatchewan, because there was only one thing *to* do there. Time. "I didn't know you were in P.A."

"Where do you think I met the axe lady, at the Winter Club?"

"How long were you inside?"

"What's the difference? A day is too long."

"Well, I see you two have been doing some catching up," Liz Borden said, re-arriving at the table. "Look Reg, I've got to run. Why don't you take Izzy down to the Project and show him around. When he sees the wonderful work you do he might not be so quick to dismiss our idea."

"*Your* idea," Reg grunted, levering his three hundred pound frame up from the table. "But Goldfarb here looks like he could use the exercise." He looked down at me from a great height. "Unless he's got other plans?"

"My dance card is wide open," I said, rising to the challenge. "Lead the way, Hulking Buffalo."

As we headed for the door the waiter arrived at our table with Lizzie Borden's order of perogies—smothered in fried onions.

11

The Core Area Outreach Project was a ten-minute walk, on the wild side, from the New Moon. While Old Market Square was getting a facelift the Main Street "Strip"—just a few blocks east—was getting its teeth knocked out. Central Main hadn't really changed just deteriorated a little further. The greasy spoons were boarded up, the cut-rate clothing stores were vacant, the movie theaters were ancient history and even the video arcades, porn parlors and poolrooms that had replaced them, were vacant. It was like walking through a war zone. The only businesses that were still thriving were pawnshops and beverage rooms. As the door to the one were passing opened the odor of stale beer wafted past my nostrils and a patron staggered onto the sidewalk and fell on his face. "Shouldn't we help him?" I said, as my Indian guide steered me around the obstruction.

"We *are* helping him. By minding our own business."

"Not a very Christian attitude."

"I'm not a Christian."

Come to think of it, neither was I. As if to remind me of this deficiency the marquee of the Gospel Lighthouse Mission announced that Jesus had died for my sins. Well, it was possible. But how could a Middle Eastern Jew have died for the sins of my fellow pedestrians? When Joshua of Nazareth was alive and preaching "sin" didn't exist in this part of the planet. It had to be imported from Europe, together with firearms, firewater, measles, syphilis, all the other wonders of Western Civilization. My train of thought was derailed by the voice of a toothless purveyor of venereal disease. "Hey handsome," she called out to a prospective customer, "want to buy me a drink?" A clean-cut kid with the chiseled features of a young warrior turned around. I assumed that when he laid his piercing black eyes on the bow-legged hag who had made the offer he would resume his journey at a quickened pace. But, to my surprise, he accepted her generous offer.

"Missed your chance, hoss" Reg said, as the odd couple disappeared into a beverage room.

"Not my type".

"How about her?"

He was referring to a willowy maiden who was tottering towards us on six-inch spikes. This fawn-like creature had the kind of face to which only a Renaissance Master could have done justice. She'd painted her lips candy-apple red, smeared gaudy rouge on her sculpted cheekbones and coated her eyelashes with an inch of black mascara but even this clown's mask couldn't hide her natural beauty. Her eyes were as black as coal, her hair like raw silk, her skin alabaster. Where did the word "redskin" come from? I wondered, as I surveyed the passing parade. There was every skin tone from polished ivory to burnished walnut but nothing even close to red. Nor could I discern any other common characteristic. In this aboriginal army, pockmarked gargoyles marched arm and arm with sloe-eyed Madonnas. The old masters and the Picassos all hung together in this Main Street Gallery—to avoid hanging separately, no doubt.

We had reached the CPR underpass, whose pitted concrete walls were spray-painted with graffiti. *THE POPE SMOKES DOPE. KILL THE PIGS. MAKE THE RICH PAY.* For what, designer bombs? Who had authored these uplifting messages? Teenage Maoists; sexually abused teens; paranoid psychopaths? Or one or two of those placid-looking dudes loitering in front of that bombed-out building? Who knew what cauldron of repressed hatred was simmering beneath those calm facades? "Well, this is it," Reg said, stopping at a storefront office.

I laughed out loud. "You're office is in Hymie's?" Times had changed. For half a century the best corned beef on rye west of Montreal had been served on these premises; now it was watery coffee in Styrofoam cups. My "recovering" guide poured several gallons of the highly sugared brew into his expanded torso as he filled me in on the organization of which he was now Executive Director. Contrary to what Ms. Borden had led me to believe "The Project" was neither restricted to aboriginals nor ex-convicts. The steady stream of "clients" that flowed through the door was made up of every age, race and background—as was the largely voluntary work force. Apart from

Reg's subsistence salary no one got a nickel. But the look in the eyes and on the faces of the workers—all former "street people"—indicated they were amply rewarded for their labors, which included teaching the illiterate to read, the chronically unemployed to take a job interview and giving those with a "past" hope for the future. Lizzie Lawyer may have been wrong on the details but she was right about one thing, Reg's work deserved public support. And I felt shitty about not being able to offer it. "Forget it," he said, tilting back in his creaking chair. "I was serious about not wanting to go on your show. The last thing I need is a bunch of do-gooders breathing down my neck and sniffing my asshole."

"But your friend said…"

"The ax lady is not my friend," he said, coming to earth with a thud. "She's a poor little rich bitch who thinks thieves and rapists are colorful—as long as they're not *her* color; a pampered Wasp chick who wants to be an Indian princess. Can you imagine what kind of impression she makes walking into court wearing that ridiculous fucking headband? Her clients start out with two strikes against them and *she's* the third."

"Aren't you being a little hard on her, hoss, she's just trying to help you cats."

"With that kind of help and six bits you can get a cup of coffee at Tim Horton. Take that kid who didn't bother showing up for his trial? You see the look on the little cocksucker's face when she was *helping* him? You think he has any respect for his so-called lawyer? Or himself? You can't help anyone who won't help himself, Smoke. Why should I pick some drunken Indian up off the sidewalk, drag him down here and pour soup down his throat. So he can crawl into another bottle the minute he's out the door? I've got better things to do with my time. I'm not a bleeding heart; I'm an ex-con. And you can't con a con. So we've been shit on for a couple centuries in our own country. Drowning our sorrow in vanilla extract isn't going to solve the problem. Neither is running to white chick lawyers, picketing the legislature for bigger welfare checks or mailing bombs to judges."

It was my cue. "What do you know about this NAAPALM outfit, Reg?"

He snorted derisively. "As much as I know about the tooth fairy."

"You saying there's no such animal?"

He shrugged his huge shoulders. "Who knows, maybe there's a tooth fairy." He took another slug of caffeine. "But finding a dime under my pillow isn't what I call convincing evidence."

"You think those letters to the Tabloid are bogus?"

"Frankly, I think that Renegade character might have written them himself."

"You're not serious?"

"Stranger things have happened."

"Why in the hell would he do a thing like that?"

"Sell papers, give the cops a hard time—our friend Renegade isn't exactly Angus Duncan's biggest fan."

"You have any idea who he is?"

"Do you?" I had my suspicions but wasn't about to voice them. "No, I don't know who he is," Reg said, after another sip of his syrupy coffee, "just *what* he is. Another shit disturbing wannabe like the axe lady."

I laughed. "You really shouldn't call her that, hoss, Lizzie Borden was acquitted."

He snorted contemptuously. "So was O.J. Simpson. Juries aren't infallible."

"You speaking from personal experience?"

There was a pregnant pause. Then he shook his head. "I copped."

"To what?"

"Voluntary manslaughter."

"Was it a bum wrap?"

Another pregnant pause. "Hard to say."

I waited for the punch line.

My old sideman looked me in the eye and delivered it in a dispassionate voice. "I killed my father."

What a coincidence—so did I. According to my mother. When I dropped out of medical school and hit the pub circuit with my high school buddy "the wild Indian".

12

There's only one thing more depressing than coming home to an empty apartment at the end of the working day—coming home to a grungy motel room in the middle of a non-working one. As I ran the gauntlet of peeling doors in search of the one with my number on it I was accompanied by odor of stale cigarettes, cheap perfume and the ghosts of all the low-rent hookers and traveling salesmen who'd worn a threadbare path down the middle of the maroon carpet. The door to my room was ajar and there was a whining noise coming from inside. I approached cautiously and looked in. A wiry chick with arms like a lightweight contender wheeling a vacuum cleaner around like she had something against the furniture. I had to yell to get her attention. "Do you think you could you make my room up a little earlier tomorrow morning?"

She didn't turn. "Some want early, some want late, I can't make everybody happy."

"No, but I'm easy to please."

She looked at me over her shoulder.

I gave her a winning smile.

She eyed me suspiciously and kept on pumping.

I hung up my jacket, took a plastic glass from her cart and poured a couple fingers of ice-breaker from the bottle I'd picked up on my shopping trip. "Join me?" I said, holding the glass aloft.

"Why," she grunted, "you coming apart?"

I laughed. "As a matter of fact I am. But I can be fixed—with a little help from a friend."

Her grin turned to a scowl. "Look, mister, I'm just here to clean so don't get any funny..."

"Please, I'm a happily married man."

She snorted, skeptically, but shut off her machine. "Well, maybe just one."

"It's twelve oh five and good to be alive!"

I forced my eyes open. I was lying on top of the bedspread, fully clothed, my nostrils swollen shut, my tongue like something at the bottom a butcher's showcase. "Just one," my drinking companion had said. One *quart*, she meant. Still it was a sound investment. Not only did Dolores agree to make up my room first thing in the morning but had bought the "undercover cop" story. It had been touch and go for a while. She assumed I was a truck driver and when I disabused of this notion she asked the obvious question.

"Well, I'm not really working right now, Dolores."

"So why do you get up so early."

"Force of habit, I'm a...farmer."

"Yeah, I'll bet. Who beat the shit out of you, a cow?"

I smiled lamely. "I fell off a tractor."

"What are you planting, snow?" Dolores, the chambermaid, could have given Angus Duncan lessons on breaking down an alibi. She was studying my battered visage like it was on a Post Office wall. "I have a feeling I've met you before, your face is familiar."

So was hers—familiar but unremarkable, like her North End accent. Then it hit me, it wasn't my face she found familiar it was my *voice*! It was the moment the moment of truth—time to blow a truly inspired cloud of smoke up her keester. I walked to the door, looked down the hall, both ways, turned back to the room and lowered my voice to conspiratorial whisper. "Can you keep a secret, Dolores?"

Not only did she agree to keep it but to leave one of her long blond hairs between the door and the jamb, when she'd finished making up my room, so I'd know if I'd had any uninvited visitors. "Just like TV," she grinned, wheeling her cart out the door.

Sure is, partner—let's just hope the series isn't canceled in mid-season.

"If you want to smile don't touch that dial!"

I didn't; I touched the "off" button. Silence descended like a shroud. I reached over and switched on the imitation bronze lamp that was bolted to the bedside table. A forty-watt bulb cast a yellow glow over the gloom.

I propped myself up on my elbows and surveyed my new home. *What a dump!* I swung my leg over the side of the bed and sat up. *Bad move.* When the pounding behind my eyeballs subsided to a dull throb I limped to the bathroom, emptied my bursting bladder and refilled it with lukewarm water straight from the tap. I came back into the room, killed the last ounce of scotch, tossed the dead soldier into the wastebasket and caught sight of Dracula staring at me above the writing table. Wedged in the corner of the mirror was a faded postcard that was supposed to depict the typical *New Moon* room. The chasm between the glossy photo and the shabby reality was as wider than the Grand Canyon. The paint was peeling from the cinder block walls, the chenille bedspreads had gray stains (I tried not to speculate on their origin) and the rest of the decor was early K Mart. For some reason they had given me a room with two beds. Above my unrumpled bed there was a rectangular frame containing a few daubs of white pigment on black velvet that was supposed to pass for a winter landscape. The same scene, in green, orange and blue, hung over the other bed. Spring no doubt. If a friend took the room next door we'd have the seasons covered.

I moved across the room picked up the remote and clicked on the television set. Maybe there was some breaking news on the bomb front. There wasn't. But a cold front was on its way from Saskatchewan. The weather was going to take a turn for the worse—twenty below zero with no relief in sigh.

The story of my life.

I switched off the set, stripped to my underwear, crawled between the paper-thin sheets and closed my eyes. But I couldn't fall sleep. My mind was racing and my heart was throbbing in my ears. *Dum, dip, dum, dip, dum, dip…* what kept it going like that? Hour after hour, day after day, year after year…when you emerged from the womb the doctor gave you a jump start and then you were on your own…like the Energizer Bunny…until the battery ran down… or… The thought that someone tried to short my circuit clutched me like an icy hand, sent a chill down my spine and squeezed the air out of my lungs. If not for a lucky accident I wouldn't be lying in motel room but a mortuary. And no one would give a rat's ass. I'd sink like a stone without causing so much as a ripple on the surface. A week after I was in the ground no one would remember I'd ever walked the earth. I had no wife, no kids…yet *someone* cared enough about my existence to bring it to an abrupt conclusion.

Could Morgan be right about this "celebrity" business? John Lennon,

William Marantz

John F. Kennedy, Mr. Justice Robert Brown and Val Virgo—what's wrong with this picture? According to three semi-reliable sources NAAPALM was a figment of someone's sick imagination—a red herring dragged across the path by some psycho with a personal score to settle. But whom could I have so greatly offended? I'd probably die of old age before Angus Duncan blundered across the answer. Twiddling my thumbs in the no-tell motel waiting for "The Bull" to get his ass in gear was not a prospect to which I was looking forward. Still, Inspector Shreck said I should lay low, not roll over and play dead. Perhaps it was time for the "investigative reporter" to do a little investigating. Hey, there's a first time for everything...

Part Three
The Merry Widow Waltz

Fritz Finkelman was *enjoying a private joke as he sipped his coffee and browsed through the morning paper. According to the Tabloid Virgo's life had been saved by his cat. Fritz smiled, ironically. "One cat less," his father had said when Fritz tearfully told him of an atrocity two playful German soldiers had perpetrated under the guise of target practice. One cat less. That's probably what the judge thought when he imposed that life sentence. Fritz had offered to plead guilty to manslaughter, and serve five years, but the Crown Attorney had wanted to make a name for himself. It was a familiar story, sacrificing an insignificant Jew to satisfy his own ambition. Fritz would never deliberately injure any innocent creature, let alone a human being, but once you were branded a "murderer" you were no longer considered a human being but an animal to be put in a cage. And tamed. Even after you were released, your life was not your own. They put a collar around your ankle so they can drag you back to the kennel if you so much as piddled in the street. But you can't tame a cat.*

Fritz Finkelman had slipped his chain. Which was no great accomplishment. He'd been living by his wits since he was twelve years old. Young Failik Finkelman had survived the slave labor camp, while older and stronger men had perished. And on the "death march" he'd escaped into the woods and lived off the land, eating frozen sugar beets and other delicacies, until Liberation. Half a century later and he was still a fugitive—a stranger in a strange land. You were only safe among your own kind—and sometimes not even then. A Jew who turned on a fellow Jew was worse than a "goy", the lowest of the low, but there were such creatures on the face of the earth. Jewish "leaders" who cooperated with the Nazis and Jewish "Kapos" who were more brutal than their anti-Semitic masters, pious hypocrites and cold-blooded opportunists who, on the day of liberation, had been slaughtered by the hefflings like the pigs they were. If you couldn't trust your own brother whom could you trust?

An oppressed people had to stick together in order to survive. That was something Fritz admired about the Indians. In the fur business Fritz had dealt with Indian trappers, who weren't bound by the game laws, and had discovered, to his surprise, that they were much more "haimish" than their white counterparts. The Indians were the "Jews" of North America. They were not only more intelligent, sensitive and humane than their Anglo Saxon counterparts they had a better sense of humor. Gallows humor. "The North American Aboriginal Peoples Army of Liberation of Manitoba". Perfect! The Indians had it worse than the Jews. The Jews weren't a "visible" minority. A Canadian born Jew could become invisible by simply changing his name. Like the big shot radio personality who was in the news. Even if you weren't born in this country you could become invisible—if you lost your accent and changed your job. In the old country you didn't have that luxury; a tailor stayed a tailor and baker stayed a baker. A Canadian could change jobs like he changed undershirts—the old one gets "dirty" you put on a clean one.

13

I parked at the curb and headed up Abigail Brown's freshly shoveled sidewalk with a queasy feeling in the pit of my stomach. I was an alien on my home turf. When I was attending the parochial school a few blocks down the street St. Johns was one of North Winnipeg's prime residential areas—a lushly-treed boulevard of stately dwellings occupied by middle-class Jews and WASPs; now it was a rooming house jungle of working class Orientals and non-working class aboriginals. Judge Brown's widow had inherited one of the few surviving single-family dwellings—a red brick dinosaur that squatted on its crumbling foundation like a dowager empress presiding over a vanished kingdom.

My prospective interviewee sounded receptive enough on the phone but my years in radio had taught me not to trust voices. Cats who came on like Gregory Peck could be one vodka away from the happy academy and chicks that sounded like Candice Bergen often looked more like *Edgar* Bergen (or Mortimer Snerd). I mean, what kind of broad would live in the Adam's Family Mansion after the lord of manor was blown away? Brown's widow was probably one of those constipated political wives who'd consumed so much rubber chicken she'd turned into plastic—an aging "Barbie" whose painted kisser had frozen into a perpetual grimace from laughing at the same jokes and smiling though the same speeches since Christ was a cowboy. Still, Honest Bob was a born-again socialist so the little lady might be one of those wide-bottomed earth mothers who's too preoccupied with saving the Newfoundland whale to bother shaving her legs. I climbed the steps with a heavy heart and rang the bell. The door opened—followed by my mouth.

"Hi, you must be Val Virgo."

Well that much was clear but who in the hell was she? Standing in front of me, in a bulky sweater and baggy blue jeans, was an athletic-looking chick with long dirty-blond hair and an impish smile who looked about eighteen.

"Yes. Is Mrs. Brown in?"

Her laugh sent a shiver up my spine. "She certainly is. But call me Abby, everybody does."

I was glad I hadn't asked for her mother. She ushered me into the vestibule and closed the door behind me. Then stood there, studying my face like it was a homework assignment. "So you're the famous Val Virgo; I was wondering what you'd look like." I hoped she'd spare me the verdict. "I know it's rude to stare but you must be used to it."

"Why should I be used to it?"

"Hey, Virgo's a big name in this town."

"But not a big face."

She frowned, thoughtfully. "Say, how do I know you're really Val Virgo, got any I.D., mister?"

You're the one who needs I.D., sister. "Don't you recognize my voice?"

"Oh I never listen to talk shows," she said, waving away an invisible fly. "I think they're an insult to the intelligence. No offence," she added as an afterthought.

I managed to keep a straight face. "How could I possibly be offended by a remark like that?"

"Sure, it's nothing personal." She turned and headed in the direction of what I assumed was the kitchen. "Take off your jacket and make yourself at home, I'll put on some tea."

I hung up my new down-filled jacket (after struggling with the zipper for an hour or so) with a much lighter heart. Maybe this investigative ghouling wasn't going to be such a drag after all. The living room brightened my outlook further. It had the ambiance of a jolly monastery—white walls, beamed ceiling and a large bay window through which the autumn sun was streaming onto sparse furnishings of unfinished wood, canvas and hemp. The only color in the room was an abundance of greenery sitting in a motley assortment of crude earthenware pots. One specimen was coiled around a ceiling beam like a python.

"That's a dieffenbachia."

I turned to see my hostess struggling with a tray of crockery that looked to have been fashioned by the same ham hand responsible for the jungle-fruit receptacles. "Any relation to the Prime Minister?" I said, moving to relieve her of the load.

She laughed. "Not that I know of. But it's very easy to grow; if you like, I can give you a slip."

"Maybe I'll take you up on the offer when I'm in the market for a roommate. How often do you have to clean its cage?"

Her laughter bubbled up like water from a mountain spring. "Oh don't worry, Mr. Virgo, it hasn't eaten a talk show host in months…no, over there on the coffee table".

"Call me Val," I panted, relieving the strain on my back.

Abby Brown sat down on the floor beside the low coffee table on which I had deposited the crockery, tucked a leg under her blue-jeaned butt and invited me to park my carcass in a canvas chair across from her. As I collapsed into it she hoisted the gargantuan tea pot and began to pour a steaming greenish liquid through a strainer into one of the gallon sized cups. "I hope alfamint is all right?"

Alfred who? "Sure, great."

"Do you like herb tea?"

"It's all I ever drink."

She looked at me dubiously.

"That's an interesting pot," I said.

"Do you like it?" she said, brightening. "I threw it myself." She waved her free arm around the room. "I threw all this stuff."

Not far enough—you fell short of the trashcan. "No kidding." Having exhausted my fund of small talk I had no choice but to take a swig of the liquid in my cup. "Mmmmm, that hits the spot," I said, choking back my gag reflex.

Smiling happily, young widow Brown poured herself a cup of the vile brew and prattled on. "I don't know how people can drink black tea, it's full of caffeine. And coffee, ugghh!" She made a face. Then took a sip of tea and smiled again. "So, how's Crosswords these days?"

"Talk."

"I beg your pardon?"

"The show is called Crosstalk—and I wouldn't know how it's doing because I haven't been on the air since my… accident."

Her face fell. "You're all right, aren't you? The paper said…"

"I'm fine. The police just think I should keep a low profile for few weeks."

"Is that why you're wearing those things?"

She was referring to my shades, which I had forgotten I was wearing. "No, these are purely cosmetic," I said, and lifted them to illustrate the point.

She cringed. "Oh my goodness!"

"It looks worse than it is," I said, stoically. If I'd known what a gratifying response a couple of shiners were going to provoke I'd have shown up on crutches. But I didn't have long to bask in her sympathy because the doorbell rang. I swore under my breath.

My hostess also didn't seem to be too pleased. "Who on earth can that be?"

It was obviously someone she hadn't seen for at least ten years. While they stood in the hallway, catching up, I used the opportunity to pour the rest of my organic swill into the nearest flowerpot. I noticed a guitar case standing in the corner and went to take a look. It was a Gibson Hummingbird, the first "serious" ax I had ever owned.

"That was my friend Sheila," young widow Brown said, bouncing back into the room. "She saw your car sitting out front..." When she saw what I was holding her cheery mood evaporated. "I'd rather you didn't play that," she said, gently taking it out of my hands and laying it back it its cradle. I had no intention of messing with her old man's baby; it was just something to do with my hands. Besides, its strings were deader than its late owner.

"You were saying something about your visitor seeing my car.

"That's right," she said, brightening. "My friend Sheila lives across the street," she gestured toward the window, "and when she saw your car parked in front of my house she thought she'd better make sure I was all right. You should have seen the look on her face when I told her who that old wreck belonged to."

I raised an eyebrow. "I'm trying to keep a low profile, remember?"

Her smile was replaced by a remorseful frown. "That's right, I forgot," she said, biting her lip. The clouds parted as quickly as they had formed. "Well, she still doesn't know what you look like. She was just *dying* to come in and meet you but I didn't feel like going through the hassle. Aren't I terrible?"

"Not really, nosy neighbors can be a pain."

Her smile evaporated. "Don't you dare talk about my friend Sheila like that. She's been just like a big sister to me since Robbie..." she bit her lip and looked away. She couldn't bring herself to say it.

And I couldn't bring myself to believe it. It was a little too theatrical. But this kid must have been a "method" actress because the tears were dribbling down her cheeks like...tears. "Look, if you'd rather I came back another time..."

"No, it's okay," she sniffed, freezing me in mid-crouch. "I don't mind talking about my husband."

Mind? When Abby Brown got onto the topic of her beloved "Robbie" her *off* button ceased to function. She talked about the guy like he'd just gone down to the corner to buy a newspaper. She prattled on, endlessly. And didn't tell me one thing that was the least bit helpful. I was hoping to get some personal information about the dearly departed on the slim chance that it might be a clue to something we had in common beside "celebrity". But his adoring young widow, to whom, I discovered, he had been married less than three years, gave me the official biography. The late Mr. Justice Robert Woodard Brown was born in Winnipeg, to lower middle-class parents, was an outstanding athlete, president of his high school, went to Oxford on a Rhode scholarship, completed his law degree at the University of Manitoba ("He won the Gold Medal, you know.") joined the Manitoba Attorney Generals Department ("...best Crown Attorney they ever had.") was drafted by the New Democratic Party to run for the St. Johns seat in the Manitoba legislature ("... won in a landslide.") served three terms in the Provincial cabinet ("Minister of Education; Minister of Northern and Indian Affairs, Attorney General...) was appointed to the bench and presided over the abortive Native Justice Commission. Did I know anything about real estate?

I looked at her, strangely. "Real Estate?"

"Yes, what's the market like?" She waved her hand around the room. "If I can't unload this white elephant I'll be stuck in this crummy neighborhood until the cows go home."

I repressed a smile. "I believe it's until the cows come home."

"Come, go, what's the difference—what does it mean, anyway?"

I laughed. "I haven't the foggiest idea."

"It's not funny," she said, petulantly. "You have no idea what it's like living alone in this creepy old place. I don't know what possessed Robbie to buy this house."

"He probably wanted to live among his constituents."

"Well, they're not *my* constituents. You should see some of the characters around here. I'm afraid to walk to the Seven Eleven for a carton of milk. If it weren't for my friend Sheila I'd probably starve to death." She moved to the window and looked out at the gloomy mansion across the street. "I'm a prisoner in my own house." As she pulled a tissue from a box that was sitting on the window sill I noticed another one on the mantle above the fireplace. And a third on the coffee table. Sarah Heartburn was prepared to have a breakdown in any part of the room. "Maybe I should just rent this place and take a trip," she continued, having wiped her eyes and blown her nose. She dropped the soggy tissue into an ashtray (or candy dish or whatever it was supposed to be). "I could sure use a vacation." She heaved a world-weary sigh, then looked at me quizzically. "How's the stock market these days—up or down?"

How the hell did we get onto the stock market? This kid jumped from topic to topic like a stone across a pond. "I have no idea," I said with a shrug.

"Aren't you supposed to know these things, Virgo? What if a caller asks you for financial advice?" She shook her head in exasperation. "My broker tells me one thing, my lawyer tells me another…" she looked at her watch. "I wonder if he's in?"

Unfortunately, he was. As I sat there, listening to Abby Brown fill her solicitor's ear with complaints about the depressed real estate market, the leaky plumbing, the rudeness of repairmen and all the other tribulations that made the life of a defenseless widow such a trial, I noticed that her teeth, though small and even, were slightly on the gray side; her hair, which had seemed so thick and lustrous, was beginning to hang rather limply and her nose had a heart-shaped bulb on the end of it. Young widow Brown wasn't quite the flawless creature she had seemed when I first walked in. Still, there was no denying she had something—even if it was just her late husband's estate. From what I could gather, the life insurance alone—with a double indemnity payoff—was in the neighborhood of half a million. Even in a depressed real estate market that wasn't exactly a slum!

As my hostess attempted to wind up her husband's affairs over the phone I didn't feel guilty about eavesdropping. Young Sarah Heartburn was obviously putting on this performance for an audience of one. Apart from the sly little smiles she kept tossing my way she kept me abreast of the proceedings with frowns, scowls, grimaces, groans and sighs. She rolled her eyes, hung her head, commanded her tear ducts to fill and pulled her adorable face into a thousand weird and wonderful shapes. It was virtuoso performance. But even the original "Divine Sarah" couldn't have held an audience with that kind of material so I finally got up, walked to the window and looked at the scenery.

I caught sight of a shadowy figure in a third floor window of the gloomy mansion across the street. "Friend Sheila" no doubt. She seemed to be watching the house. I moved away from the window and began to browse through the framed photographs that were hanging on the wall. My eyes came to rest on a confident looking dude in cap and gown with shoulder length hair, a blond mouser and a disturbingly familiar face. I was still trying to figure out where I had seen it when Abby Brown came bouncing back into the room.

"Well, I guess I told him a thing or two! They're all the same...lawyers, accountants, bank managers...just because you're a widow they think they can lead you around by the...oh, you've found Robbie's graduation picture." She came over to help me admire it.

"Is this your husband?"

She smiled, proudly. "Isn't he handsome?"

"When was this picture taken?"

"When Robbie was at law school. Y'know he won the Gold..."

"No, I mean what year."

She looked at me, curiously. "1980, why?"

"I think I know your husband from somewhere."

"Well, I should hope so."

"No, I don't mean I know Judge Brown, I mean I know the young man in this picture."

She took it down and studied it. Even an adoring widow could see the hirsute young lawyer was a far cry from the balding, jurist who'd recently been elevated to that great Court of Appeal in the sky. She looked at me, intrigued. "You think you knew Robbie when this picture was taken?"

I nodded. "Would you mind if I borrowed it?" *Mind*? Why didn't I just ask for her right arm? "I'll guard it with my life," I promised. "I just want to keep it for a few days."

She clutched the sacred icon to her modest bosom and narrowed her eyes, suspiciously. "What for?"

"To refresh my memory."

"Robbie and I had no secrets. Why can't I refresh it?"

Because a picture is worth a thousand words, honey, and the portrait you've been painting bears as much resemblance to a human being as those clay abortions do to functional pottery. "Look, I have a friend who's a professional photographer. I'll get him to make a copy of the picture today and bring back the original tomorrow."

She considered the offer for several seconds. "All right, but you better take good care of it." She picked up the framed photograph, turned and left the room. When she returned, a few minutes later, she was carrying a large Manila envelope. She reluctantly held it out. But, as I reached for it, she suddenly had second thoughts. "You're not going to say anything about this on that stupid radio show?"

"I've been grounded, remember."

She nodded. "That's right, I forgot." She released the envelope, which felt like it contained a cardboard protector in addition to the photo, and brought me my jacket. I put it on and prepared to take my leave. Which isn't as easy at it sounds. "What's the matter is the zipper stuck?"

"It's all right," I grunted. "I'll have it in a minute." But I didn't; it had me. I pushed and pulled and muttered and sweated and managed to embed the flap a little more firmly into the teeth.

"Is there anything I can do?"

Yes, you can stop looking over my shoulder while I make an ass of myself.

I gave the tab a vicious yank and the zipper finally broke free, with a sound that made my heart sink.

"Oh my, you've torn your jacket."

"That's okay, it's an old one."

"Looks pretty new to me. Take it off, I'll mend it."

"Don't bother."

"It's no bother, I'm a very good seamstress. If you come home with your jacket in that condition your wife will have a bird."

"I'm not married."

She looked at me curiously. "Divorced?"

I nodded.

She frowned. "I don't believe in divorce." Or even remarriage. "I'm a one-man woman," she informed me, gravely. Well, she certainly didn't seem to be pining for the one that got blown away, I mused, as she bounced out of the room with my torn jacket. When she returned, several minutes later, I could see that my less-than reliable source hadn't exaggerated about one thing—young widow Brown *was* a hell of a seamstress.

14

The same hard-bitten dick was pecking away at the great Canadian police procedural but he gave me a much warmer reception. "Hey Virgo, how's it going?"

"Can't complain, Stan."

"Good to see you back on your feet."

"They hardly laid a glove on me, Stanley. Is the inspector busy?"

"Never too busy for you, champ."

Yeah right!

"I can only spare a few minutes," Duncan said, intercepting me at his office door and ushering me into an empty interview room. He closed the door and we sat down on opposite sides of a table. "So, what brings you down here?"

"This." I handed him the envelope with Brown's graduation picture.

He opened it, slipped out the photograph, looked at it, then at me. "Why are you carrying around Justice Brown's picture?"

"You recognize him?"

"Of course I recognize him, why wouldn't I?"

"It was taken over twenty years ago."

He looked at me strangely. "So where did you get it?"

"From Abby Brown."

"You *know* her?"

"I do now." I described my semi-successful excursion into the world of private sleuthing. My new colleague was less than impressed. "Look Virgo, I thought I told you.."

"To lay low until the dust settles. Give me a break, inspector, what's the point of twiddling my thumbs in some motel room when I might be able to help you get to the bottom of these bombings? You were the one who suggested there might be some connection between the victims so I wanted to see if Judge Brown's widow could tell me anything about her late husband that rang a bell."

He glanced at the photo. "And this did?"

"Loud and clear. Well, maybe not too clear. But I'm sure I had some dealings with Brown around the time it was taken."

"But you can't remember what kind of...*dealings*?"

I shook my head. "But I have a feeling it's connected to the bombings."

"A *feeling*?"

"Well, yes."

"What *kind* of feeling?"

"Kind of a...queasy feeling."

"A queasy feeling?"

We should have used his office; this one had an echo. "You know, the kind you get when you recall an unpleasant experience. Or, rather, an experience that you *don't* recall."

Duncan turned his attention back to the photo. "About how old would you have been around the time this was taken?"

In 1980 I turned eighteen. Assuming Brown sported the latter-day hippie look for a few years I would have been anywhere from my early twenties to my early thirties when our paths had crossed.

"You weren't in any trouble with the law?" Duncan wondered out loud.

"Apart from the odd speeding ticket, no."

"What were you doing for a living around that time?"

"Pounding salt."

Duncan looked at me quizzically.

"I was a country singer."

Did I detect the trace of a smile? Duncan looked at Brown's eight by ten glossy for a few seconds then moved onto a different track. "How about Abigail Brown, she ring any bells?"

I grinned.

Duncan grimaced. "I'm not interested in your fantasy life, Virgo, is there any chance you might have met the woman before?"

"Not unless I didn't recognize her without her diapers. She looks young enough to be Brown's daughter."

Duncan didn't comment, just studied the photo again. "You're sure you had some association with Justice Brown around the time this was taken?"

"I didn't say I was *sure*; I said I had a feeling. There's something spooky about that photograph."

He looked up. "Spooky?"

There it was again, the echo. I nodded. Duncan heaved a resigned sigh and slipped the photo back into the envelope. "Okay, sometimes it's better not to try and force these things. Just go about your business and maybe it'll come back to you." He handed me the envelope and got to his feet. "If you remember anything give me a call." He opened the door. "In the meantime let me do the detective work, you stick to broadcasting."

"But you told me to keep a low profile."

He looked at me incredulously. "And you thought I meant you couldn't go back to work?"

"Well...yeah."

Duncan heaved a weary sigh. "You know, Virgo, for a guy who's so free with his advice you're pretty clueless. No one in his right mind is going to go after you under the nose of an army of witnesses. When I said to keep out of circulation I meant when you were *off* the air. " He fixed me with the death ray. "You didn't tell anyone where you're staying?"

"Just my producer—in case she has to get in touch with me."

"Will she keep it under her hat?"

She doesn't wear a hat, inspector, just an armband and jack boots. "Yes, I think so."

Angus Duncan had enough to worry about without upsetting him with the truth.

15

Sheldon Kurtz, Artist Photographer read the legend on the glass door. *Legend? Fairy tale is more like it.* It was like stepping into a time warp. It must have been twenty years since I'd paid a visit to my buddy, Phote, and nothing had changed, not even the receptionist. "Well, stranger!" she cried, as I came though the door. The old doll must have been pushing seventy but her hair was barely tinged with gray, her pearly whites looked like the genuine article and her skin was as smooth as a baby's butt.

"Hello, Mrs. Kurtz, how are you?"

"Don't ask," she said, and rattled off a list of chronic (and probably imaginary) ailments.

"Well, we all have our problems."

"That's right," she said, suddenly realizing she was talking to a fellow invalid. "When we heard you were in the hospital Shelly was so upset that he ran right out and bought you," she began to rummage around in a drawer, "here it is." She took a square white envelope out of the drawer and handed it to me. I opened it and took out a Hallmark card. It had the usually saccharine get well message and was signed "With best regards, Shelly" in his mother's handwriting. "By the time we found out what hospital you were in it was too late to mail. You'd already been discharged. And we didn't have your address…"

"That's okay, it's the thought that counts," I gave her my sincerest phony smile.

"That's right," she said, nodding sagely. Then she looked at me with obvious concern. "How are you feeling now, Izzy?"

"Oh not too…"

"Shelly," she screeched, over my shoulder, "come see who's here!"

I turned just in time to see a cherubic face pop through the door to work area. The boy photographer hadn't changed any more than anything else in his tidy little world. His frizzy blond hair (which he'd been worried about losing since he was twelve) wasn't noticeably thinner, his moon face still had its youthful glow and his ear was still glued to a telephone receiver. "Mood," he beamed, covering the mouthpiece with his chubby nail-bitten fingers. "C'mon in. I'll be through in a minute,"

I moved a little deeper into the time warp. A camera the size of the Hubble Telescope was still sitting on its ancient tripod and the dusty wooden floor was covered with the same snakelike cables, empty film boxes, jugs of developing fluid and the other photographic detritus that was essential to the family business my boyhood friend had inherited at the tender age of seventeen. The oak filing cabinets no doubt contained the same glossy monochrome proofs Shell had shuffled through the last time I'd visited, in search of the publicity photo he'd taken of me "for practice" when he'd stepped into his father's ill-fitting shoes. As my mother often reminded me, he was a "good son". Having laid his bets, Shell hung up the phone, trotted over and clasped my hand warmly. "Talk about a blast from the past," he chortled. "How you doing, Mood?"

"Can't complain, you?"

"Don't ask," he said, his face puckering into a familiar pout. "I don't know how I'll ever catch up. Weddings, bar mitzvahs…"

"Poker, gin rummy…"

He laughed, boyishly. "Same old Mood."

"Same old bitcher. If you're so busy, asshole, why don't you get some help?"

He waved a dismissive paw. "Ahhh, you hire someone to help you and right away he wants to be a partner."

"And you've already got a partner."

He followed my eyes to the door to the outer office and laughed his innocent laugh. "Same old Mood." It was like an Abbot and Costello routine—same stupid questions, same stupid answers—Phote and Mood, appearing daily at St. Johns High. I suppose I may have seemed a trifle moody in those days—especially to someone who was as sunny as a summer's day (and as shallow as rain puddle)—but the nickname had never caught on. The kid who coined it was the only one who ever used it. "So," he grinned, "what brings you down here?"

"I want to ask you about a picture." I took Brown's photograph out of the envelope and handed it to him.

He studied it with a professional eye. "Nice looking guy, who is he?"

"You don't recognize him?"

"Should I?"

"You took it."

He looked at the logo on the back and shook his head. "Not me, we haven't used this stamp since my dad died."

"So there's nothing you can tell me about that *nice looking* guy."

"Well, maybe if you tell me who he is…"

"The late Judge Brown."

"Who?"

I was less than amazed that Shell drew a blank. The only paper he ever opened was the *Morning Digest* and the only thing he ever watched on television was the NFL. Of course he had never watched an entire football game in his life, just skipped from channel to channel to get the scores. "The judge who was blown away before the mad bombers got around to me."

The dawn broke. "Say, that's right. I couldn't believe it when I heard you were in the hospital. Did you get my card?"

"Your mother just gave it to me, thanks."

"Forget it."

I'll do my best. "So, do you think you can check your files to see if there's something helpful you can tell me about this picture?"

He made a petulant face. "Gee, Mood, I'm really jammed up…"

"So unjam yourself. You can call your bookie back *after* you've attended to business. I'm not asking for a favor, I'm willing to pay for your time."

It did the trick. He would give me the friendship rate—no more than he charged anyone else who had walked in off the street. He took down the details of Brown's no longer vital statistics, scanned a quick copy of both sides of the photograph and handed me back the original. "Come back at two." I turned to leave but he put his hand on my arm. He hesitated. "Do you think you could pay me now?"

I looked at him incredulously. "You think I'll stiff you?"

"No, but…" His baby blues shifted to the front office.

"Oh yeah, I forgot about your partner." I handed him a double sawbuck.

"Make sure you stick it in your sock so she won't find it when she goes through your pockets."

He grinned his foolish grin. "Same old Mood!"

"Same old Phote!" I grinned. You just couldn't get mad at the guy. I carefully slipped Abby Brown's keepsake back into the envelope and headed out the door for what I was sure would be a less pleasant reunion.

Absence doesn't make the heart grow fonder, cliché fan, it makes the memory grow dimmer. As I languished in my grungy motel room, feeling sorry for myself, the DBC had begun to take on a rosy glow in the rear view mirror. But the instant I stepped back inside the building gloom descended like a fog. This wasn't a radio station; it was a rest home for semi-retired civil servants. The atmosphere of ennui was so thick it hung in the air like a debilitating gas. No one was in a hurry to go anywhere. Or do anything. But drink innumerable cups of watery coffee, play chess in the basement cafeteria or drift through the halls like disembodied spirits. Or dispirited bodies. The only person who showed a spark of life was the oldest person in the building. "Mr. Virgo," Santa's clone cried, as I stopped at his makeshift desk beside the switchboard to sign in, "long time no see!"

"I've been under the weather, Pop."

The old security guard's face fell. "Yeah, I read about it." He shook his head and pulled at his white beard. "I don't know what the world's coming to when a person isn't safe in his own home."

"Hey, if the world was too safe you'd be out of a job, kid."

The twinkle returned to his crinkly eyes. "Never thought of that. You want me to warm up your car? They're predicting twenty below."

"I think we better cool it on the car warming for a while, Pop. The police don't want me handing my keys around." He flinched. "Besides, I'm not going to be here very long," I said, closing the barn door. "I just came down to talk to my Producer. Do you know if she's in?"

Pop dutifully scanned the door sheet. "She hasn't signed out," he mumbled into his beard.

I headed for the elevator feeling like warmed-over shit. If they had a Nobel Prize for Diplomacy Val Virgo would be shoe-in. He'd managed to alienate the only friend he had in this hostile territory.

Compared to the rest of the building the Current Affairs Department was a beehive of activity. As I ran the maze of cubicles in search of my quarry, my colleagues didn't seem to notice my presence let alone rise to greet me. They were too busy cannibalizing the latest crop of news fodder for the electronic tapeworm. News, like history, doesn't repeat itself; newsmen repeat each other—over and over and over...I heard the hesitant click of computer keys coming from the Girl Wonder's cubicle. My producer—a lead-footed writer but a lightening word processor—must have sprained a wrist patting herself on the back. I poked my head around the partition and discovered what the problem was. Or, rather, *who* the problem was. "Yo, Cringer, what's up?"

Lloyd Cringely sat bolt upright, a rabbit frozen in the headlights of an oncoming car. "Oh, it's you Val," he said, when his heart started beating again. He removed his headphones, brushed a lock of greasy hair from his shifty eyes and gave me weak smile. "You gave me a start."

"Sorry Lloyd, I guess I should have coughed or something."

"That's all right, I'm a little on edge today."

Yeah, right, and Donald Trump is a trifle vain. Lloyd Cringely reminded me of an old dog that was beaten as a pup. He always seemed to be wondering where the next blow was coming from. The Cringer was the kind of dude who made you feel guilty for being semi-competent. In the course of a long and undistinguished career he'd been kicked up and down the broadcast ladder (from script assistant, to announcer, to producer, and back again) without finding a niche small enough to contain his lack of talent. "So how's the world been treating you, Lloyd?"

"Can't complain." He picked up a tarnished cigarette case and, with trembling, nicotine-stained fingers, removed a roll-your-own, inserted it into an amber holder, lit up and sucked the orange glow half way down.

"What are you working on?" I said, as he expelled a cloud of blue smoke.

He brightened. "It's for tomorrow's show, want to see it?"

I didn't, but the printer was already spitting it out. He handed me what looked like a script for a radio drama. "What is this?" I asked after reading a bit of the dialogue.

"An interview with Harry Epps." Epps was the Minister of Agriculture. Or Mining. Or something. "We taped it this morning."

"So why are you transcribing it?"

"He's going to be on tomorrow's show."

"I thought you said Patricia interviewed him today."

"She did, after the show. They're going to do it tomorrow."

"Do what?"

"The interview."

I stood there, trying to figure out what the hell he was babbling about. Then, with a sinking feeling in the pit of my stomach, I thought I did. "Let me get this straight, Lloyd, Patricia and Epp are going into the studio tomorrow morning," I held up the script, "and *perform* this?"

Bingo! The Girl Wonder was going to read Epp her questions and he was going to read back his answers. "But the interview ran a little long," Cringely said, brightly. "So I'm editing the transcript."

I could feel a migraine coming on. "Why don't you just edit the tape and play that?"

The Cringer looked at me like I'd just dropped in from the planet Ork. "Val, you know Crosstalk is a *live* show."

Unfortunately the standards weren't quite that high for the zombies who were now in charge. The only thing that kept me from laughing in his face was the thought that my star was hitched to his broken wagon. Fortunately, his days were numbered.

He read my mind. "Say, what are you doing here, anyway?"

I didn't have the heart to tell the pathetic jerk the truth. "Oh," I said with a hollow laugh, "just dropped in to see how the working stiffs are doing. You didn't happen to see Patricia around?"

"Isn't she in her office?"

"Apparently not."

It took a few heartbeats for the penny to drop. "Oh, this isn't Patricia's cubicle. She moved into your office, to free this one up for me."

Lady Bountiful wasn't in *our* office; she must have gone for lunch. The desktop was buried under a litter of correspondence so I sat down and occupied myself by browsing through it. The bulk of it was addressed to "Val Virgo"—rather than "Crosstalk"—but it was all new to me. Apparently my producer had decided to pass on only the poison pen letters, in an effort to guard me from the pernicious effects of vanity. I opened the drawer and found dozens of other letters I'd never seen, dated as far back as the beginning of the season. In a lower drawer I found a scrapbook of newspaper clippings about the bombings, including every word "Renegade" had written on the subject. I was perusing one of his more vitriolic attacks on the local constabulary when the notebook was unceremoniously yanked out of my hands. "I'll thank you to keep your paws off the things in my desk."

I looked up into the glowering face of my erstwhile producer. "*Your* desk?"

She flushed. "Well, temporarily," she said, putting the scrapbook into her brief case and locking it.

"What's the big secret, Patricia, you planning on writing a book?"

"Never mind what I'm doing, what are you doing here?"

"I work here, remember."

She looked confused. Or was it disappointed? "I thought Inspector Duncan wanted you to stay off the air until..."

"Hell freezes over? No such luck, my dear, there was a breakdown in communication. Apparently no one's allowed to blow me away as long as I'm on the air. It violates the DBC's code of ethics or something."

"Well, you should have given me some warning. You can't expect to just drop in out of the blue and pick up where you left off."

"Okay, where can I pick up?"

She gave it some thought. "How about the beginning of next month?"

"How about the day after tomorrow?"

"That's not enough time."

"For what? You and the Cringer to scare off what's left of the listening audience?"

If looks could kill, I would have left the building on a slab. "Is that so?" my producer snarled. "Well it may come as a shock to you, hotshot, but Crosstalk has managed to limp along without the great Virgo. Since you've been snooping around my desk you may have noticed that listener interest," she picked up a handful of paper and shook it in my face, "hasn't exactly dropped off."

I was struck dumb. Was she really that clueless? "Patricia," I said, softly, "most of those letters are from people who want to know if I'm still alive."

She seemed to regret her lack of tact, if not sensitivity. "How do you know?" she said, sulkily.

"Because I read them, that's how. I also read some of the others you've been keeping for your private collection. Whoever told you it was a producer's job to censor the mail?"

The fire came back in her eye. "Don't tell me about my job, Virgo, you just worry about *your* job. If you expect go back on the air you're going to have to reconcile yourself to a few changes."

"Such as?"

She began shuffling the correspondence into a neat stack. "This is neither the time nor place to discuss it; I have a show to prepare."

You mean rehearse. "So name a time and place."

She looked up, thoughtfully. "What are you doing for lunch tomorrow?"

"Eating might be a viable option."

"Fine, I'll meet you at the Union Center at twelve-thirty."

I could hardly wait. The Union Center chef was famous for his crow.

On my way out of the building I stuck my head into the DBC commissary and saw Neil Bannerman sitting at a back table, nursing his lunch. As usual, his head was buried in a skin magazine, a cup of coffee growing cold at his elbow, an unfiltered cigarette making an ash of itself over the edge of the arborite. I took my ptomaine on rye over to his table. "Catching up on a little T and A, Bans?"

He looked up blankly. Then his bloodshot eyes came back into focus. "Well, I'll be fucked," he said and sprang to his feet. Since my hands were otherwise occupied he greeted me with a slap me on the back. "How you doing, buddy?"

"Still truckin'," I said, putting my sandwich, coffee and manila envelope on the table. I pulled up a chair and Bans sat down and closed his glossy magazine. Contrary to my expectations the cover didn't feature a scantily clad bimbo but a naked forty-four magnum. The Great White Technician hadn't been reading *Penthouse* but a more hardcore type of pornography called *Guns and Ammo*. He extinguished his butt, shook a fresh one out of his pack and offered it me.

I shook my head. "Trying to give 'em up." And *Export Plain* was a little strong for my taste—as was the guy who chain-smoked them. Unlike the rest of his DBC colleagues Neil Bannerman didn't give me the cold shoulder yet I'd never been able to warm up to the guy. He came on a little too strong. Bans reminded me of those over-friendly cats who send drinks to your table then shout obscenities if you don't get to their "requests" promptly enough—hard drinking gentiles with bad teeth and little piggy eyes who tell dirty jokes that aren't funny and say "you people" because it wouldn't be polite to say "fucking Jews".

"Man, you're a sight for sore eyes," Bans said, slapping me on the shoulder again. "If I have to spend one more morning in the same booth with that brain-dead Cringer I'll strangle the fucker."

"Your joy is premature, Bans, I've just had a heart-to-heart with coach *Sinjin* Hog. It seems I'm going to have to play myself back into the line-up."

Bans swore under his breath. "That frustrated.... You know what she needs, don't you?"

I shook my head. "No, that's not her problem."

Neil Bannerman's scowl turned into a leer. "Don't tell me you've had some experience in that area?"

I wasn't about to tell him. I had no experience worth gossiping about. When Val Virgo was still the DBC's fair-haired boy and The Girl Wonder was just learning the ropes she invited me to her place for a little shoptalk over a glass of Beaujolais Nouveau. The glass became a bottle and the shoptalk became a boozy lament about the father who never loved her—a "legendary journalist" whose career she was trying to live up to. It was such a heartrending tale that I made a sympathy pass and found myself on the floor, with my hostess straddling me and unzipping my fly. At the moment of truth she paused to ask the million dollar question.

"Making love with a safe" an old poolroom acquaintance used to say "is like taking a bath with your socks on." And since I had no desire to get mired in this particular swamp, with or without socks, I told my passionate script assistant that I'd left my rubbers in the closet and asked for a rain check. Which convinced her that I didn't have the balls to host a radio talk show.

A few weeks after this debacle my Producer, Morgan Riley, delivered the bad news. The Union had filed a grievance on behalf of brother Garth Grenfel. Old lard tonsils—ably assisted by Patricia St. John Hogg—had belatedly discovered a clause in the Announcers collective agreement that required the DBC to "audition" existing staff before hiring a freelancer for an on-air position. The DBC brass promptly did an about face. Since it was a little late to close the barn door the boys in Toronto suggested a compromise: Garth would be my announcer (and heir apparent), Patricia "Sinjin" Hogg would replace Morgan as Producer of the show and he would be "promoted" to Executive Producer. Morgan had been lured from private broadcasting with the assurance that he would have a free hand to bring up the DBC ratings and he was assured that would still have a free hand to determine the course of the show—as long as he could do it with both of them tied behind his back. So Captain Morgan did the honorable thing. He jumped ship, leaving his first mate standing at the end of the plank with the sharks circling.

"No Bans, I did not sleep with Patricia. I just know that her problem isn't sex. It's gender. Apparently her father was a hotshot journalist who wanted to have a *son* follow in his footsteps."

Bans snorted smoke through his nostrils. "Tell me about it."

"You've heard the story."

"Heard it? I lived it. Louis Hogg is the fucker who broke me into this business. And *broke* is the right word. You think Patricia has a chip on her shoulder; you should have tried working with her old man. He was the most insufferable little prick who ever walked into a studio."

"He's a small man?" I said, taken aback. From Patsy description of the intrepid war correspondent I picture "Papa" as Canada's answer to Ernest Hemmingway.

"Small? He's a fucking Munchkin. That's his problem—he has a Napoleon complex that won't fucking quit."

"Where is he now?"

Bans shrugged. "Who knows? When the DBC fired his ass he went into politics. He was an MLA for about a hundred fucking years but when the leader of the NDP stepped down and the party refused to anoint King Louis, he quit the party and ran as an independent. And got one fucking vote, his own." Having unburdened himself of an obviously painful memory Bans sucked his coffin nail to within and inch of its life and lit a fresh one. As he stubbed out the spent butt he noticed my manila envelope lying beside the ashtray. "What's this," he said, picking it up, "one of the Cringers scripts?"

I shook my head. "A picture."

"Of what?"

"Take a look."

He did. "Who is it?"

"The late Mr. Justice Robert Brown."

"Yeah, right."

"I'm serious, it's his law school graduation picture."

Bans looked at me curiously "So what the fuck are you doing with it?" Suddenly, it hit him. "Say, this doesn't have anything to do with your... accident?"

"It wasn't an accident, Bans, someone tried to kill me."

He grinned, sheepishly. "Yeah, but I figured you might be a little paranoid about it."

"Even paranoids can have real enemies, Neil."

"I guess. Well, I better boogie." The Great White Technician packed up his guns and ammo, crushed his coffin nail under his heel and rose. "You need a lift? I'm going right by the New Moon."

My heart skipped a beat. "Who told you where I was staying?"

Bans shrugged. "I don't know—why, is it a secret?"

"Not any more," I said, packing up *my* (blank) ammo.

The "Artist Photographer" lived up to my expectations. He hadn't started looking for the file yet. For which I couldn't blame him, it was an exercise in futility. Well, I hope he picked the right team—I'd hate to think that twenty bucks was a total loss. Dinnertime was approaching when we hurriedly locked up—he was on his way to "The Club"—and since I was on a nostalgia trip I decided to treat myself to a Kelekis hot dog. Kelekis Restaurant—a one time French fry wagon that a Greek paterfamilias had built into a North End institution through the sweat of his five semi-beautiful daughters' brows (his only son became a lawyer) was just a stone's throw from the New Moon so it really wasn't out of my way. When I walked in Mary (the eldest) was behind the counter. She greeted me semi-warmly and gave me extra fried onions but it wasn't the same greasy spoon of my youth even though my photo was still on the "wall of fame" beside other semi-famous local luminaries. When I emerged back onto Main Street, burping Pepsi fumes, I thought, since I was in the neighborhood, I might as well drive by Abby Brown's place and drop off her hubby's photo.

The downstairs lights were on but I didn't see any sign of life so I circled the block and drove by again. On my third pass I was rewarded by a glimpse of Abby Brown moving from the living room to the dining room. I slowed to a crawl and fingered the manila envelope on the seat beside me. It was kind of late for "I just happened to be in neighborhood" to sound convincing. She was bound to suspect my motives. On the other hand, she might welcome a little company. She'd made no secret of the fact that she hated living all alone in that haunted house. But she'd also made no secret of the fact that she was a "one man woman"—who preferred the company of her husband's ghost to a live talk show host. I was passing the old brick dinosaur for the fifth time—or maybe the sixth. The debate was over. The living room lights were off and the bedroom lights were on. Well, the night wouldn't be a total loss—Rumpole was on PBS.

16

I flushed the toilet, padded back to bed and crawled between the sheets. It was my third trip to the john in the past hour. Or was it my fourth? My bladder empty, I resumed my fruitless reflection. Angus Duncan was right. You couldn't squeeze out a memory like toothpaste from a tube; you had to let it form like a bubble on the side of the glass then, with a gentle nudge, it might rise to the surface and burst on your consciousness. I closed my eyes and tried to let the bubble form.

Yeah, right! How do you *not* think of something?

I sat up and turned on the bedside lamp. Brown's picture was lying on the floor. I must have knocked it from its perch on one of my trips to the john. I leaned over and picked it up. Thank God I hadn't stepped on it. Abby Brown would emasculate me.

Or would she? You never knew which way that chick was going to jump. Weeping and wailing for the departed saint in one breath, calculating the interest on his life insurance the next. "Tell me Robbie, old sport, is your child bride for real?" He didn't answer—just looked back with the same inscrutable stare. I put the photo back on the night table and picked up the paper. The news hadn't changed since the last time I'd read it, an hour ago. I tossed the paper on the floor and opened the night table drawer. Maybe the Hooker Hilton provided its patrons with some inspirational literature, like *Teenage Mutant Ninja Cheerleaders*. No such luck—I had to settle for The Gideon Society's offering. I turned to Ecclesiastes to see what counsel "the wisest man who ever lived" could offer. No matter how dire your circumstances you could always count on jolly old King Solomon to cheer you up:

Vanity of vanities, all is vanity. What profit hath a man of all his labor which he taketh under the sun...the eye is not satisfied with seeing, nor the ear with hearing... There is no remembrance of former things; neither shall there be any remembrance of things that are to come...

On that reassuring note I drifted off.

And Abigail Brown stepped into my dreams.

The telephone woke me. I looked at the clock radio. I'd overslept—half a bottle of scotch will do that to you—the show was over and the Girl Wonder was back on my case. I picked up the receiver and broke out my most conciliatory tone. "Hello, sweetheart, I was just thinking about you."

Dead silence. Then, hesitantly, "Is this Val Virgo's room?"

I sat up, abruptly. "Yes..."

"Hi, it's Abby Brown. I didn't wake you, did I?"

"That's okay, I overslept."

"Lucky you I was awake all night. Some pervert kept driving past the house. I swear he must have gone by a dozen times."

Why did women exaggerate? It wasn't more than half a dozen. "He was probably just looking for a house number. I'm sure he was harmless."

"Harmless? What planet do you live on, bub? Do you have any idea how many degenerates are running around loose in this city?"

Oh, there aren't that many of us. "You didn't happen to notice what kind of car he was driving?"

"Are you kidding? I wouldn't even have known he was out there if my friend Sheila hadn't phoned. Why don't you get them to install a few streets lights around here Virgo? I thought you had some pull in this one horse town."

I laughed with relief. "I'll see what I can do."

"Look, have you made a copy of that picture yet?"

"Yes..."

"Good, when can you bring it back?"

"What time would be convenient?"

"Eleven-thirty."

"Today?"

"Well, twelve thirty at the latest. Do you like sole?"

"Music?"

"Food. Since I'm making you drive all the way out here thought I'd give you brunch. I'm a very good cook you know."

"And you specialize in soul food?"

"No, dummy, *fillet* of sole. I make it with a wine and mushroom sauce. Is that all right?"

"It's all I ever eat."

For someone who hadn't slept a wink Abby Brown was remarkably bright-eyed and perky. She was wearing a different bulky sweater but the same baggy jeans, impish smile and well-scrubbed look. "Well, you're prompt," she said, and relieved me of my manila envelope and jacket.

"Tell that to my mother. She says I'll be late for my own funeral."

It wasn't the happiest choice of words but young widow Brown didn't seem to notice. "You can't even see it," she said, admiring her handiwork.

"Nope, just like new."

She smiled happily and hung the jacket up. "Are your parents alive?"

"Just my mother."

"Does she live in the city?"

"No, she moved to the promised land."

"Israel?"

"Florida."

My hostess frowned with disapproval, but didn't have time to scold. Sole is an extremely delicate and impatient fish.

The dining room table looked like a layout from *Better Homes and Gardens*. The meal was equally professional. Having seen Abby Brown's artwork I figured she was exaggerating her culinary skill—most chicks with her physical endowments didn't bother to cultivate the domestic arts—but I had misjudged her again. "That was delicious," I said, as I washed down the last morsel with a modest but cheeky Sauvignon Blanc. "You *are* an excellent cook."

She smiled modestly. "I had a good teacher."

I wonder who? The table talk wasn't quite as satisfactory as the meal. She dragged her beloved "Robbie" into the conversation at every available opportunity but the person she described did not resemble an ordinary mortal, let alone one with whom I might have had something in common. The more she talked the fuzzier the picture became. I helped her clear the dishes and she put on the kettle. "Do you prefer chamomile or alfamint?" she asked, reaching for the tea canister.

"Frankly, I prefer coffee," I said with an apologetic smile.
She made a face.
"Yeah, I know, it's poison. What did I have last time?"
"Alfamint."
"Okay, I'll have the other stuff."
She laughed. "Go sit down in the living room, and I'll bring you your caffeine fix."

I adjourned to the drawing room, feeling rather mellow. Since my hostess had barely touched the wine I'd been forced to drink most of the bottle myself, so as not to offend her. I sat on the futon looking out the picture window at a Christmas card. A fresh fall of snow blanketed the ground, sunlight sparkled on sugar-coated evergreens and smoke curled languidly from the chimney of the stately "white elephant" across the street. Why was my hostess so anxious to pull up stakes? It was a nice neighborhood—if you discounted the neighbors. I yawned, contentedly. Maybe I should catch a quick forty winks. I lay my head back and began to drift. The doorbell brought me back to earth with a thud. "Could you answer that, please?" Abby called from the other room.

The old frump in the doorway looked about as happy to see me as I was to see her. "Is Mrs. Brown in?" she said, studying my face like it was in a police lineup.

"Is that you Sheila?" Abby sang out from the kitchen.

"Yes it is," the visitor sang back. "I just wanted to make sure you were all right."

"I'm fine," Abby said, sticking her head around the corner. "Come in and take off your coat; we were just going to have a cup of tea. Or coffee, if you prefer."

"Oh no, you have company," the old biddy said, still giving me the fish eye.

"That's right, you two haven't met have you?" Abby said, coming into the hall. "Val, this is my friend Sheila. Sheila, this is the famous Val Virgo."

Friend Sheila was less than astonished—she probably had a thicker file on me than Angus Duncan. She offered me a limp hand but didn't move her butt from the open doorway, through which frigid air was billowing like smoke.

Abby shivered. "Now come on in before we freeze to death."

The reluctant dragon didn't budge. "No, I don't want to be a third wheel."

"A third wheel?" Abby screeched. "Don't be a goose, Mr. Virgo just came to return a picture of Robbie that I let him borrow. Now close the door and take your coat off."

Or we'll have to put ours on.

"Well, just for a minute," the spy said, and, finally, came in from the cold.

Friend Sheila's "minute" was the kind you recorded on a calendar. Having disposed of the weather we moved on to other small talk. Small? It was miniscule! I could picture us still sitting there, a year from now, covered in cobwebs, three characters in search of a Victorian novel. *Tea, Mr. Darcy? Just a spot, Miss Haversham. How's David Copperfield these days? Oh, top notch. Well, pip, pip and tally ho!* I snuck a glance at my digital. Surely we couldn't have been sitting there for only ten minutes. I scoured my excuse file for a graceful exit line. A sudden headache…a pressing appointment…a previous… It hit me like a sucker punch! I didn't have to make something up; I had a legitimate excuse to jump *out* of the frying pan.

17

The Union Center, a modest three-story structure across Portage Ave. from the DBC building, where, among other things, you could get a good meal without taking out a bank loan, was built in the early fifties as a recreational haven for the honest workman. But the denizens of "The Peoples Network" used it anyway. Where, but in the midst of all those plumbers and machinists, could an empty suit that intoned the daily news feel like a show biz personality? My DBC colleagues had the best of both worlds, "artists" with job security. As I scanned the sparse lunchroom crowd it wasn't difficult to single them out, in their blue jeans and elbow-patched corduroys, from their fellow proles. But the face I was looking for wasn't in the crowd so I walked back across Portage Avenue and found her busily shuffling papers at "our" desk. She greeted me with a charming scowl. "Well, if it isn't the *late* Mr. Virgo."

"Sorry Patricia, a personal matter came up at the last minute and I clean forgot about our lunch date."

"Well, maybe you'd better get back to your personal matter," she said, resuming her paper shuffle. "I wouldn't dream of taking up your leisure time with anything as trivial as work."

"You aren't taking up my leisure time, you are *creating* it. I was ready to go back to work yesterday but you had to have a summit conference. Though what there is to confer about is beyond me. I've been hosting a talk show for so long I can do it in my sleep."

She looked up and pinned me like a bug, with her eyes. "Maybe that's the problem."

"Would you care to elaborate?"

Care to? She was licking her lips—and not just to remove the trace of cheesecake she'd had for dessert. The days of Val Virgo flying by the seat of his pants were over. The People's Network was not going to have a repeat of the debacle that had almost cost me my life. If I didn't care about my own security that was my business, but if I expected to go back on the air I'd not only have a female co-pilot but a flight plan that was carved in stone. I sat there, with a sinking heart, listening to the new "security" precautions. All calls would be screened, all scripts rehearsed and, where possible, interviews would be taped and edited prior to airtime. Anything that wasn't properly embalmed by the time red light went on would go back into the DBC vault for further aging. Including yours truly. "You don't have to make a decision today," my replacement said. "Take all the time you need. It's a big change and you'll want to consider your options."

Only I'd have to consider them somewhere else. Having appropriated my relatively upscale digs The Girl Wonder generously allowed me to share her former rat hole with Lloyd Cringely. I slunk out the door of my former office and down the hall with my tail between my legs to consider whether on not I wanted to participate in this groundbreaking experiment in creative taxidermy. I sat there for hours with Hobson's choice stuck in my crop like a rancid peanut. I couldn't decide whether to choke it down or spit it out. I was screwed either way. I was dying to pull a Johnny Paychek, but couldn't afford the luxury. My stock on the country music circuit had sunk even lower than old Johnny's. Besides, that was obviously the move she was trying to goad me into. I knew she was dying to get rid of me but never suspected that she wanted to host the fucking show herself! She couldn't even wait for the body to get cold. *Just something I came up with off the top.* Yeah, right, she just happened to have a pound of shrimp on standby, waiting to be fried. Patricia St. John Hogg never made a spontaneous move in her life. She must have been planning the ridiculous on-air "anniversary party" for...a spider crawled down my back.

No, it was preposterous. Who murders a guy to get his job? Especially when she's in a position to make his life so miserable he'll quit of his own accord? My emotions were clouding my judgment. Still, I couldn't get over the look on her face when Duncan asked if she recognized the voice of the phantom caller. The Great White Technician always looked a little shifty-eyed, so I could be mistaken about him, but the Girl Wonder was as subtle as rhino. I could read her like a Harlequin novel—with large print. She looked like someone who had just soiled her panty hose. She *knew* who that drunk was; I'd bet my life on it. *Bad choice of words.*

A scenario began to play itself out in my head. It's a few weeks before the Angus Duncan interview and The Girl Wonder is in the control room doing a slow burn as I piss away *her* show talking to some "nobody". Suddenly her scowl is replaced by a fiendish grin. What's so funny? Neil Bannerman wonders. She lets him in on the gag. Bans grins. If she's serious he can set it up. Patricia has second thoughts. Is it worth the risk? What risk? It was a piece of cake. They could get an "outsider" to make the call—some Main Street wino who wouldn't remember his own name, let alone the call, an hour after he'd make it and with the two of them controlling "the board" there was no chance of it going over the air—it would remain an in-house joke.

Patsy's pipe dream begins to take a more solid form. This could be her ticket to broadcasting immortality. She'd be a legend in her own time. The author of a classic prank her DBC colleagues would be laughing about for years. Even "Papa" might sit up and take notice. This was the type of practical joke he and his journalist cronies used to pull in the good old days when reporters pounded out their daily copy on manual typewriters with a cigarette dangling from their lips, a fedora perched on the backs of their heads and devil-may-care attitude to life. Hard working, hard drinking newshounds who indulged in crude horseplay to insulate themselves from the human misery they confronted on a daily basis. The Girl Wonder's imagination goes into overdrive. Why stop at a bogus threat? Why not give the arrogant Mr. Virgo something to really make him wet those threadbare blue jeans. He lived in the same building, for heaven sake, it was like fate. She turns to her confidante. Could Bans make some kind of smoke bomb; a harmless explosive that wouldn't do any physical damage, just make enough noise to scare the living shit out of the famous talk jock? A walk in the park! Mr. *Guns And Ammo* dazzles her with his expertise. But his bible isn't written for amateur practical jokers but professional mercenaries and he has to improvise. But he wants the biggest bang for his buck and uses a little too much of this, not quite enough of that...

"Oh, it's you, Mr. Virgo."

I snapped out of my reverie. It took my eyes a few seconds to adjust.

"Pop, you gave me a start."

"Sorry, I didn't think anyone was still working up here."

"Just doing a little research."

"In the dark?"

I laughed. "Mental research—otherwise known as woolgathering." I consulted my watch. "Funny, how time slips away?"

"Willie Nelson."

"Hey, Pop, I didn't know you were a country music buff."

The old boy smiled like Santa. "There are lots of things you don't know about me, Mr. Virgo."

Yeah, like your name. "Pop" wasn't even a nickname it was a stereotype: a condescending epithet the DBC security guard shared with the faceless army of senior citizenry who might as well have been invisible. By thinking of him as "the old guy who sits at the door" I had sold him short. He wasn't a Santa clone, there was a human heart beating under that blue uniform and a unique individual behind that white beard. An individual who had likes and dislikes, faults and virtues and who had always gone out of his way to be friendly and helpful. "You know, Pop, I think we've know each other long enough to drop the formality. It's Val."

He nodded. "Okay...Val." There was an awkward silence as I waited for him to reciprocate. When the silence became unbearable I looked at his nametag, *H. Frobisher,* and asked what the "H" stood for. He looked even more embarrassed. "Harrison," he mumbled.

"Harrison Frobisher, that's quite a mouthful. Do you mind if I call you Harry?"

He smiled uncomfortably. "Frankly, I prefer Pop."

So much for good intentions. As my failed experiment in public relations hobbled out the door I thought of another project I could undertake. With, hopefully, better results.

"Hello."

Her voice sent a little shiver over my skin. "Hi, it's Val."

Dead silence.

"Val Virgo..."

"I know your full name, Mister Virgo, what is it?"

I laughed uncomfortably. "Well, I just thought I'd call and thank you for that lovely lunch; I really enjoyed myself."

"Is that why you shot out the door like your pants were on fire?"

"But I explained..."

"That you had a previous appointment; an important meeting you

117

conveniently forgot about until my friend Sheila showed up. I was never so embarrassed in my life. My best friend, and he treats her like she has a…social disease. I don't know how you were brought up, Mr. Virgo, but where I come from it's considered the height of rudeness to eat and run."

"You're right," I said, lamely. "But I was hoping you might let me make up for my rudeness by taking *you* to dinner."

This generous offer was greeted a silence so deep it could have been used to store nuclear waste. When Abby Brown finally broke it I almost got frostbite. "You seem to forget you are talking to a woman who has just lost her husband. He eats my food, insults my friends and now he's trying to hustle me."

"No, I'm not," I protested, feebly. "I mean, it's just that you went to so much trouble for me…"

"That you thought I'd be dying to go out with you. I don't believe this guy; just because he's on some crummy talk show—that nobody listens to— he thinks he's…Larry King!"

Larry King! Just how old did she think I was?

Before I could recover from this low blow she blindsided me again. "Where are you going to take me?"

"Take you?"

"For dinner. And it better be a gourmet restaurant, Virgo, because that sole cost me an arm and a leg." I grinned, happily. I guess Kelekis was out. "And for goodness sake, when you come to pick me up don't park that broken down jalopy in front of the house."

18

You must think I'm awful."

Abigail Brown was propped up on an elbow, looking down at me, a curtain of hair hanging over her face, tickling my chest. Was it a dream? Surely I couldn't be sleeping in Abby Brown's bed. Well, it wasn't exactly *her* bed; she insisted we use the guest room. Did I think she was awful? Well, all's well that ends well. We had eaten dinner at the Swiss Inn. Or was it the Swiss Chalet? Well, it was the *Swiss* something. The attraction wasn't the food, which was mediocre, but the waiters who were from Europe not Quebec. Abby, an upscale "army brat" who'd attended finishing school in Geneva (*or was it Berne?)*, seldom got a chance to speak "real French" anymore. Well she got her chance. Having flirted outrageously with the guy waiting on our table she waxed indignant on the drive home about how the Francophone grease ball kept ogling her "boobs". Young widow Brown's bosom isn't spectacular but when you wear a silk blouse and no brassiere you get more than your fair share of oglers. Since she had ignored me all evening I expected my dinner companion to blow me off as soon as I pulled up to her back door—as per instructions—but, to my astonishment (and delight) she asked me in for a "cup of tea."

While she put on the kettle I was assigned the task of building a fire. By the time she arrived back in the living room, lugging the infamous tray, I had disproved an old axiom—where there's smoke there is not necessarily fire. "Oh for goodness sakes," she said, putting down her load, "are you trying to asphyxiate us?" She rearranged the logs, newspaper and kindling, the way Mr. Eagle Scout had taught her, took the single match that was still left in the box and in five minutes we were sitting in front of a cozy smokeless fire. (I think opening the flu might have helped.) She poured me a cup of tea and picked up the polite conversation we were having before my precipitous departure.

"So how come your wife dumped you?"

I laughed. "How do you know I didn't dump her?"

"Did you?"

"No, but you might have considered the possibility."

"Quit stalling, Virgo, what did you do to alienate the poor girl?"

"It's a long story."

She snuggled a little deeper into her canvas chair. "So make it a bedtime story."

It was an offer I couldn't refuse so I made the long story short. "I guess she felt an endless series of beverage rooms was no place for a nice Jewish boy to be spending his married life."

Abby Brown looked at me curiously. Then smiled, impishly. "What kind of a name is Virgo for a nice Jewish boy?"

"You don't think I was born with that stupid name?"

"Well I can't imagine anyone choosing it—is that your sign?"

"My cross." *Or Star of David.*

"I don't know much about astrology, who would be a typical Virgo?"

I was tempted to say "Sean Connery" but didn't want to appear immodest so I searched for a more typical example. "Peter Falk...Bill Murray...Felix Unger..."

"Who?"

"You know, that dude on the *Odd Couple*."

"The sloppy one."

I shook my head. "The hypercritical one."

She looked at me, dubiously. "I can't see that."

Don't judge a talk jock by his cover story, toots, under this carefree exterior beats the heart of a nitpicker. "You're not looking hard enough."

"Robbie was a Leo; is that a good sign?"

Not for me, it wasn't.

"He played the guitar too, did I tell you that? At least he tried." She sighed and shook her head. "I used to lie in bed and listen to him plinking away down here for hours."

"He wasn't very good?" I said, hopefully.

She rolled her eyes. "Poor Robbie, he loved that guitar." She heaved a nostalgic sigh.

My spirits rose a little higher. "Well, you know what they say, 'you always hurt the one you love.'"

She laughed until the tears came. It wasn't mirth but hysteria seasoned with grief. When the storm abated she plucked one of the ubiquitous Scotties, wiped her eyes and blew her nose. "How about you, Virgo, were you any good?"

"If I was any good I wouldn't be talking on the phone for a living."

"Oh pooh". She left the room and returned with her late husband's axe, holding it by the neck like a chicken. "Here," she said, thrusting it at me, "play me something."

I was an offer I couldn't refuse, so I starting tuning up. "What would you like me to sing?"

She was taken aback, and impressed. "You sing too?"

"I don't play well enough *not* to sing." *Or sing well enough not to play. It's an old magician's trick called 'misdirection'.* I wasn't only describing the technique but employing it. While dazzling her with my witty repartee I'd stumbled through a few rudimentary chords to get my chops into a semblance of working order. "Of course the pipes are pretty rusty," I said, clearing my throat. "I'll have to lubricate them with something a little stronger than herbal tea."

My hostess frowned. "Don't you know that stuff is..."

"Yeah, I know, poison. But if you want to call the tune..."

Young Widow Brown heaved a resigned sigh.

Her late husband had very good taste in poison. After warming the cockles of my throat with a few fingers of Black Label I laid a little novelty number on my one-woman audience. "That was great," she cried, clapping her hands. "Did you write it?"

"Guilty."

"Don't be childish; false modesty is not the least bit becoming. An adult should know how accept a compliment graciously."

She was right, especially if the adult was pushing forty—from the top. But I hadn't had much practice accepting compliments lately, graciously or otherwise. This was my first command performance and it was kind of refreshing to have such an uncritical audience.

"Do you know any waltzes?"

"Sad songs and waltzes aren't selling this year."

She wrinkled her adorable forehead. "I don't want to buy one, I just want to hear one."

I laughed. "That's the name of a song."

"Sure it is."

There was no point going up that blind alley so I illustrated my point.

Her response was more subdued but equally enthusiastic. "Did you write that?"

I shook my head. "Willie Nelson."

"Play me something else of yours. But not that silly stuff, another waltz."

"How about a hurtin' song?"

"What's that?"

"Just what it sounds like." I took another shot of liquid courage and jumped in with both feet. When the last painful note died away there was a moment of reverent silence. Staring into the fire, with a faraway look in her eye, Abby Brown asked the sixty four thousand dollar question.

"Who's Helen, is she a real person?"

"That's a matter of opinion." She waited for the other shoe to drop. "Helen is my ex's name."

Abby Brown was not amused. "Do you have to make a joke out of everything?"

It was a good question—one I'd asked myself many times. But when you don't have the stomach for small talk, or the guts to say what's on your mind, or in your heart, humor is the only alternative. Well, *almost* the only one.

"How can you drink that stuff, don't you know what it's doing to your liver?"

"Of course I do, I used to be pub musician, remember."

So why did I drink it?

"Because a grown man isn't supposed to suck his thumb."

She giggled in spite of herself, then made a face as I drained the glass. "Doesn't it burn?"

"Only at first—then numbness sets in."

She heaved a world-weary sigh. There was an awkward silence as I poured myself a refill. Then, gazing into the fire, "Give me a little taste."

And now she was asking another million dollar question. Did I think she was awful? Well she wasn't great but the first time seldom is. And I was hardly in a position to throw stones. The liquid courage I'd used to put my inhibitions to sleep didn't exactly perk up the old anatomy. And the cold-blooded ritual of walking upstairs to the guest room—she didn't want to soil the futon, let alone the conjugal bed—taking off shirt, pants, underwear, shoes, socks…virtually mugged what was left of my libido. Our lovemaking was so awkward my partner cried when it was over. I felt like a child molester. I started to offer a tentative apology but she put her hand over my mouth. "No, it's not you," she sniffed. "You were very gentle. It's just that it's been so long…" Now, *she* was on a guilt trip.

"You must think I'm awful," she repeated.

"I think you're great." I gave her thigh a little squeeze.

She squinted at me but it was too dark to see the expression on my face. "Do you really?"

"Have I ever lied to you before?"

"Probably," she snorted. Then laid back down and snuggled up. There were several seconds of blissful silence as we lay there, sharing the warmth of each other's body, and listening to the floor creak. "You know what my friend Sheila says?" I waited, less than breathlessly, for the punch line. "Sheila says that when a Jewish boy goes with a gentile girl it's for only one thing."

"With friends like that, I don't need any enemies."

Abby sat up and glared down at me. "Don't try to weasel your way out of this, Virgo, are you taking advantage of me?"

"Well, *somebody* had to do it."

She laughed so hard I thought she was going to wet the bed. After she had calmed down, wiped her eyes and blown her nose, I told her the facts of life. "Abby, when a *gentile* boy goes with a gentile girl it's for only one thing."

"I don't believe you," she sniffed. "Robbie wasn't that type of person." She tossed the soggy tissue in wastebasket beside the bed and snuggled up again. "And neither are you."

"How do you know?"

"He told me."

"Who told you?"

"Robbie—I wouldn't have gone out with you if he didn't tell me you were a nice person."

It was my turn to sit up. Since I couldn't see her face I didn't know if she was pulling my leg so I said, gingerly, "You *talk* to your husband?"

"Sure. Robbie always used to tell me what to do; he was my guru."

And now he was her guardian angel! One of these days I was going to get involved with a chick who *wasn't* a fugitive from the Twilight Zone. Still, any port in a storm. I lay back down and snuggled up. I felt snug as a bug in a rug lying in the Adams Family Mansion, naked under a down quilt, listening to the radiator clank, the floors creak, the walls groan and the window panes buzz as the chill wind whistled impotently outside. Then, suddenly, I felt a draught.

"Okay bub," my bedmate said, stripping the covers from my loins, "time to hit the road."

"You want me to leave?" I said, lamely.

"Well, I hope you don't expect me to feed you breakfast."

The thought had crossed my mind. "Have a heart, Abby, it's still pitch black out."

"Duh."

"Yeah, right." *Can't have friend Sheila alerting the media.*

Fortunately there was an electrical outlet beside the parking area next to the garage so I was able to plug in the old Valiant and it started on the first crank. I pulled into the back lane and made my getaway as silently as possible. Rather than head back to the no-tell motel, so I could lie in bed for another few hours listening to my stomach growl and the toilet flush in the adjoining room, I dropped into an all-night grease pit to refuel. Fortified with three fried eggs, a rasher of bacon, hash browns, two pieces of toast, three cups of coffee and the morning edition of the *Winnipeg Tabloid*, I was ready to face the day.

There was only one problem, it wasn't day and there was nothing to face—other than my "options". As I drove down Main Street, in the dawn's early darkness, the day yawned before me like Death Valley. The wandering Jew was not only homeless but on the precipice of joblessness. Then I thought of a fellow traveler whose career was also unceremoniously terminated. This was the perfect opportunity to keep the promise I'd made to *my* guardian angel for delivering me from the valley of the shadow and the hands of my enemies. Whoever they were...

19

Welcome back to the Health Sciences Center. As I circled the block for the third time, looking for the "Rehab" building, I could recall my youth when this sprawling medical complex was a single building called the Winnipeg General Hospital. But the word "hospital", like the term "police station", has been stricken from the lexicon as being too *negative*. Police stations are for criminals and hospitals are for sick people. But who can argue with "safety" and "health"? Not to mention "science". While churches and synagogues are being turned into parking lots the temples of modern medicine are springing up like mushrooms. We have a separate building for every disease and a new disease every month. The era of mumps, measles and chicken pocks is beginning to look like "the good old days." Today it's Cystic Fibrosis, Muscular Dystrophy, Acquired Immune Deficiency Syndrome—we're dying of disease we can't even pronounce, so we have to use acronyms; horrible parasitic viruses and genetic abnormalities that attack the unborn and suck the life out of the living—leaving a pulsating hulk that the health scientists hook up to their machines—space age afflictions of which our "ignorant" ancestor couldn't conceive in their worst nightmares.

Yet our medical gurus insist that we are on the road to a disease-free Utopia. With sufficient funding they can cure all our ills, physical, mental and spiritual. And we believe them. Having dismissed as superstitious twaddle everything our forefathers held sacred we are prepared to accept any scientific "miracle" as long as the prophet who proclaims it has been anointed by the College of Physicians and Surgeons. We don't want pie in the sky, we want immortality *now*—while we're still *healthy* enough to enjoy it.

Still, as I headed down the hall to my destination I had to admit that technological medicine was rising to the challenge of all human malfunction rooted in pure mechanics. Fiberglass limbs, stainless steel joints—no one seemed to be operating with his or her original parts. I poked my head in the door of room 402 and saw a ruddy-faced dude sitting in a chair watching television. Could the rumors of the maimed and mutilated mailman's impending demise have been exaggerated? Except for the missing right hand this guy looked healthy as an ox.

"Is this Leon Coleman's room?"

The ox turned. "He's in therapy (*terapy*). Be back in a few minutes."

I sat down to wait. The minutes dragged by. My attention kept wandering to the missing right hand of Coleman's roommate. Apart from a few ragged teardrops of skin the stump was clean as a whistle. He caught me looking. "Chain saw," he said, raising his invisible hand. "Doctors are giving me a prosthesis." He flashed an embarrassed smile. "That's what they call them. It's not just a hook, like the pirates used to have, but looks and works like a real hand." He sighed, gratefully. "Amazing what they can do nowadays."

"Sure is." It would have been cruel to point out that the technology that made his bionic limb possible is what had made it *necessary*.

"Well, we have a visitor!"

I turned to see a buxom nurse pushing a wheelchair through the door. When I looked at what was in the chair I couldn't help wonder of what Leon Coleman's "therapy" had consisted. Blinking? He looked like a rag doll with most of the stuffing torn out. "Are those for us?" the nurse enthused. She took the flowers from my hand and shoved them in her patient's face. "Look at the nice flowers our friend has brought us," she fairly shouted. Coleman didn't respond. Or, at least, look at them—his eyes were locked on me. They were the only part of him that still seemed animated. "I'll just put these in some water," the nurses said, and headed out the door. When she returned, five minutes later, her patient was still trying to memorize my features. His face had escalated from gray to pink. "Oh my goodness, just look at that color!" The nurse turned to me, excitedly. "I think he recognizes you."

That makes two of us, sister.

20

Stan the Man wasn't working on the Great Canadian Police Procedural, he was busy on the phone. Still he looked glad to see me. No, overjoyed would be the better word. "Never mind, he just walked in." He hung up. "Thank Christ you're here, Virgo, I've been phoning all over the city."

My heart skipped a beat. "Has there been a break in the case?"

He hesitated. "Well…a new development. The Inspector will fill you in." I headed for his office. "Not here," Stan called after me. I stopped and turned. "At the New Moon."

Boy this must be some development! "Inspector Duncan went to my motel?"

He nodded and smiled, grimly, "What's left of it…"

21

It hit me the instant I stepped into the building, the same sickening odor that permeated my bombed-out apartment, only stronger. I fought back a wave of nausea and headed for my room. There was no door, just a charred frame and a gaping hole. An army of rubber-gloved forensic types were crawling over the remains, like ants at a picnic site, taking photographs and picking through the rubble. The king of the hill greeted me with his usual cordially. "Where in hell have you been hiding?"

"I'll tell you later, Inspector, what's the story here?"

It was deja vu all over again. Only this time the "device" was detonated by a simple push/pull mechanism attached to the door and the person who had taken the bomb with my name only had one life to give for her—*partner.* "She must have triggered it when she came in to clean up your room," Duncan grunted. "What time did you leave this morning, Virgo?"

I didn't reply, just headed for the john and tossed my breakfast into the toilet bowl. I cleaned myself up with some toilet paper, reached for the toilet handle, then had second thoughts. "Is it okay if I flush it?" I said, turning to Duncan who was watching me from the door.

"Be my guest," he said with utmost sincerity.

"Poor Luba," I said, rejoining him.

Angus the Bull looked like he'd been pole axed. "You knew her?"

"Well, she wasn't a personal friend." I was not inclined to tell him about my little scam but didn't have much choice. To my surprise he took it quite well. Rather than booking me for impersonating an undercover cop he complimented me on my ingenuity. "How about you, when you left the room in the morning did you leave *her* any kind of signal?"

I shook my head. "Didn't think of that."

"Doesn't matter, whoever planted that explosive had an extremely narrow window of opportunity. Lets see if we can narrow it a little further. When time did you get back to your room last night, and what time did you leave in the morning?"

"I didn't sleep in my room last night," I mumbled.

"What?"

"I said…"

"I heard what you said; where *did* you sleep?"

"With a friend."

"Does your friend have a name?" he asked, with admirable self-restraint.

"What difference does it make?"

The self restraint went out the window. "What difference does it make?" he snarled. "There have been two attempts on your life, a woman is dead as a result of one of these attempts and you want to know what difference it makes who you spent last night with? In case you haven't noticed, Virgo, I'm conducting a multiple murder investigation so will you please cut the bullshit and spit out that name."

I took a deep breath and bit the bullet.

Duncan didn't have a coronary, which wouldn't have surprised me, just struck dumb. When he finally found his voice it was icily calm. "Does your girlfriend know you're staying at the *New Moon*?"

"She's not my girlfriend."

"Yes, I know, you're just good friends; now answer the question."

"For God sake, Inspector, you don't seriously believe Abby Brown could have had anything to do with," I waved my hand at the carnage, "this?"

"Never mind what I believe, just answer the question."

"The question implies that she's a suspect in these bombings. A woman whose husband was the first *victim*."

"And who stands to collect a bundle on his life insurance."

"I don't believe this, she worshipped the ground the guy walked on!"

"Yes, I see how she's grieving." It was a cheap shot and Duncan regretted it. "Look Virgo, I have no interest in your sex life, and that goes double for Brown's widow. Maybe she's not a serious suspect but she's a woman and women talk. If you told her you were staying here she might have told someone else and that someone else might have told someone else. So please answer the question, did you or did you not tell Abigail Brown you were staying at the New Moon?"

I heaved a resigned sigh. "No I didn't tell her but she knew. She phoned me yesterday."

"Where the hell did she get the number?"

I didn't know, but I could make a pretty good guess.

Duncan leveled the ray. "You said she'd keep it under her hat."

I shrugged. "Like you say, she's a woman..."

Angus Duncan rubbed his eyes and pinched the bridge of his nose with the sausages he used for fingers. He looked like he was auditioning for an Excedrin commercial. "Well, it was bound to come out sooner or later. But we can't have you moving into another place that's empty all day. Don't you have any family you can move in with?"

"Not in town."

"How about friends, surely there's someone who will put you up for a while?"

"Put up with me, you mean."

He snorted. "Maybe Mrs. Brown has a spare room; she seems willing to put up with you."

I smiled. "Only to a point, she kicked me out at four a.m."

Duncan looked at me, strangely. "So where were you all morning? I called the DBC and your Producer said she had no idea of your whereabouts."

Suddenly I remembered *my* new development. When I delivered the good news Angus Duncan got as excited as I'd ever seen him get—he raised a shaggy eyebrow.

"What makes you so sure Coleman recognized you?"

"Because I recognized *him.*"

Both eyebrows shot up. "From *where?*"

I smiled, sheepishly.

Angus Duncan looked like he'd contracted Excedrin Headache number 937. He massaged his temples for a few seconds, heaved a sigh, studied my face like it was on a space alien and asked, more in sympathy than in anger, "Virgo, by any chance were you dropped on your head as a child?"

It was a rhetorical question and I gave him the obvious answer. "I don't remember."

22

A penny for your thoughts."

It was the second best offer I'd had all night. Well, the first wasn't so much an offer as a demand. There was nothing wrong with Abby Brown's libido that a little hysteria couldn't cure. When she discovered that her "hospitality" had kept me from joining her late husband in the land from which no bedmate returns she didn't know whether to laugh or cry so she did both. She ranted and raved about the incompetence of the police and the insensitivity of men who put themselves in harm's way with no concern for the women who's lives they disrupted and then made love to me as if it was the last chance she'd ever get. She had another chance less than an hour later—and not in the guest room but the conjugal bed. My "endangered lover" status had bumped me up from Tourist to First Class.

"Save your money, they're not worth it."

"I'll be the judge of that," Abby said, playing with my chest hair.

"You'll have to go to law school first." *Like your beloved Robbie.* That's who I'd been spending my pennyworth of thoughts on—the late "Honest Bob" Brown and the barely viable Leon Coleman—without getting any return on my investment. What could a politician/judge, a mailman and a country artist/talkjock possibly have in common? Besides an enemy?

"So I'll be the jury."

"Juror." *And I don't think there's room for another eleven people in here. Ten, maybe.* Abby Brown's bed was just slightly smaller than my motel room. Well, former motel room.

"Okay, Mr. Nitpicker, I'll be the juror." She idly plucked a few of my chest hairs.

"Hey, that hurts."

She giggled and plucked a few more.

"Will you cut that out!"

"Not until you tell me what you were thinking about."

"What do you think I was thinking about."

There was a moment of silence. Then, softly, "I'm sorry."

"Not that. I was thinking about your late husband and Leon Coleman and where we all know each other from."

She sat up and studied my face. "You're sure you know them from somewhere?"

I nodded. "Pretty sure." I was also pretty sure that our relationship was the key that would unlock the door to these bombings. That aboriginal terrorist business always smelled kind of fishy, now it stunk to high heaven. Morgan said I shouldn't take the attempt on my life "personally", that I was just a "symbol", but you don't go after the same *symbolic* target twice. Whoever planted that bomb in my motel room wasn't trying to make a political statement but a room-temperature talk show host. "I think this NAPAALM business is bogus, Abby. There's no aboriginal organization behind these bombing just some psycho with a personal score to settle."

Her face turned grave. "With you and Robbie?"

"And Coleman."

"You don't think he was just collateral damage?"

I smiled to myself. She was "army brat" all right. "Not any more."

"But why you three—what's the connection?"

"That's the billion dollar question." *The only three things we have in common are location, location, location.* "The only connection I've been able discover is St. Johns Tech," I said, referring to the high school a few blocks away. "Coleman was just two years ahead of me, so I might have known him casually, but your husband was long gone by the time I got there. And after graduating we all went our separate ways. I hit the road to become an unsuccessful country singer, Coleman bummed around, doing odd jobs, until he landed that post office gig and your husband went straight up the ladder to the top."

Abby shook her head. "It doesn't make sense, Val. Robbie had to deal with all these horrible criminals, that was his job, but what could you and Mr. Coleman have done to make anyone this angry at you?"

"Good question."

There was a thoughtful silence. "What does inspector Duncan think?"

"That I was dropped on my head as a child."

She laughed for what seemed like ten minutes. "Well, we have something in common," she said, reaching for a tissue. After she performed her ablutions she lay back down but didn't snuggle up and play with my chest hair, just put her hands behind her head and studied the ceiling. "He's not a very nice person is he, Val?"

"He's all right—it's his job that's not very nice. You can't do police work very long without developing a rather cynical attitude towards your fellow man."

Abby heaved a long sigh. "It's not going to be much of a Christmas is it?"

"Not for you."

"What about you?"

"Jews don't celebrate Christmas, dummy."

She elbowed me in the ribs. "Don't call me dummy."

"Jews don't celebrate Christmas, sweetheart."

"That's better. Don't you do anything at all?"

"Such as?"

"I don't know, put up a tree?"

"No just light candles. We have a holiday called Chanukah that coincides with Christmas." I gave her a brief rundown of the "Festival of Lights" and got up to relieve myself.

As I was flushing she got a bright idea. "Say, isn't that Mr. Coleman Jewish?" she called from the bedroom.

"Yes, he is," I said, coming back into the room.

"So maybe that's where you know him from. My friend Sheila says..."

"All Jews stick together. What about Robbie was he Jewish too?"

She took the question seriously. "No, but he had lots of Jewish friends; half his law school classmates were Jewish."

"Jewish lawyers? Get out of here!"

"No, really, I'll show you." She jumped out of bed, left the room, and returned with a framed photograph. She handed it to me. "Take a look maybe you'll recognize someone."

It was a black and white class photograph and I only saw only one semi-familiar face—stereotypically WASP. "Who's this?" I said, pointing.

Abby leaned over, her hair tickling my arm. "The future Mr. Justice Kilgore."

"Maximum Jack?" I said, taken aback.

Abby giggled. "Robbie used to call him that too. He didn't have much respect for him. Especially after that remark he made about all native people being alcoholics."

That wasn't *exactly* what Kilgore had said but it was close enough for the media vultures to turn him into lunchmeat. "You know, Abby, if this NAAPALM business was legitimate your husband would still be around and Kilgore would be history." No sooner were the words out of my mouth than I wanted to call them back, but it was too late—her eyes were filled with tears.

"Oh God Val, why did he have to die?," she said in a choked voice. "He was so young. He had his whole life ahead of him." She fell into my arms, sobbing. I held her tight and let her cry herself out. When the shaking subsided I reached across her body, plucked a few tissues from the box and handed them to her. She sat up, blew her nose, and wiped her eyes. Then we both lay back and stared at the ceiling. After several minutes she broke the silence.

"Where are you going to live now, Val?"

"You owe me a penny."

She rolled on her side to face me. "What?"

"For my thoughts. You read them."

"And…"

I shrugged. "I'm open for suggestions."

She made a face. "Well, I certainly wouldn't recommend going back to that crummy motel. I don't know why you went there in the first place."

"It was Duncan's choice." *Or maybe Hobson's.*

"Some choice."

Suddenly something hit me. I tried to sound casual. "How did you know I was staying there?"

"You told me."

"No, before that, when you phoned?"

"Oh, some woman at the DBC gave me your number." She made a sour face. "I've never dealt with such a rude person in my life! She gave me the third degree. Who was I? Where did I live? What was the nature of my business—she treated me like I was some kind of…criminal."

I laughed. "Welcome to my world, sweetheart. That was The Girl Wonder."

"Who?"

"My Producer."

"Why do you call her The Girl Wonder?"

"Because sometimes I wonder if she's a girl."

Abby giggled. Then, sobering up, "This isn't a joke, Val, you have to find a safe place to live. Doesn't inspector Duncan have anything to suggest?"

"Yeah, that I should move in with you." Oops!

She reacted like shed been stung by a bee. "You *told* him about us?"

I looked up into her glowering face and smiled, lamely. "Somebody planted a bomb in my room last night, Abby. And I wasn't there. So I didn't have much choice but to tell Duncan where I spent the night. Or, at least, part of it."

She didn't return my smile, just laid back down, with her back to me. I heaved a sigh and turned to face the opposite wall. As I lay there listening to the moaning wind the chill in the bedroom matched the outside temperature. Still, I was not looking forward to the pre-dawn when I'd be evicted from my temporary cocoon and be back wandering the streets in search of some other flophouse.

"Would you like to?"

Who was she talking to, the wall? "Like to what?"

"Move in."

I rolled over to face her—back. "Are you serious?"

She rolled over, still glowering. "I wouldn't have said it if I wasn't serious, Virgo. You think I enjoy living all by myself in this spooky old place?"

"But I'm practically a stranger." I suppose I could have found a more offensive word, if I'd had a Thesaurus.

My bedmate reacted like a scalded cat. "A stranger," she screeched. "He eats my food, he sleeps in my bed…" she yanked the covers from my naked loins and pointed to the bedroom door. "Get of my house, you…*stranger!*"

The floor was like ice. I groped around, found my shorts and pulled them on. Then I sat down on the side of the bed and pulled my socks on. Then I rose to find the rest of my clothes.

"Where are you going?"

I turned and tried to sound as pathetic as possible.

"You told me to get out of your house."

"I know what I told you," she said, sulkily. Get back in bed, you rat."

She didn't have to ask me twice. Now that I was back under the covers I had to get back in her good graces. "I didn't mean that the way it sounded, Abby, I was just thinking of how it would look to...other people. You just met me a few days ago. I didn't want you to make a hasty decision you would live to regret."

"I'm over eighteen, Mister Virgo."

I grinned. "Not by a hell of a lot, Ms. Brown."

"Pardon me, grandpa, I didn't notice your walker."

"It's parked outside, next to your tricycle."

She tried to think of a comeback but the cupboard was bare. In the ensuing silence I considered her ill-considered offer. It might be fun playing house with the adorable little airhead. But would it still be fun when the bloom was off the rose? When the fires of passion began to cool would her "refreshing innocence" begin to seem like invisible ignorance and her "charming prattle" like the clang of an ill-tuned cymbal? Was I ready for this kind of commitment? More to the point, was she? How long would it take for her to regret her generous impulse and rue the day she betrayed the memory of her golden Goy for a roll in the hay with an aging Yid who couldn't keep his end up? And there was a more immediate problem..."What about your friend Sheila?"

"Fuck my friend Sheila."

I laughed out loud. "Thanks, but she's not my type." Grinning like a fool I snuggled up to my new landlady.

Part Four
Shelter From the Storm

23

It was the best of times, it was the worst of times, it was the season of light, it was the season of darkness, it was the spring of hope, it was the winter of despair…okay so it's not original. When you're a novice at this scribbling game you need all the help you can get—and I believe in stealing from the best. After spending my life on the sidelines I'd suddenly been yanked off the bench and thrust onto the field of battle when the game was on the line. The score was Mad Bomber 2, Virgo 0, and time was running out. No, running isn't the right word—time may fly when you're having fun but it stands still when you're waiting for the other shoe to drop. As I hunkered down in my bunker, with my new housemate, or in my soundproof booth, with my new co-hostess—waiting for minute hand on the DBC's outdated clock to jerk forward—every minute was an eternity.

Having accepted the Girl Wonder's ground rules I would drag myself to work every morning and receive the daily flight plan, which I wouldn't look at it until we were airborne. Patricia's meticulously-timed scripts left no room for so much as a spontaneous belch but my shit detector would occasionally force me to transpose a section of her stilted prose into something resembling spoken English—which would invariable result in a few seconds of "dead air" while my co-pilot frantically scanned the flight plan to find our location. Poor Patricia, I almost felt sorry for her. She was chained to those wooden scripts like a suffragette to a lamppost. Why would a chick whose lack of spontaneity was equaled only by her lack of interest in the opinions of anyone who didn't hold public office have such a burning desire to host an open-line show? Good question. It was almost as big a mystery as why a cat who had lost whatever interest he'd had in the gig would keep on truckin'.

If it was a mystery to me, it was an enigma to my live-in landlady. Why didn't I quit "that stupid job" she would wonder, with monotonous regularity. Abigail Brown couldn't understand why I had ever given up my non-career. I didn't give it up, I tried to explain; it had given up on me. You only got one try for the brass ring. She said this was nonsense. (Or, as she delicately put it, "Oh pooh!") It was never too late to start over. I had the talent I just lacked ambition, drive and discipline—like you-know-who? Since I obviously needed someone to build a fire under my butt she was going to rub the sticks together. Every night, after dinner, Sergeant Major Brown would hand me Robbie's axe and issue a one-word command: "play". Gradually my rusty chops began to get lubricated. I even started writing some new songs. My creative juices, dammed up for so long, began to flow. The trickle became a flood. My radio career was swirling around the toilet bowl, my life was on the line, but I felt like a young Roger Miller. The worst of times had become the best of times. I had something to live for.

And someone—my live-in muse. Contrary to my misgivings Abby was an endless source of delight and inspiration. She was the light at the end of my tunnel vision, a beacon of hope that kept me from foundering on the rocks of despair and sinking into a sea of depression. We were two shipwrecked survivors clinging to each other to stay afloat. We didn't need faux French food and a night at the Grand Old Opry, just gourmet home cooking and hot-off-the-griddle semi-palatable county songs. Eating in the kitchen, washing the dishes, taking a walk in St. Johns Park—it was heaven on earth. The simplest things we did together were my profoundest pleasures. Seeing the world through her eyes gave it a new luster. She was sunshine incarnate. Every morning she awoke to a world that had been created the night before. Nothing could crush her resilient spirit or dampen her appetite for life.

But old mortality was always there, lurking in the shadows. On one of our Sunday walks my guardian angel stopped to muse on the plight of a sparrow vainly pecking at the snow-covered ground.

"Don't they fly south, Val?"

"Apparently not."

She looked up with concern in her innocent brown eyes. "How do they survive the winter?"

She was asking the wrong guy.

The key to my survival, I felt, was locked in Leon Coleman's impenetrable memory bank. Every day, after work, I'd drop around to the Rehab Center and the instant I walked in the door his eyes would lock on mine and his whole body would tremble. But he remained as wordless as his writing pad. My visits didn't seem to be doing either of us much good. I might have discontinued them if his nurse hadn't assured me they were "therapeutic". My entry into her patient's life had re-awakened his will to live. He was actually holding the pencil on his own now. Did I have any idea what he was trying to write? *Probably the name of the nut who's trying to blow us away, Florence.* I didn't take Ms. Nightingale into my confidence—what she didn't know wouldn't hurt me—or her patient. I continued to hold my tongue and Coleman continued to hold his pencil stub, in a death grip, while the notepad in front of him remained as blank as his face—and my memory. Until one morning I arrived to find his bed empty. That was not unusual but something was else was missing. I was standing there, trying to figure out what it was, when a voice intruded in my thoughts.

"You looking for the patient who was in that bed?"

I turned to see a candy striper wheeling a tray of fruit juice through the door and suddenly realized what missing from the bed—the side rails.

"Was?"

She nodded. "He died last night." She cracked her gum and moved to a chair that held a lanky, one-legged guy with an eye patch. "You want orange or apple today, Mr. Silver?"

"He didn't leave a note did he?"

She turned and frowned. *He didn't commit suicide,* her eyes said.

"Get a move on Sally, you're ten minutes behind."

We both turned to see a white-capped sourpuss standing in the doorway.

"I know," Sally shot me a dirty look, "but this man was asking me about a patient. He thinks Mr. Coleman..."

"Might have written me a note."

The battle-axe glowered. "Are you the one responsible for that nonsense?"

"Well, his nurse thought it might be good therapy..."

"Therapy," she sniffed. "Straining to make those pathetic chicken tracks might have contributed to his cerebral aneurysm."

My heart stopped. "You mean he actually wrote something?"

"If you call that writing."

"Can I see it?"

The old witch almost smiled. "If you like."

All I had to do was dig to the bottom of the hospital trash bin, of which nothing is trashier. After wading through a rainbow of scarlet gauze bandages, yellow puss pads and green phlegm balls, I hit the pot of gold, crumpled up in a tight ball. I held my breath and uncrumpled it with rubber-gloved hands. And my heart sank. I'd risked contracting fatal diseases for *this*? "Chicken tracks" was a charitable description. It could have been "JU" or "JV" or "UJ" or "UU" or none of the above. Poor Coleman had given up the ghost trying to deliver an undecipherable message. Well, his troubles were over, mine had just been compounded. Still what purpose would it serve to disclose my putative role in my fellow victim's untimely demise to Inspector Shreck?

I decided to let sleeping bloodhounds lie.

24

We bring nothing into this world and it is certain that we take nothing out.

I was browsing through the Gideon bible I'd "borrowed" from the New Moon, to get myself in the proper mood, when my "date" finally materialized in what she considered a "suitable" ensemble. Abby had not only ditched her baggy sweater and blue denims in favor of a skirt and blouse but had washed her hair and done her nails. "I've never been to a Jewish funeral," she said, happily bouncing down the stairs.

You'd think we were on our way to a wedding. "Frankly, I don't know why you're going to this one."

"For the same reason *you* are." Her frown turned quizzical. "Why *are* you going?"

I laughed. Ostensibly to look for a familiar face, one that might reawaken the memory of a long-lost acquaintance who was now irretrievably lost, but it was basically a guilt trip. I felt vaguely responsible for Coleman's death—just as I did for the "collateral damage" that had taken two bullets with my name on them. "It's a mitzvah."

"A what?"

"Mitzvah…blessing…good deed. Something you do to get brownie points with," I pointed to the ceiling, "the Man upstairs."

Abby grinned. She probably thought I was talking about her late husband. "Are you very religious, Val?"

"Not so you'd notice—but I need all the brownie points I can get."

She handed me a beige coat, which seemed rather flimsy for the time of year. "Robbie wasn't religious either," she said, turning around so I could help her on with it. "But he didn't do good deeds to get *brownie points* but because it was the right thing to do." Not anxious to pursue the subject of her late

143

husband, to whose memory I couldn't possibly live up, I suggested she might want to put on something a little warmer. She tossed a familiar scathing look over her shoulder. "This coat is *boiled* wool, Virgo!"

"Oh." I hadn't the foggiest notion what boiling was supposed to do to wool but arguing with Abigail Brown was not the most productive activity in the world. If she wanted to her freeze her adorable buns—and then chew me out for "dragging" her on this arctic expedition I was prepared to live with it. I helped her on with her "boiled wool" and we went merrily on our way to Leon Coleman's going away party.

The mood evaporated when the princess arrived at her chariot. "Why don't you get a new car, Virgo?" she grumbled, as I unplugged the old Valiant and wound the extension chord around the radio antenna.

"I can't afford a new car."

"Don't give me that baloney, you're just too cheap."

I opened the door for her. She got in, reluctantly. I closed the door went around to the driver's side and got behind the wheel. "And there's nothing wrong with the old car," I said, as it coughed into action.

"Sure, it sounds like a tractor. Well, at least you've got a decent deck," she said, admiring my top of line Alpine. As we waited for the car to warm up she shuffled through my CDs and MP3s, found one that suited her and went to insert it. I put out a restraining hand. "I'd rather you didn't use it." I smiled apologetically. "It drains the battery."

"I don't believe this guy. He buys a sound system that's worth more than his whole car put together and I can't use it because he's too cheap to get a new battery. Turn off the motor, Virgo. We're taking Robbie's car."

"People in tin Fiats shouldn't throw stones," I said, as I backed out of the garage.

My passenger scowled. "What's wrong with Fiats?"

"You know what FIAT stands for don't you?"

She shook her head.

"Fix It Again, Tony."

She laughed in spite of herself. "Well, that doesn't apply to Robbie's car," she said, sobering up. "My friend Charlie fixes it."

We both laughed.

Her "friend Sheila", her "friend Charlie"...everyone was her *friend.* Not only her nosy neighbor and the neighborhood gas pump jockey but her bank manager, lawyer, accountant…the adorable flake couldn't believe anyone she dealt with could possibly be motivated by anything as crass as self interest. Or idle curiosity. They were all doing their jobs, practicing their professions, spying on her house and sticking their noses into her business as a personal favor.

As we proceeded south down Main Street, past the kosher meat markets, ethnic book stores and onion-domed cathedrals that were the remnants of the neighborhood's past, Abby took it all in like a tourist from another planet. "Is this the Jewish district?" she wondered out loud.

"Not any more. There are still a handful of old Ukrainians living around here but the Chosen People have long since emigrated to the Promised Land."

"Florida," Abby said, proudly.

I shook my head. "Suburbia."

She rolled her eyes and heaved a resigned sigh. "Did anyone ever tell you, you have a very strange sense of humor, Mr. Virgo?"

"No, Mrs. Brown, you're the first. Well, this is it." I pulled up in front of a lugubrious single story brick building that was wedged between *The Carpathia Credit Union* and *Our Lady of Fatima* like a lonely Jewish petunia in a Ukrainian onion patch.

"Is that the temple?" Abby said, slightly crestfallen.

"Cheery little place, isn't it?"

"Oh it's not so bad," she said, getting out of the car.

I joined her on the sidewalk and we headed up the worn stone steps. "But it's not the temple, that was destroyed a couple of thousand years ago."

"What are you talking about, Virgo, my friend Rebecca belongs to a temple."

"Where does she live?"

"Santa Barbara."

"In the States Jewish people call their synagogues *temples*."

Abby paused on the sidewalk and looked at me curiously. "Why?"

I shrugged. "Sounds less…Jewish."

"So this is a synagogue."

"No, it's the Chessed Shel Emmes." I pointed to the words engraved on the corner stone in both Hebrew and English.

Abby couldn't pronounce them in either language. "What does it mean?"

Good question. *Emmes* meant "truth" and I was pretty sure *shel* meant "of" but what the hell was a *chessed*? House? "I'm not sure, it's the place where they prepare the bodies for burial."

"You mean embalm them and stuff like that?"

"Jews don't do 'stuff like that'—just a cotton sheet and a pine box."

Abby nodded with approval. "Robbie didn't believe in all that stuff either. He was cremated, you know." I didn't. Nor was I anxious to pursue the subject. Fortunately, my companion's nimble mind had skipped to another square on the hopscotch pattern. "Do all Jewish people have their funerals here?" she wondered as we climbed the worn stone steps.

I shook my head. "Just the ones who don't belong to a synagogue."

"Do you belong to a synagogue, Val?"

I shook my head. "No."

"Well, I guess you'll be coming here someday."

On that cheery note we entered the clearinghouse for Jewish cadavers. The temperature was appropriately that of a meat locker. The handful of mourners scattered about the cavernous chapel were wearing overcoats, parkas, fedoras, fur hats and babushkas. As I steered Abby to an empty pew a few vaguely familiar faces turned in our direction but none rang any serious bells. Coleman hadn't drawn much a crowd for his farewell party. He'd even come up short in the pallbearer department—one of the eight folding chairs flanking the cloth-covered casket at the top of the center aisle was empty. Again, a few of pallbearers looked vaguely familiar. Across the aisle, two yentas were gabbing away as if they'd just dropped in to pass the time of day. The one closest to me had a wart on her chin with white hairs growing out of it and no teeth. She chewed her words, like a cow chewing it's cud, trying to gum the last drop of nourishment from each morsel of gossip before passing it on. The other one, who had a droopy eye, kept nodding her kerchiefed head like one of those ornamental dogs you see in the back window of a passing car. I strained my ears and got the impression Coleman's parents had written off their only son as a "goy". Still they were giving him a proper Jewish funeral. The family was sitting in the front row and I couldn't see anything but the backs of their heads. Every so often someone would walk up and offer his or her condolences.

"I'll be right back."

"That was very thoughtful," Abby whispered, as I slid back in beside her.

I didn't disabuse her. Coleman's mother and father, two orthodox Jews who spoke broken English, were complete strangers. The two old yentas were still gabbing. What did they find to talk about after all these years? The dearly departed? Not likely. They were just recycling the gossip they had heard at the last funeral. Or wedding. Or bar mitzvah. I glanced at my rosy-cheeked companion and tried to imagine her at the same age as the wrinkled old crones across the aisle. Before I could get the picture in focus the voice of Death whispered in my ear.

"Are you going to the cemetery?"

I turned to see a parchment-faced dude leaning over the back of the pew. He was wearing a pin strip suit that smelled of cigarettes and formaldehyde. He bared his yellow teeth in a ghoulish smile, adding cheap rye to the cocktail, and said, "We could use another strong young man." He nodded at empty chair beside the casket.

I began thumbing through my excuse file

"Yes, we are."

I turned to the helpful little idiot and muttered, under my breath, "He wants me to be a pall bearer."

"So? Somebody has to do it."

But why did it have to be me? As I headed up the center aisle the answer became obvious. Some of the mourners I passed looked more like they should have been in the box rather than carrying it. I sat down in the empty chair with a heavy heart. This was a more of a mitzvah than I had bargained for. It was a pretty sad commentary on your life when a stranger has to carry you to your last resting place. Then, suddenly, I realized I wasn't the only one who had been drafted for this mitzvah. The boy photographer was grinning at me from the other side of the casket.

The cemetery was a few miles north of town, at the edge of the open prairie, and the wind was gusting so fiercely I could barely open the car door. Fortunately I only had to open the driver's side. While I would bear Leon Coleman to his final resting place my passenger would remain in the car, snuggled in her boiled wool coat, with the heater running. Having volunteered me for this suicide mission Abby decided her presence was not required at the graveside.

As my fellow bearers and I, teeth chattering, followed the chanting rabbi down a narrow path in the snow the freshly dug grave, surrounded by a green carpet of plastic grass, was steaming like an open wound. We were steaming like a team of Clydesdales. By the time we had transferred the coffin to the canvas straps strung across the steaming hole, icicles had formed on our eyebrows and nose hairs. As the straps began to unwind and the casket began to descend, with a creak, and the rabbi, rocking back and forth, raced through the graveside service the wind whipped granular snow pellets into my eyes like frozen salt. I wiped the tears from my eyelids before they froze shut. The rabbi had finished chanting and the creaking had stopped. Coleman's stoop-shouldered father began to mumble the *kaddish* as a cemetery worker unhitched the straps and pushed a button that rewound them. Coleman's father, having finished the brief mourner's prayer, moved to a mound of earth beside the grave, picked up one of the shovels and, with considerable difficulty, dislodged a few frozen clods and shoved them into the hole. They made a hollow sound, bouncing off the casket. He handed the shovel to the first pallbearer and we each took a turn. The John Deere backhoe, which had been waiting patiently off to the side, revved up its motor and two burly gentiles begun to roll up the plastic grass. By the time Shell and I had trotted back to our cars the wound in the earth was being sealed up.

After Shell, who's coat was even flimsier than Abby's, had started his car he got into the back seat of our car to warm up while his car was warming up. After I'd introduced him to the car's owner he asked me a question that had obviously being bothering him since I'd sat down on the other side of Coleman's casket. "What are you doing here, Mood?"

"I was about to ask you the same question, where do you know Leon Coleman from?"

"Who?"

I always knew the Boy Photographer wasn't the brightest light in the studio but no one could be *that* dim. "What do you mean *who*, you just helped me bury the guy!"

"Oh, you mean Frosty!" He grinned his foolish grin. "You know I played poker with him every Wednesday night for about twenty years and didn't know his first name was Leon until yesterday."

I was wrong, there *was* someone who could be that far out to lunch. "That's nothing, Shell, I didn't know until five seconds ago."

25

What's in a name? Plenty—a Rose Kennedy by any other name would *not* smell as sweet. When you're born into a family dynasty you have the golden key that can open a lot of doors and keep the others from being slammed in your face. But when your parents have just stepped off the boat, wearing a nametag they can't pronounce, let alone read, you have to make a name for yourself. Or have one conferred upon you by your peers. Leon "Frosty" Coleman was one the "bums" who hung around the *Nordic Billiard Parlor*, the *Unicorn* (gambling) *Club*, and other institutions of lower learning I had occasionally frequented in my misspent youth. Some nicknames are not descriptive but simply remnants of schoolyard games. But Leon Coleman had gotten his the old fashioned way—he had earned it. *Frosty The Snowman* was a jolly happy soul who could sell refrigerators to Eskimos.

"So the mystery is solved," Abby said, snapping me out of my reverie. She was at the dining room table sorting and folding clothes—for a change. I'd fallen into the clutches of "Mrs. Clean". My live-in landlady wouldn't even let me wear the same shorts two days in a row.

"I guess," I said, looking out the picture window at the Christmas lights. The only housefront that was dark, apart from the one I was living in, was the one directly across from us.

"How did he end up in the Post Office," Abby wondered out loud, as she sorted clothes.

According to Shel, his father-in-law, who worked at the Post Office, got him the job. Frosty was so crazy about Irene Davidow (I'd had kind of crush on her myself) that he cleaned up his act—quit gambling, rambling and staying out late at night. Then "Goodnight Irene" left him for another "bum" and it was a blow from which the iceman never recovered. He kept his day job but resumed his all night poker sessions at the Unicorn Club, which, rather than a source of income became a bottomless pit into which he tossed his semi-hard-earned wages. Lady Luck, like his bride, had given him the brush. Then Old Man Fate delivered the final insult—the cool "con man", who had never been at a loss for words, was reduced to…

"What's this, Val, do you need it?"

I looked up to see the Maytag lady holding a crumpled piece of note paper.

"Where did you get that?"

"From the pocket of your dirty jeans."

"They aren't dirty."

"You've been wearing them all week."

"But they aren't *dirty*."

"Look, Virgo, maybe you don't care if your clothes stink but I'm the one who has to smell them. Now do you need this thing or not?"

"Not." Abby began to crumple it up. "No wait…" I put down my axe and went into the dining room. "Here, give it to me." I held out my hand.

Abby looked at me, oddly, then at Coleman's Last Will and Testament. "But there's nothing on it but a couple of smudges."

"I know, but I don't want you to throw it out."

"Why not?"

"I just don't."

Abby shook her head and heaved a resigned sigh. "You know, Virgo, sometimes I wonder about you." She looked at both sides of the note, then smoothed it out on the dining room table and examined it closely. "What is it supposed to be?" I could see that she wasn't going to relinquish it without an explanation so I told her the whole grisly story. "And you've been walking around with it in your *pocket*?" she cried. "Why on earth didn't you give it to inspector Duncan?"

I smiled, lamely. "I told you why."

"I don't believe this guy, someone's trying to blow his head off and he's afraid of a…scolding!" She held up the crumple paper. "This is *evidence*, Virgo."

Yeah, of brain damage. "Of what, it's completely illegible."

"To you, maybe, but the police have handwriting experts."

I managed to keep a straight face. "I wouldn't describe that as handwriting, sweetheart, and I already know who wrote it."

Abby looked at me like I was the one with brain damage. "Look, bub, if you don't take this thing to inspector Duncan I will."

I heaved a resigned sigh. "All right, I'll go and see him tomorrow, after the show."

"You'll go and see him right now."

"Gimme a break, Abby, it's Sunday night."

"So call him at home, I'm sure he won't mind."

She was right, he didn't mind—because he wasn't home. A woman whom I presumed was his wife asked if I would like to leave a message. No, it was rather urgent; did she know where I could get in touch with him? There was a moment of silence.

"May I ask whose calling, please?"

"Val Virgo. "

"Oh… You might try the Law Courts Building, Mr. Virgo."

Angus's old lady wasn't as efficient as she sounded, she didn't even know where he worked.

"You mean the Public Safety Building."

"No, the Law Courts Building—on Broadway."

As I drove across town I wondered what Angus Duncan was doing at the courthouse. His wife wouldn't say. I didn't even know the building was open on Sunday. As I pulled into the parking lot I saw several cop cars and a grim-faced cop was guarding the entrance.

"What's your business here, sir?"

"I'm looking for Inspector Duncan."

The young cop looked at me suspiciously. "May I have your name please?"

"Virgo. Val Virgo."

Open Sesame! Being a semi-famous victim wasn't all roses but it did open doors. I headed for the light coming from a doorway at the end of the dim marble corridor. As approached, Angus Duncan emerged from a door marked *Queens Bench, Judges Chambers*, with a distracted look on his craggy mug, and almost barreled into me. He stopped in his tracks. "Virgo!" He clamped a vice-grip on my right elbow and steered me to a neutral corner. "What the hell are *you* doing here?"

Believe me, Angus, it was not my idea. "I have something to show you."

I dug the crumpled note out of my shirt pocket and handed it to him. As the blood flowed back into my arm he squinted at the illegible scrawl, then looked up, impatiently. "Alright, I'll bite, what is it?"

I shrugged. "Your guess is as good as mine, Leon Coleman's nurse found it clutched in his hand when had that fatal stroke."

Duncan's jaw dropped. "And you've been hanging onto it all this time?"

"I didn't see any point in bothering you—like you say: *what is it?*"

He withdrew a pair of rimless glasses from his breast pocket, moved into the light from the doorway and took a closer look. Then his expression changed to something almost approaching excitement. "My God, take a look at this, Virgo." I came over and looked. He pointed at the first chicken track, "that looks like a *j*" he moved to the second one, "and that could be a *u*. *J-u-* Coleman might have been trying to write *judge*. Or *Justice*."

"I guess it's possible, but what's the significance of those words?"

Duncan looked up. "Well it's a long shot but Coleman might have known who the next victim was going to be."

"What do you mean the next victim, Justice Brown was the *first* victim."

"For Christ sake, Virgo, are you being deliberately difficult or are you really that dense? I'm talking about *Kilgore*."

It hit me like the acrid smell that was drifting through the door from which he had emerged. I suddenly realize what Angus Duncan was doing at the Law Courts Building on his day off.

26

Abby left the hall light on but when I came into the bedroom she was snoring, softly, like a purring cat. I undressed as quietly as possible so as not to wake her. A country song was drifting from the I-pod that was plugged into a player on her night table. Abby had fallen asleep doing her *homework.* When I slipped under the covers she stirred, then snuggled her warm backside against my cold leg. "Hi."

"Go back to sleep."

"I wasn't sleeping." She rolled over to face me. "You know I can't fall asleep till you get home," she yawned. "What took you so long?"

"I was talking to inspector Duncan."

"About that note?"

"Um hum."

"So, what did he think?"

"That it might be the beginning of a word."

"See, I told you, what kind of word?"

"Lie down. I'll tell you all about it in the morning."

No point in ruining *both* our night's sleep. Not that anyone was likely to lose much sleep over "Maximum Jack" Kilgore's untimely demise. Kilgore was a "Law and Order" Justice who had one minor flaw; he didn't know the law. His lack of legal acumen was exceeded only by his lack of restraint. During his short tenure on the trial bench his tendency to shoot from lip generated so much heat, and so little light, that he was hastily "elevated" to the Court of Appeal where he would have no witnesses to intimidate, juries to confuse, or journalist to delight with off-the-cuff comments that might bring the entire justice system into disrepute. But the best-laid plans often fall prey to capricious fate. On a slow news day a local muckraker happened to wander into the Court of Appeal when a defense lawyer was urging the learned Justices to overturn the conviction of an aboriginal offender because the only Crown witness was his accomplice, who admitted to being intoxicated at the time of the offence. To which Justice Kilgore replied: "If we had to disregard the evidence of every drunken Indian who testified in these cases we'd have to overturn them all."

Needless to say these remarks, which appeared on the front page of the *Daily Tabloid*, did not endear Justice Kilgore to the aboriginal community or his judicial brethren. Since removing a Superior Court Judge is just slightly less difficult than kissing your elbow The Chief Justice invited his colleague to take a little vacation until the controversy died down. Apparently Kilgore's leave of absence did not make the public's heart grow fonder. Still, a week after he returned from Bermuda he had joined the most exclusive club in town...posthumously.

"You'll tell me *now*."

It was a tone I had learned not to trifle with. So I didn't trifle.

"Thank God," she said and hugged me so hard I saw stars. I didn't expect her to be devastated but this was a little over the top. Realizing the inappropriateness of her joy, she smiled sheepishly. "I know it's terrible to be happy when something like this happens but it's such a relief that it's..." She hesitated.

"Not me."

Tears welled up in her eyes. "Oh, Val, I've just been holding my breath since that bomb went off in your motel room and now...it's like a dark cloud has moved away from our house to someone else's." She smiled through her tears. "Aren't I terrible?"

I hugged her. "No, sweetheart, just honest." She wasn't the only one who was relieved to see a break in the pattern.

"Besides, he wasn't a very nice man was he, Val?"

"Judge not lest ye be judged."

"But what about those awful things he said about Indians?"

"He was probably just saying what a lot of the other judges think but are too diplomatic to say. According to Inspector Duncan Maximum Jack Kilgore didn't have anything against Indians, he treated every one who appeared before him exactly the same." *Like dirt.*

"Anyway, this kind of shoots down your theory. "

"Kind of." Angus Duncan didn't seem to think there was any significance in Jack Kilgore and Robert Brown being law school classmates and, frankly, neither did I. And his theory about Frosty Coleman's "note" was somewhere on the border between wishful thinking and fantasy. I still had a feeling that there was some connection I was missing but wasn't about to re-open *that* can of worms. If the mad bomber (or bombers) were prepared to move on, so was Izzy Miller.

"Who's that singing, Val?"

"Waylon."

"All right *wailing*. Do you have to correct everything I say?"

I laughed. "I'm not correcting you, Toots, the man's name is Waylon Jennings."

"Don't call me Toots, I'm not your wife."

A hint? Or a threat? I wasn't hostile to the idea but wasn't prepared to plan for the future until I was sure I was sure I *had* one. As usual with her pregnant silences, this one gave birth to a new thought. "You know, Val, that was a nice funeral."

"I'm glad you enjoyed it."

"Don't be rude. I didn't *enjoy* it; I just thought it was..." she couldn't think of the word.

"Exotic?"

"Well, it certainly was different from Robbie's. His funeral was so formal and cold. I didn't feel a thing, even during the eulogy. It was like they were talking about a stranger."

"You were probably numb from the shock."

"Well, maybe. But Mr. Coleman's funeral really got to me. I felt like such a ninny, crying over someone I hadn't even met, but when the rabbi started to sing, or whatever you call it, it was just so moving. Do they do that at all Jewish funerals?"

"I suppose, I've only been to a few."

"Is being Jewish very important to you, Val?"

"In what way?"

"Well, if you had children, would you want them brought up as Jews?"

Something dropped inside me. "I hope the question is academic."

She giggled. "Well, I did miss my period."

"When were you due?"

"Two days ago."

I started breathing again. "Big deal; sometimes my ex-wife was over a week late."

"Well I'm not your wife, bub, I'm as regular as clock work."

"Aren't you taking anything?"

"Such as?"

I shrugged. "The pill…"

You'd have thought I was accusing her of snorting coke. "The pill," she screeched, sitting bolt upright. "Do you believe this guy? I've just lost my husband and he thinks I should be back on the pill." She turned from the invisible jury to the defendant. "What kind of a person do you think I am, Virgo?"

It was a good question—laughing one minute, crying the next, you never knew in what direction she was going to jump. I'd fallen into a bed of roses but the thorns were keeping me awake. "I think you're the best landlady I've ever had," I said, squeezing her delicious thigh.

"Yeah, sure, because you don't have to pay any rent." She got back under the covers and snuggled up. Then, with a yawn, "What shall we call her, Val?"

"Call who?"

"The baby. How about Rebecca? That's a nice Jewish name."

"Very funny."

"Of course it might be a boy. Lets see…" she bit her thumb, lost in thought. "I've got it, Hymie! Hymie Miller." She sat up and looked down at me. "How does that grab you, dear?" I held my silence. Her smile escalated to a fiendish grin. "What's the matter, Izzy, you look a little green around the gills, you aren't pregnant are you?" It wasn't a laugh, it was a shriek of triumph. Young widow Brown was seized by such a paroxysm of mirth I thought she was going to wet the bed. By the time she managed to get a grip on herself tears were running down her cheeks and her nose was running like a tap. "Well, don't just sit there," she said, with a hiccup, "get me a tissue."

I pulled one out of the box and handed it to her. "Did anyone ever tell you you have a strange sense of humor, Mrs. Brown?"

"Sure." She blew her red honker and leaned across my body to toss the soggy tissues into the wastebasket, which she insisted stay on my side of the bed. "Robbie used to tell me all the time."

And look where he is now. Maybe the wound had healed sufficiently to do a little probing. "Look, sweetheart, I don't want to upset you, so if you don't want to discuss it, just say so, but would you mind telling me something about the day Robbie…well, you know."

She looked at me quizzically. "Like what?"

I shrugged. "Just some of the details. For instance, do you know what kind of a package it was?"

"Just a plain brown paper package with his name on it."

"Did you see it?"

"Of course, I took it into the house."

"It came to the house?" I said, taken aback. "I thought it was mailed to his office."

She shook her head. "No, it was left on the doorstep. Robbie had just suspended that horrible inquiry…you remember when that policeman shot himself and everybody said it was Robbie's fault…well the poor baby was so upset that I thought I'd take him out to lunch at someplace fancy but when I phoned him he said he was too busy; he'd meet me at the Norquay Building cafeteria which is just across the street from the courthouse. Have you ever eaten there?"

"No…"

"*Don't*; the food is plastic and there's all these lawyers and civil servants sitting around, smoking their heads off…"

"Sweetheart, do you think you could cut to the chase?"

She gave me a "who's telling this story?" scowl but took the hint. "Well, to make a long story short, when I got home there was this package on the doorstep. It was addressed to Robbie but there were no stamps on it, or any of those courier stickers, so I figured someone from his office had dropped by with some documents or something and left them between the doors, because the package was too big to fit in the mailbox, but when I called Robbie he said he wasn't expecting anything and I should open it. So I did."

My heart skipped a beat. "You opened it?"

She nodded.

"What was inside?"

"A bunch of crumpled up newspapers and this tacky lamp, one of those Scales of Justice things, it was bronze or iron, or something, and had a blindfolded woman holding up one of those old fashioned scales and I certainly didn't want it in my living room. But when Robbie came home he thought it might look kind of cute on his desk. You know, sort of a conversation piece. A judge isn't supposed to accept gifts but it wasn't much a gift, and we couldn't send it back because there was no return address. Robbie thought it was probably some of his lawyer friends who did it for a joke."

"It had no return address?"

"It didn't even have *our* address, just Robbie's name, in black marker."

"Can you remember the exact words?"

She closed her eyes and bit her lip. "The Honorable Mr. Justice Robert W. Brown." She opened her eyes. "Did you know Robbie's middle name was Woodsworth. He was named after the man who started the C.C.F.?"

"No kidding," I said, as if it made a difference. "And there was nothing else on the package? No address, postal markings…?" She shook her head. "You're positive?"

"Of course I am, you think I could forget something like that? Why are you cross-examining me, Virgo?"

"Because it doesn't make sense to *personally deliver* a package like that. How much would it cost to mail it, ten bucks? Whoever's behind these bombings may be a psycho but that doesn't mean they're crazy. Why walk up to your doorstep in broad daylight and take a chance on being spotted by a nosy neighbor?"

Abby glowered. "Like my friend Sheila?"

I smiled, apologetically. "Look, sweetheart, I know she means well, but every time I look out the living room window I see her watching the house."

"You liar, you can't even see her living room windows from my house. Those spruce trees are in the way."

"I'm not talking about her living room windows. I'm talking about that little window on the third floor."

Abby smiled triumphantly. "That's not Sheila, dummy, that's her husband." She made a face. "He's a horrible little man, sits up in that rat hole he calls a studio, day and night, spying on the whole neighborhood. Sheila says he won't even let her in to dust. I don't know why she puts up with him. He treats her like a servant. If Robbie talked to me the way Louis Hogg talks to his wife it would have been goodbye …"

"Sheila's married name is Hogg?" I fairly gasped.

Abby frowned—she did not appreciate being interrupted in mid-diatribe.

"Wash your ears, Virgo, I just introduced you to the woman a couple of days ago."

"You introduced her as your *friend Sheila.*"

"Well, she *is* my friend," rejoined little Miss Non-Sequitur.

"She's also The Girl Wonder's *mother.*"

Abby looked at me, thunderstruck. "That horrible person you work with?"

"Otherwise known as Patricia St. John Hogg."

"Well, she certainly takes after her father, he's the rudest man I ever met. Just because it's named after one of his ancestor, or something, he thought he owned this riding." She smiled, smugly. "But Robbie beat the pants off him."

"Louis Hogg used to be the MLA for St. Johns?"

She looked at me, incredulously. "You didn't know *that* either, Mr. Talk show host?" I smiled, sheepishly. "What planet do you live on, Virgo?"

I was beginning to wonder.

27

Mmmm, that looks so good I think that's what I'll have for lunch." The pretty dark-eyed young waitress set the Greek Salad down in front of me and turned to my companion. "And yours was the hot roast beef sandwich." She put down the plate and held up the coffee pot. "Can I freshen you up?"

Morgan Riley put his hand across the top of his half-full cup and the pretty dark-eyed waitress bounced off to another table. "Don't you hate it when they do that?"

"Do what?"

"Put on that friendly act."

"You think it's an act?"

"Don't you?" It wasn't a rhetorical question; he was soliciting my opinion. Morgan trusted my "shit detector" just as I trusted his. In all the time he was my "boss" we hadn't had a single argument. Not that we always agreed. His worldview was darker than mine. Compared to old "Morgue" I was Pollyanna. I assume the girl at the cash register really *wants* me to have a nice day—unless I detect a "fuck you" in her tone of voice. I was prepared to accept friendliness as genuine until people did something *unfriendly*. Like plant a bomb in my room.

"No, I don't, Morgan. I think she's one of those rare individuals who actually *enjoys* what she does for a living."

"Well, maybe," he said, unconvinced. Any pretty young thing that didn't treat you like a potential rapist must be after *something*; like a big tip. Of course tipping wasn't my lunch companion's responsibility—I was the one who asked *him*. But Morgan knew there was no such thing as a free lunch. "So," he said, attacking his chips and gravy, "what's this all about?"

"Louis Hogg."

Morgan paused with a gravy-soaked French fry halfway to his mouth. "What about him."

"What do you know about him?"

The French fry resumed its journey. "What makes you think I know *anything* about him?"

"You know something about everybody, Mr. Editor. Besides he's a colleague of yours?"

Morgan paused in mid-chew. "Who told you that?"

"The Girl Wonder. Over a bottle of wine, she spilled her guts about her father's legendary journalistic career."

Morgan seemed to relax. He finished his mouthful of French fries and speared a few more from his plate. "When did this historic meeting take place?" he said, cutting into his gravy-soaked hot beef sandwich.

"When I was young and foolish." I started on my salad. The waitress was right; it *was* good.

Morgan, who had polished off his sandwich in two or three bites, began buttering a roll. "So why this sudden interest?"

"He's going to be a guest on the show."

Morgan raised an eyebrow. "Oh?"

"At least that's the plan," I said, spitting out an olive pit. "I'm going to see him tomorrow."

"Save yourself the trip," Morgan said, shoveling more fuel into the hopper. Where did he put it? He was one of those infuriating bastards who ate like a horse and stayed as thin as a whippet. "Louis St. John Hogg is a very private person. There's no way you're going to get him out of his house, let alone into a DBC studio."

"Look, getting Hogg to come on the show is *my* problem, all I want is some help getting my foot in door."

"What make you think I can help you with that?"

Time to put my cards (well, book) on the table. I put down my fork and opened my briefcase. "This."

Morgan picked up the weighty tome and studied the dust jacket. "Where'd you get this from?"

"The library." It wasn't exactly a lie—I'd found it in Abby Brown's library. *Robbie bought it because he felt sorry for the old crank. Nobody else was buying his stupid book.*

"Did you find it interesting?" Morgan said, evenly.

"I didn't get past the title—but I certainly found *that* interesting." Louis Hogg's magnum opus was entitled *One Man Majority; Memoirs of a Political Renegade.*

Morgan continued the bluff. "Yes, it's from Thoreau: *"Any man more right that his neighbor constitutes a majority of one."*

"I take it old Louis marches to his own drummer?"

"Well he's willing to put his ass on the line for what he believes in. Journalism is his trade but military history is his passion. He's a throwback to the old soldier-scholar. He writes poetry, paints, cooks, plays the piano..."

"And crawls on his belly like a reptile. If he's such a Renaissance dude how come the DBC dumped him?"

"It's a long story."

"So give me the Reader's Digest version."

"Why don't you ask Patricia?" Morgan averted his eyes to his plate—alas the cupboard was bare. Something occurred to him. "She has no problem with him as a guest?" he said, suspiciously.

You can't have a problem with something you don't know about. "Okay, Morgan, let's cut the bullshit, I promise not the blow *Renegade's* cover if you level with me."

It took him several seconds to decide whether or not he could trust me. But what choice did he have? Better to take a chance on me keeping my word than giving me no reason to keep his secret. "What do you want to know?"

"How to get through his shell."

Morgan took a swig of coffee, wiped his mouth with his napkin and said, "Ask him about the Lonechild case."

"And?"

"He'll take it from there."

"Can't you give me a hint? In case I have to prime the pump."

"You don't remember the case?"

I shook my head. "The name rings a bell..."

"It should, it was in the news for months. Lonechild served twenty years for a murder he didn't commit."

"Like the Millgard case?"

Morgan nodded. "And half a dozen others. But this one tops them all. John Lonechild was a seventeen-year old Indian kid who was accused of stabbing his best friend in St. Johns Park. When the police questioned him he denied even being in the park but when a witness said he saw him there, on the night in question, Lonechild came up with a new story. That was so bizarre that if you put it in a novel nobody would publish it. He and his buddy were having a few innocent beers when a total stranger walked up and stabbed his buddy through the chest with some kind of sword cane. He described the killer as an old man with a white goatee and an eye patch."

I smiled. "Maybe it was Long John Silver, risen from the grave."

Morgan nodded. "That's exactly what the police thought. Needless to say the jury was also less than enchanted by this fairy tale. Lonechild was convicted of non-capital murder and sentenced to life imprisonment."

"When was this?"

Morgan made a brief mental calculation "Around Nineteen fifty-eight. Which would have made him eligible for parole around nineteen sixty-eight. But they won't parole you unless you show some remorse and Lonechild continued to protest his innocence."

"He stuck to his story?"

"Like shit to a blanket. In Lonechild's case it looked like "life" really *meant* life. And that's where Louis Hogg comes in. In the seventies he had a DBC radio show called *The Court of Last Resort.* By the time he became aware of the case John Lonechild was yesterday's news. Nobody seemed to give a damn that he was languishing in Stony Mountain, least of all the authorities. But Louis Hogg was convinced that Lonechild was innocent and did what Lonechild's lawyers neglected to do, tore the prosecution's case to shreds—over the air. Why would Lonechild kill his best friend? What was his motive? If it was a drunken fight, as the prosecution suggested, why were there no bruises or abrasions? How could you stab a man to death without getting a drop of blood on your hands or clothing? And where was the murder weapon? The police hadn't found a shred of physical evidence tying Lonechild to the murder. He was convicted solely on the fact that his explanation of the crime was hard to believe. But why would a guilty man make up such an unbelievable story? And then stick to it even though it was keeping him in jail?"

"Good question, but he'd already changed his story. He didn't come up with the mysterious stranger until the police blew his first story out of the water. When they picked him up he denied even being at the scene of the crime."

"What would you have done in his place? You're a teenage Indian whose friend has just been murdered in a way you *know* the cops aren't going to buy. The police made absolutely no effort to find the guy Lonechild described; their entire investigation consisted of trying to browbeat a confession out of him. They made up their minds he was guilty before he opened his mouth." Morgan drained his cup and scanned the room for the waitress. "Just like a cop, never around when you need her." He eyed the last roll in the basket. "You going to eat that?" I shook my head. He broke it open and proceeded to butter it. "Louis Hogg did the police's job for them."

"He found the mysterious stranger?"

Morgan shook his head. "The guy was already dead but he found the mythical sword cane. Or, rather, it dropped into his lap. An old wino brought it to him. Said a flophouse buddy who was dying of emphysema gave it to him just before he shuffled off his mortal coil; an old character with a white goatee and shoulder length hair everyone called "Pirate Bill". The sword cane was his most precious possession. He claimed he'd once killed someone with it; a young punk who tried to mug him in St. Johns Park."

"Jesus Christ!"

Morgan smiled, grimly. "Well, he may have had something to do with it. Pirate Bill wanted to meet his maker with a clear conscience and since a priest wasn't available he told the nearest available body. His father confessor didn't know whether to believe him or not. Pirate Bill was always bragging about his prowess with the sword cane and everybody took his stories with a grain of salt."

"And a swig of Muscatel."

"Exactly. Pirate Bill's wino friend was not about to walk into the police station with a cock and bull story about a twenty year old murder. So he just stashed the sword cane in his duffel bag and went about his business. Then he heard Louis Hogg talking about the Lonechild case and decided to do his civic duty."

"And possibly make a little beer money."

"Possibly. But Louis Hogg wasn't about to go public with crucial evidence in a murder case so he took the wino straight to the police. And got a very chilly reception. The case was closed. Lonechild had been convicted by a jury of his peers and the police couldn't reopen the investigation, even if they were so inclined."

"And they were not so inclined."

Morgan shook his head. "And neither was the prosecution. Louis went to the Attorney General and hit the same brick wall. Lonechild had exhausted his legal remedies. He'd appealed his conviction and it was dismissed by the Court of Appeal."

"But not by the Court of Last Resort."

Morgan grinned. "Those smug bastards didn't know who they were dealing with. Louis St. John Hogg is a bulldog—once he sinks his teeth into what he feels is a miscarriage of justice he hangs on like grim death." The thought of his journalistic idol sinking his teeth into the backside of the Establishment put a fresh edge on his appetite. "How about some rolls?" he asked, as our waitress materialized with a pot of coffee. She picked up the basket and returned, within seconds. Morgan picked up a roll and the thread of his story. "Since they didn't consider Louis' revelations to be evidence," he mumbled over a hunk of roll, "he felt free to reveal them to the public. If they were prepared to keep an innocent man in jail for life, because it was too much trouble to re-open a file, the voters should know about it. He put so much heat on the government that the Attorney General had sudden change of heart."

"He picked up the case?"

"And tossed it to the Court of Appeal like a hot potato. After months of deliberation the learned Justices decided that Lonechild was entitled to a new trial."

"A new trial?" I was incredulous. "Why not just release the poor bastard?"

"That would be too simple," Morgan said, polishing off his roll. "Needless to say Louis was not exactly thrilled by this decision. He'd held his fire while the Court of Appeal was deliberating but now he climbed back on the soapbox and kept up the barrage, even as the jury was being picked for the new trial. The Attorney General got the presiding judge to issue a restraining order. Louis ignored it. The DBC was dragged into court to show cause why it should not be held in contempt of court. 'Because we've closed the barn door, your Lordship,' they said."

"They fired him?"

Morgan shook his head. "Reassigned him—from The Court of Last Resort to The Sedentary Gourmet."

"You're kidding?"

Morgan laughed. "Yes, I am. I don't remember what the show was called and I'm sure Louis has done his best to forget it too. He grudgingly took up his new assignment but as the trial dragged on he broke under the strain. One day he got a little too deeply into the vintage and not only expressed his opinion of the wine he was sampling but the ancestry of the judge who had robbed him of his editorial freedom. Not to mention the DBC bureaucrats who had gone along with the gag order."

I laughed. "And *that* was the end of his radio career?"

Morgan smiled affirmatively.

"What happened at the second trial?"

"Lonechild was found guilty of manslaughter."

"What?"

"Lonechild was…"

"I heard what you said, I just don't believe it. How could any jury convict him after hearing what that wino had to say?"

"He never took the stand. The judge ruled that his evidence was hearsay and since he was the only witness who could connect the sword cane to the murder it wasn't allowed in either. The only new evidence came from Lonechild, who admitted that he hadn't told the police the whole truth, Pirate Bill hadn't attacked him and his buddy out of the blue but after they asked if he could spare a few bucks."

"And the second jury didn't find the revised version any more convincing than the original story?"

"Can you blame them?"

I shook my head. "Without the evidence of the wino and the sword cane the trial was a travesty."

"Exactly what Lonechild's lawyer successfully argued before the Court of Appeal. They held that the wino should have been allowed to testify—Pirate Bill's confession was a "dying declaration" which is an exception to the hearsay rule. They quashed the conviction and ordered a new trial."

"*Another* trial? Lonechild must have died of old age before it was over."

"No such luck, he hanged himself at the Remand Center."

There were several seconds of thoughtful silence as my luncheon companion conscientiously cleaned up the gelatinous mess of gravy that had congealed on his plate with the remnants of a crusty roll.

"And then Louis Hogg went into politics."

Morgan looked up from his plate. "With a vengeance. For twenty years he was the most high profile cabinet member in the province and when Ed Shreyer accepted the job of Governor General Louis was the obvious choice to succeed him as Premier. But his colleagues thought he was a little too radical so he lost out to Howard Pawley."

"By a majority of one?"

"By acclamation," Morgan said with a pained smile. "Louis had alienated a number of the younger members of the party. In the next election he wasn't even nominated to run in his old district. His track record should have been enough to get him in by a landslide but he was nosed out by a high profile newcomer."

"The late judge Brown."

Morgan nodded. "And to add insult to injury he moved into the house right across the street."

"Tell me about it."

Morgan smiled, ruefully. "It's a small world, Muddy."

And getting smaller all the time, Morgue.

As I headed back across town, to rendezvous with my reclusive neighbor, I didn't realize how claustrophobic it was about to become.

28

As the crow flies Hogg Manor is fifty yards from Abby Brown's house; as the Virgo walks it was in a different galaxy. Louis Hogg's house was on the sunny side of the street but, thanks to two towering evergreens on the front law, was in perpetual shade. Nevertheless all the curtains on the main floor were drawn. According to Morgan, when "King Louis" ruled the riding, as if by divine right, his stately home had been the social and political hub of the constituency but the "safe seat" had been under an alien rump for over a decade and its perennial MLA was an embittered recluse whose decaying palace was a relic of a bygone era. *Louis Hogg doesn't live in this house*, I thought, as I climbed the crumbling steps, *he haunts it.*

I pushed the doorbell and heard a chime intone what sounded like the first four notes of *Rule Britannia.* My imagination was working overtime. Before the last note faded the door opened and I did a double take. Standing in front of me, in a maroon cardigan, was a replica of The Girl Wonder, as she might look after being entombed in the family vault for a decade or two. The cadaver surveyed me with a baleful gleam in his sunken eyes and pissed-off sneer on his thin-lipped mouth. I started to introduce myself but he cut me off in mid-introduction.

"I know who you are, c'mon in."

When he shut the door behind me the gloom enveloped me like a shroud. Compared to this place the DBC was invigorating. Unlike Abby Brown's refurbished museum piece, the interior of Hogg Manor was as cheerless as the facade. No wonder Patricia St. John Hogg was such a ray of sunshine; her childhood home had all the warmth and charm of a funeral parlor; a musty mothball factory in which a window had not been opened nor a piece furniture replaced since it's proprietor had retired from public life.

"Hang up your jacket. We can talk in my study."

All we had to do was climb three flights of stairs. Hogg's "study" made my cubbyhole seem spacious. I had to duck my head to get through the door. The slanting walls were lined with books, except for an area on the south wall where a lead-glass window was doing its best to shed a little light onto an enormous oak desk that looked like it was probably brand new—when Queen Victoria's secretary had used it. The surface of this gargantuan antique was buried under a sea of paper, in the center of which stood an incongruous island of modern technology. A Mac Computer, an HP All-In-One printer fax copier scanner and an unidentified modem with blinking yellow lights. Well, my reclusive host and I had one thing in common: an electronic umbilicus to the outside world.

"Have a chair," he said, moving behind the desk.

Since there was only one, a leather club chair of roughly the same vintage as the desk, I sank into it gratefully. For a zombie Hogg was surprisingly spry. He had fairly sprinted up those three creaky flights and wasn't even winded. The little shrimp was not only in better shape than I was but, suddenly, taller. That stenographer's chair must have been screwed up as far as it would go. And since I was virtually sitting on the floor I found myself looking up at him. Which suited him right down the ground. "I understand you're a Henry Miller fan," he observed, from his lofty perch.

It wasn't the opening gambit I had anticipated but I wasn't inclined to look a gift horse in the mouth. "That's right," I said, brightly.

"How can an intelligent person read that filth?"

The horse's teeth were obviously worn to the gum. I gave him a disarming smile. "What makes you think I'm intelligent?"

"You're *not*—if you admire that juvenile trash. What do you think of Hemingway?"

I took a second to consider my response. The fate of the interview could hang on the answer to this "leading" question. Diplomacy was the watchword. "Frankly, I'm not too familiar with his work."

"What have you read?"

I scoured my memory. "A Moveable Feast…The Sun Also Rises…Islands In The Stream…a couple of short stories…"

"What did you think of them?"

"The stories?"

"Stories, novels, what do you think of Hemmingway's work."

I smiled apologetically. "It isn't really my cup of tea."

"Why not?"

I was backed into a corner. Not an unfamiliar feeling. The secret of Izzy Miller's lack of success is his habit of telling people what they aren't exactly dying to hear—the truth. But with my life on the line, rather than just my career, one would think I'd have enough sense to come up with a diplomatic fib.

And one would be wrong.

"Because I don't believe a word he's written. To me Hemmingway's so-called realism has a hollow ring. His characters are more like heroes in a Spaghetti Western than human beings. They're constantly mouthing profundities and striking attitudes. And so was Hemmingway. In my opinion he was too concerned about his image as the "Great American Novelist" to reveal any unflattering truths about himself. He uncovers the top layer and buries the rest under a load of literary rubbish." I bit my tongue and braced myself for the counter-attack.

"You're right, Hemingway was a fraud." Louis Hogg had outflanked me. "War correspondent!" he snorted. "Hemingway drove an ambulance for a couple of months in Spain, before the *real* war broke out then went back to Paris to drink cognac in some bistro. Same with bullfighting. And big game hunting. Hemmingway was a dilettante." Hogg directed his sneer in my direction. "But at least he wasn't a pornographer."

"You've got the wrong idea about Henry Miller. What have you read of his?"

"Nothing. I *tried* reading Tropic of Cancer; couldn't stomach more than a few pages."

"Try The Colossus of Maroussi," I said, baiting the hook.

"Never heard of it."

"It has no sex at all. It's a combination memoir and travel book." The fish showed a spark of interest. Time to reel him in. "Miller got out of Paris just before the Nazis marched in and on his way back to the States he stopped off to visit his friend Laurence Durrel, who had a villa on the isle of Corfu. And Miller fell in love with Greece."

"A lot Henry Miller can tell me about Greece," Hogg grunted. "I was there for the duration, Virgo. And not in some fancy villa, or a luxury hotel as a guest of the government, but up in the hills with the partisans. There was none of this buddy-buddy with the enemy business in those days. I didn't have a camera crew just an old wire recorder that would break down if you looked at it the wrong way. If the Nazis had gotten their hands on me I'd have been shot as a spy. But I got the message out. 'The Voice of the Greek Resistance'—that's what they called me on the radio."

I nodded. "I listened to a few of the broadcasts."

"You must have been in diapers," Hogg said, trying not to sound too pleased.

I shook my head. "The same pants I'm wearing today, they're in the DBC archives."

Hogg snorted. "I'm surprised they haven't burned them. I'm persona non grata around that place, you know? I was a little too honest for those pusillanimous paper pushers." He pointed a bony finger at me. "Let's get one thing straight, Virgo, if you want me to come on your show I go on live or I don't go on at all. You tell that daughter of mine to forget about that cut and paste journalism. No one edits…"

"Louis, dear?"

I turned to see Sheila Hogg standing in the doorway.

Her husband didn't return her smile. "Can't you see I have company?"

"That's why I came up, dear, I thought you and your guest might like some tea."

"Well, you thought wrong." Her smile didn't waver. She was obviously used to her husband's bark and knew it was worse than his bite. He turned his scowl on me. "You drink wine, Virgo?"

"Occasionally—with a meal."

"You don't need a meal to enjoy a glass of wine. My wife can bring us a little brie or something. Ever try Retsina?"

"Once."

He waited for the punch line.

"It was like sucking a pine cone."

I didn't do any better in the return of smile game than Hogg's wife. "Bring us a bottle of Beaujolais," he snapped at her. "The ninety one." She scurried off to the wine cellar and Hogg climbed back onto the soapbox. "Retsina's an acquired taste. The ancient Greeks used to seal their wine casks with resin and got used to the flavor. So now they add resin to the finished product. That's why it's called Retsina."

"Is that right?" I said, as if it was a revelation from Delphi.

The Oracle gave me a scornful smirk. "I'm surprised you didn't know that, Virgo; didn't your friend Miller mention it in his travel book?"

"I don't remember," I said, truthfully. *I might have come across that hoary pine nut in my Dick and Jane reader.*

"What was the name of that book again?"

"The Colossus of Maroussi."

Hogg took out a pad and fountain pen. "How do you spell Maroussi?"

It was a good question—and I was sure *one* of us knew the answer. Fortunately the other one was saved by the arrival of the refreshments. "Put it on the desk," King Louis grunted, as his cupbearer lugged in a silver tray with a bottle of red wine, two long-stemmed glasses and an abundant cheese platter. She set the tray down and made her exit without waiting for (or receiving) any thanks from her husband. He was working on the wine before she was out the door. After deftly peeling the foil from the neck of the bottle he picked up a two-pronged implement that he identified as a "cork remover". This precision instrument, he informed me, as he inserted the unequal prongs on either side of the cork, was superior to your garden variety corkscrew because it prevented stray particles of cork from impairing the taste and purity of the wine. Fitting deed to word he withdrew the cork, "virgo intactus", without so much as a pop. Then he sniffed it, set it on the silver tray and, with an expert twist of the wrist, poured a sample of ruby liquid into one of the wine glasses—without spilling a drop. He picked up the glass, spun his chair around to face the window, examined the wine against the light, swirled it around, tilted the glass and watched it run down the side to see if it was—I don't know what. Whatever he was looking for, he seemed to find it because, after sniffing the bouquet, he took a sip, swished it around in his mouth, chewed and, at long last, swallowed. He smacked his thin lips, topped up his glass, filled the other one and watched like a hawk as I raised it to my lips.

"Very nice," I said, after taking a short swig.

If my host was disappointed in my failure to chew my wine properly, before swallowing, he didn't show it. "It should be," he harrumphed. "For the price they charge. I remember when you could get a good Beaujolais for under two dollars. But the Pepsi generation doesn't have the patience to lay a wine down so they'll pay the earth for one that's drinkable the minute you get it home. . Beaujolais Nouveau is the latest fad, Virgo. Your Yuppie friends have driven the price through the roof. The day the new crop hits the market you young people line up like hippies at a rock concert." Having gotten a bit of a dry throat delivering this oration Professor Hogg knocked off his second glass in one long swallow. As he refilled it, I tried to lure him off his current tangent and back to the previous one.

"You were saying that you're not too welcome at the DBC."

"That's right," he said, picking up his cue. "Louis St. John Hogg was a little too outspoken for those pusillanimous bureaucrats. They kicked me off the air because I refused to be muzzled. I said there was a law for the white man and a law for the Indian. It was true then and it's still true."

"You mean the Lonechild case?"

He gave me a searching look. "What do you know about the case?"

"Not much."

"Well let me enlighten you." He fortified himself for the task. "John Lonechild was an Indian, a Communist and he wouldn't keep his mouth shut; in short, he was an ideal victim for the big shots. When the big powers make up their mind to get you, Virgo, nothing will stop them. I know; they made up their mind to get me. Read my book, it'll open your eyes." Before I had a chance to give him the good news, he turned to the door and bellowed. "Sheila!"

Her bland face popped through the door. "Yes, dear?"

"Are there any copies of my book around?"

She shook her head. "You gave them all away."

"Well phone that Farr woman and tell her to send over a dozen more. Virgo here wants to read it."

Sheila Hogg hesitated. "She won't give us any more." She smiled awkwardly. "She said you didn't pay her for the last batch."

Hogg turned beet red. "I'm not going to pay for my own bloody book. She should pay *me* to take them off her hands—she's got boxes of them gathering dust down there. And doesn't do a damn thing to sell them."

"We'll it won't hurt to give her a call," his wife said, and beat a hasty retreat.

Hogg consoled himself with another pull on the vintage. "Never write a book, Virgo. Or go into politics," he added, with a soft belch. "They'll make you pay for that too." Having refilled his glass he moved to top me up. When he saw that my glass was still half-full he looked at me darkly. "I thought you liked it?"

"I do. But I have to pace myself. If I drink more than a glass of red wine without eating a meal I get a headache."

Hogg gave me a superior smirk. "Maybe I should ask my wife to brew you a pot of herb tea."

It was the opening I was waiting for. "You don't miss much do you?" I said with a smile.

"Not in this neighborhood."

I stood up, moved to the window and pretended to admire the view. "I see what you mean." Then, after a suitable pause, "I don't suppose you noticed anything suspicious out there on the day judge Brown's was killed?"

Hogg looked up at me, suspiciously. "What do you mean suspicious?"

I resumed my seat. "Oh, I don't know, any unusual characters hanging around his house."

Hogg tossed off the remainder of his wine and neatly reversed his field. "I don't pay any attention to what goes on out there. I broke my neck for this constituency for twenty years and what thanks did I get? Some opportunist parachutes into the riding and they desert me like…" He didn't like the metaphor so he broke off to refill his glass, muttering to himself. "The two-faced bugger didn't even buy that house until they handed him my seat on a silver platter." He turned back to face me but seemed to have trouble focusing his eyes. Purple blotches had broken out on his face and he was beginning to slur his words. "My grandfather built this house in 1919, Virgo, year of the Winnipeg General Strike. Now some Jewish gentleman wants to turn it into a rooming house. I don't mind telling you, when those ungrateful buggers," he pointed a shaky finger in the general direction of the window, "stabbed me in the back, I almost packed my bags. But then I heard my father's voice. *You're running away.*" He retrained his bleary eyes on me and resumed his own voice. "A St. John Hogg never runs from a fight, Virgo. I was damned if I'd let some Johnny-Come-Lately run me out of my own home." He turned to the window and heaved a world-weary sigh. "When I'm gone the slumlords can do what they want with this place." He turned back to me and tried, in vain, to refocus his eyes. "I'm the last of the Mohicans, Virgo."

"What about Patricia?"

King Louis didn't acknowledge the possibility that a female might be in the line of succession, let alone inherit his castle. He had more important matters to attend to. The bottle had run dry and his lady in waiting was no longer lurking in the hall. He had to bellow himself hoarse before she finally huffed and puffed into the throne room. "Well, it's about time." Hogg held up the dead soldier. "Bring us another bottle of Beaujolais."

Sheila's face fell. "But Louis, you know what the doctor..."

"But me no buts," Hogg snapped. "Just bring it."

His wife gave him a sick smile. "How about a nice white? You have some very good Chardonnay..."

"If I wanted a Chardonnay," the troll roared, "I'd have *asked* for a Chardonnay! For once in your life can't you just do as you're told without an argument?"

Sheila Hogg looked like she was about to cry. "Oh dear," she said, biting her lip. "I don't know why you insist on drinking red wine when it gives you such terrible migraines."

The Girl Wonder was no slouch in the blushing department but her old man could have spotted her fifty blood pressure points and beat her to a cerebral hemorrhage. From the way Louis Hogg's temporal vein was bulging I thought it might suddenly spray Beaujolais-saturated gore all over the room. To avert this possibility his chief cook and bottle washer hurriedly retrieved the dead soldier and scurried out to find a live one. Hogg turned to me and belched. His voice was so thick I could barely understand him. "Never marry a nurse, Virgo, they'll nurse you to death."

I had no intention of marrying a nurse; I had another candidate in mind. As my host licked the dreg from his empty glass, I drank to her health with an empty feeling in the pit of my stomach. I would have helped myself to a slice of Jarelsburg but I might have thrown it up. "You were telling me about Judge Brown's political background," I forced myself to say.

"What political background?" Hogg slobbered. His purplish lips curled into a sneer. "Your girlfriend's husband was a rank opportunist, Virgo. Honest Bob Brown, The Great White Father! I was fighting for native rights when that two-faced bugger was still..." He paused in mid diatribe as his wife scurried in with a fresh bottle. "Well, it's about time," he said, snatching it from her. Before she was out the door he was working on the foil. He was trembling so violently the bottle kept slipping out of his hands. When he finally managed to wrestle it to a draw he attacked it with his designer corkscrew. After several near misses (which resulted in a few minor flesh wounds) he managed to insert the prongs and yanked out the cork. He sloshed the wine into his glass, spilling a few drops on the desk. He wiped them off with his sleeve and gulped the ruby liquid greedily, without nary a sniff or a chew. A bit of wine dribbled down his chin onto his cardigan where it disappeared without a trace. Maroon was definitely his color. It even matched his complexion. "Your friend Brown was a parlor socialist," he slurred, sloshing wine in the general direction of his glass. "There are more important things than winning an election. Things like truth…integrity…" He drank a toast to truth and integrity. Then refilled his glass. He didn't offer to refill mine. He'd obviously written me off as a drinking buddy. In fact, he seemed to have forgotten I was in the room as he sat there, cradling his wine glass in trembling blue-veined hands, staring glassily into space, muttering semi-coherent platitudes. Louis St. John Hogg was no longer addressing me but posterity. And I was no longer listening to his words of wisdom. But his voice was still ringing in my ears as I stumbled down the stairs and out the front door.

You're next you two-faced bugger!

29

I was greeted at Abby's front door by a familiar boyhood smell and decided to wait until morning to give her the good/bad news. Why spoil her surprise? "Hi, it's me," I said, hanging up my jacket.

"Hi you," she called from the kitchen.

I found her at the stove, spooning potato pancake batter into a frying pan. I came to look over her shoulder. "Get your nose out of here, Virgo" she said, pushing me back with her butt. "Unless you want it splashed with hot peanut oil."

"Is it Chanukah already?"

She nodded. "Tonight's the first night."

I laughed. "How do you know?"

"A little birdie told me."

"The birdie's initials don't happen to be G-O-O-G-L-E?"

"Don't ask so many questions. Just go wash your hands; we have to light the candles."

"You bought candles?"

"Well we have to do *something* to celebrate the season. And you're too cheap to buy me a Christmas tree."

Abby had not only obtained a box of colored candles but a nine-branched candelabra and a card on which the Hebrew prayer was printed in phonetic English characters. As I lit the "shamus" and then the "first candle" she did her best to sing the blessing along with me but her best was none too good. She tripped over the words and fell flat on the melody. The would-be Jewish housewife had a heart of gold but her ear was pure tin. Still, she did cook a mean Chanukah latke. "These are delicious," I said, shoveling in my fifth or sixth.

"As good as your mother's?"

"Are you kidding? You could have used my mother's for curling stones; these are light as a feather."

Abby grinned, mischievously. "It's Malka's recipe."

"Who the hell is Malka, one of your imaginary friends?" That's what Abby called her computer buddies 'imaginary friends'.

She laughed. "No, she's a *real* imaginary person. I found a website that had all sorts of Chanukah stuff on it and read this cute story called Malka's Recipe, that actually had a potato pancake recipe. So I printed it up and that's what you're eating."

"The recipe?"

"Very funny." She got up, went to the stove and flipped over the pancakes that were sizzling on the frying pan.

"So you spent the day surfing the web and grating potatoes?"

"No, I had a visitor."

"So what else is new?" I said, reaching for the yogurt—which was "healthier" then sour cream. Actually, it was also better on potato latkes.

"Well you've certainly changed your tune, when I told you I was late, you almost had a bird."

I looked up and felt a wave of relief. "Oh, you mean your period? I thought you were talking about your friend Sheila."

"Wasn't she at home?"

"Not when I first got there. At least, I didn't see her."

"She was probably hiding from the slave driver. So, how did it go; did he see anything?"

"If he did, he's keeping it to himself."

"I told you, you were wasting your time."

"I'm used to it, that's what I do for a living."

"For goodness sakes," Abby said, returning to the table with a fresh batch. "If you hate the job that much, why don't you just quit?"

"Because I've developed this bad habit," I said, helping myself to a few more golden beauties. "It's called eating."

"Don't give me that baloney, Virgo, you haven't given me a nickel since you moved in."

I paused with my fork half way to my mouth. "I *offered* to share expenses, and you practically bit my head off!"

"I don't need your money, Virgo. My husband left me very well provided for. I just want you to shape up. Decide what you want to do with your life and go ahead and do it. Not just drift with the tide like a jellyfish. I'm not used to living with a wishy-washy man."

"Don't worry, stick with me and you'll get used to it."

Her scowl darkened. "That's your answer to everything? A joke. You'd rather tear yourself down than pull your socks up. Has anyone ever told you, you have a very low self-image, Mr. Virgo?"

I looked up from my plate into her scornful gaze. "In the last ten seconds you mean?"

She smiled, in spite of herself. Then her eyes softened. "What am I going to do with you? You have everything going for you, brains, personality, talent…if Robbie had your musical ability he'd probably have given up law and become another Bruce Cockburn. He'd have given anything to play the guitar like you do." She heaved a nostalgic sigh. "Poor Robbie, I'd lie in bed and hear him plunking away down here for hours. He tried so hard and never seemed to get any better." She turned with an accusatory glower. "But he kept trying. He didn't just…give up."

I reached over and took her hand. "Abby, I can't tell you how much I appreciate your confidence in me. But sometimes you have to come to terms with your own limitations. Just because I play the guitar a lot better than your late husband doesn't make me Chet Atkins. There are a hundred young pickers in this town who can play rings around me, and who will never rise high enough in the country music world to quit their day jobs. "

"That's the worst load of defeatist rubbish I've ever heard. For goodness sakes, Virgo, what are you afraid of? It's not like I'm asking you to support me. Robbie would never have stuck with a job he didn't believe in, just because it paid well."

I felt the potato pancakes backing up on me. Victim or no victim, I'd just about had my fill of the Ghost of Christmas Past. "Sweetheart, I don't want to speak ill of the departed, but isn't it possible you're looking at the past through rose-colored shades? There are some people who don't seem to share your admiration of your late husband."

"Like who?" Abby said, narrowing her eyes.

I gestured toward the front door with my head. "Like your friend across the street."

Abby reacted like a scalded cat. "You liar. Sheila thought Robbie was the greatest…"

"…thing since sliced bread. I'm not talking about Sheila I'm talking about her lord and master. Did you know Louis Hogg hated your husband's guts?"

Abby came down from the ceiling. "Oh, him. The little twerp never forgave Robbie for beating the pants off him in that election. Not that he needed a reason, Louis Hogg hates everybody."

And shortly, everyone would hate *him*.

After we had done the dishes Abby went up to bed, as per our routine, and I stayed downstairs to hone my chops. But I didn't do much honing, just ruminating. If I expected Angus Duncan to call Louis St. John Hogg, former cabinet minister, in for a little chat I'd have to give him something more tangible than my suspicions. And something else was bugging me. After an hour of playing the same three chords, which I wouldn't have been able to name, I thought of a way to kill two birds with…two stones. I'd vent my spleen and hedge my bet.

Reasonably sure that Abby was asleep I went into the den, closed the door, and punched in Morgan's number. When he came on the line I came straight to the point. "I've been thinking about our lunch date, Morgan, and something's been bugging me. When you came to visit me at the hospital why didn't you tell me, right then, that The Girl Wonder's father works for you?"

There was dead silence on the other end of the line. "He doesn't," Morgan said, finally.

I was familiar with his double-speak. Louis Hogg didn't work for him because Morgan didn't own the paper. As editor he had the power to hire and fire, but, theoretically, he was not Hogg's employer. "Let me rephrase that. Why didn't you tell me Louis Hogg is the Tabloid's phantom editorialist?"

"Is that what he told you?"

"Just answer the question, Morgan. Did it, or did it not occur to you that keeping that information from me, and the police, might have been putting my life in danger?"

"No comment."

"I'll take that as a yes."

"That's your privilege."

"It's also my privilege to ask Hogg himself, when I get him in front of a microphone."

Pregnant silence. "He's agreed to come on the show?"

"Are you kidding, pass up the opportunity to blow his own horn? And he insists we go *live* so none of his pearls end up on the cutting room floor."

"When did you speak to him?"

"This afternoon. We had a nice long chat about how he made the world safe for democracy. In spite of all the capitalist big shots that are out to get him."

"Was he...drinking?"

"What makes you think he was?" *Two can play this game.*

The silence was more prolonged this time. When Morgan finally broke it there was an uncharacteristic note of urgency in his tone. "Look Val, I'm going to be honest with you..."

"Hold it, I want to hide my wallet."

"...Louis Hogg is a sick man."

"You mean an alcoholic."

"He has a drinking problem, yes, but he also has a medical problem—that's aggravated by his drinking. He's over eighty and his blood pressure is dangerously high. He's under doctor's orders to cut down on the wine, and avoid stress, but you've met him so you know how bull headed he can be. He's his own worst enemy." *Not as long as I'm around, Morgan.* "So his friends, and he doesn't have many left, have to protect him from his own excesses. Writing that column under a pseudonym wasn't his idea; it was mine. In fact I made it a condition of his employment. If word got out that Louis Hogg was Renegade the media attention would probably kill him. "

I managed to choke back my tears. "Thanks for sharing that with me, Morgan, but it's a little late to close the barn door. Why didn't you tell me this weeks ago?"

"I don't know. I suppose I didn't..." he searched for a diplomatic phrase.

"Trust me?"

"Well, God knows, that show of yours needs *something* to liven it up."

"So you thought I'd be prepared to risk giving Louis Hogg a stroke—to gain a few rating points?"

"Well he's not *your* friend, Val. Even if you didn't do it deliberately you might accidentally blow his cover. And I wasn't prepared to risk that. The stakes are too high. I haven't even revealed Renegade's identity to his colleagues at the Tabloid. Louis has never set foot inside the building. I bought him a computer and taught him how to use it so he could send his stuff directly to my personal laptop over a modem. Weaning him from a manual typewriter to a word processor was no walk in the park but it's a sacrifice I was willing to make to keep him alive. It's the only outlet he has for his creative energy."

"And pent up rage."

"That too." Silence. "So, now that you know the whole story what are going to do?"

"What would you do in my place, Morgan?"

There was dead silence on the other end of the line.

I kept the treacherous weasel twisting in the wind for a few seconds and then said, "Relax, I'm not the dedicated newshounds you are. I'm going to call up your friend right now and tell him I've had second thoughts about booking him as a guest."

"What excuse will you give?"

"I'll think of something."

I had, in fact, been thinking of nothing else for the past hour. When I phoned Hogg's house, as expected, Sheila answered. She was in the midst of telling me her husband was "indisposed" when his drunken voice broke in on an extension line. I pushed the "memo" button on the answering machine and broke the bad news. As expected, he did not take it very well. Somehow, in his addled brain, he got the idea that his old nemesis, the late judge Brown, was behind this conspiracy to silence him. I let the drunken troll rant and rave to his vindictive heart's content. When he finally ran out of gas I hung up, rewound the tape, removed it from the answering machine, broke the tab and replayed it on my cassette recorder. It was hardly broadcast quality— Louis St. John Hogg's raspy drunken voice was barely coherent. But it was music to my ears.

30

Now I knew what it felt like to be Lloyd Cringely. As I sat in my semi-comfortable chair, on the other side of the glass, waiting for the show to start, I was as jumpy as a cat on a hot tin roof. My heart was in my throat, my stomach was in a knot and Angus Duncan's voice was echoing in my head. "Virgo, I'm doing this against my better judgment so don't make me regret it; not a word of what you see or hear is to leave this room." I was already regretting having shrugged off his generous offer. "I suggest you to go the john because you won't get another chance. I don't want you in any other part of the building until the show is over. Until then this room is your home."

Actually, I felt kind of at home in that broom closet. The walls and ceiling were acoustic tiled, the furniture (except for a couple of wooden chairs) was nonexistent and it had a window through which I could observe my producer and operator writhing in agony. But our positions were reversed, this time they would be the "lab rats"—and I had chosen today's "guest".

At least, that was the plan. Hogg might not show up. And if he did, he wasn't likely to live up to my advance billing. Louis Hogg was a drunk but he was nobody's fool. If he showed up for this "interview" he'd probably be cold sober. Well, there was no use fretting over things you can't control. Que sera, sera. I settled into the spectator's seat and waited for the three-ring circus to begin. It was taking a hell of long time to get the show on the road. And the longer it took the more nervous I was getting. I didn't even have a program to thumb through, just an empty stage to stare at. It wasn't much of a set: a table, three chairs, two tape recorders. One chair was behind the table, facing the door, one was directly opposite, facing a blank wall, and the third was at the far end of the table. The tape recorders—one cassette, one reel-to-reel—were sitting in the middle of the table, rather conspicuously.

My bladder contracted another notch as Angus Duncan walked into the room and sat down in the chair facing the door. After a few seconds I heard a muffled voice say, "Right in here," and Neil Bannerman sauntered into view. From the bemused smile on his pockmarked face I could tell he felt right a home in the cop shop. Angus was his kind of guy. And the respect seemed to be mutual. At their first meeting Duncan had treated The Great White Technician with far more deference than he'd shown either Patricia or me. But now he was all business. "Shut the door behind you, Bannerman."

A shadow passed over Neil Bannerman's countenance. It wasn't the cordial greeting he had anticipated. He closed the door. Duncan nodded at the chair on the other side of the desk.

"Sit down."

Ban's left hand reflexively moved towards his shirt pocket. "Do you mind if I smoke?"

"Yes, I do."

Bans smiled lamely and dropped his hand into his lap. Then he noticed what was sitting on the table. "Are you going to tape this?" he asked, hesitantly.

Duncan shook his head and bans took his seat. "I just want you to listen to something." Duncan reached over and depressed the *play* toggle on the larger machine. As the reels began to spin he kept his eyes riveted on Neil Bannerman's face. It was déjà vu all over again.

"You're next you two-faced bugger."

Duncan punched the stop button and silence fell like an asbestos curtain. "Do you recognize that voice, Bannerman?"

Bans looked at him, strangely. "It's that nut that called the show."

"Does that nut have a name?"

Bans smiled, weakly. "I suppose."

"Do you know what it is?"

Bans couldn't look him in the eye. "I told you before, Inspector…"

"I know what you told me, I want you to tell me again." Duncan leveled the ray. " Do you or do you not recognize that voice?"

Bans tried to re-establish eye contact but fell a few inches short. "It's hard to say," he informed Duncan's necktie. "I've heard it so many times now…"

"That's it's hard for you to remember." Duncan reached for the cassette recorder. "Well, maybe this will refresh your memory." He hit the *play* button and a tinny voice spilled from the speaker.

"I know what you're afraid of Virgo, that I'll spill the beans on your girlfriend's beloved husband, Honest Bob Brown, the Great White Father! You know what that two-faced bugger did before he became..."

Duncan punched the *stop* button.

This time the silence was almost palpable.

Neil Bannerman had turned to stone.

"Well, Bannerman?"

Bans almost jumped out of his chair. He cleared his throat and tried to find his voice. Apparently he thought it might lying somewhere around his ankles. "Sounds like Louis Hogg," he muttered at the floor.

Duncan looked astonished. "And you had no trouble recognizing his voice?" The silence that greeting this rhetorical question was so thick you could have stuffed a mattress with it. "Do the words obstruction of justice mean anything to you, Bannerman?"

Bans looked up, abruptly. "Obstruction of *justice*?" He looked like he had just soiled his underwear. "I wasn't trying...I mean, I didn't think...Inspector, the last person I would try to protect is that fucking little..." he bit his tongue. "I'm sorry..."

"You needn't apologize, Bannerman," Duncan said, coldly. "I'm not offended by your language, merely your attitude. You seem to think a murder investigation is some sort of game. That you can choose what to tell the truth about and what to lie about?"

"It wasn't my idea," Bans whined. "Patricia Hogg worships her father. And I knew he was just a harmless drunk who likes to shoot his mouth off so I agreed to keep his identity secret. What choice did I have? She's my boss."

It was bullshit. At the DBC a Producer had virtually no control over a technician, let alone the power to hire and fire. But Bans was no longer merely a technician; he had been bumped up to "assistant" Producer of the show, which was probably the price he'd exacted for his silence. I'd had no idea Bans lusted after the Girl Wonder's job but then I'd had no idea that she had dibs on mine. Apparently everyone working on that lousy show wanted to do something else—including the host.

"Okay, thanks for clearing that up."

Ban's groveling came to an abrupt halt.

Duncan came around the table and opened the door.

"Send Miss Hogg in."

The color drained from Neil Bannerman's florid face. As Angus Duncan returned to his seat Bans watched him like a rat watching a cobra. Ignoring him, Duncan produced a file folder and began to thumb through it. The seconds dragged by. Finally, without looking up, Duncan broke the silence. "Don't let the door hit you in the ass on your way out, Bannerman."

There was little chance of that; Ban's shot out of the hot seat like a human cannonball.

But he wasn't quite fast enough. When the Girl Wonder stepped into the ring I could tell, from the disconcerted look on her face, that she'd seen just what Angus Duncan wanted her to see. She'd passed her co-conspirator on the way in, with no opportunity to compare notes. In showbiz, timing is everything.

"Come in, Ms. Hogg." Duncan rose to greet her with an avuncular smile on his meaty mug. "I'm sorry for calling you down on such short notice but I'll try not to keep you too long." He closed the door and nodded at the chair Bans had just vacated.

The Girl Wonder took it, gingerly sitting on the edge.

Duncan moved back behind the desk. "Can I have someone get you a cup of coffee, or a soft drink..."

"No, thanks," Patricia said, firmly. "What is this all about?"

"Duncan idly toyed with the file folder. "Well, certain information has come to my attention concerning the person who made that telephone call to your show on..." he opened the file folder, flipped through a few pages, and, after a pregnant pause, read off a date and time he could have recited in his sleep. He looked up and smiled, pleasantly. "I have reason to believe you know the identity of that caller."

Patricia's face turned scarlet. She looked at her lap and mumbled something I couldn't hear. The concealed mike wasn't sensitive enough to catch it. Apparently Duncan, who was sitting less than three feet away, didn't catch it either.

"I beg your pardon?"

Patricia raised her eyes—and her voice. "What gives you reason to believe that?"

Duncan's eyes twinkled. "A reliable source."

Patricia's flush deepened and her eyes blazed. Mr. Reliable Source could kiss his Assistant Producing career good-bye. "Did he say who he thought the caller was?"

Duncan smiled playfully. "How do you know my source is a *he*?"

Patricia bit her lip and her eyes began to fill. Not with tears of sorrow but frustration.

"Yes, your colleague had some thoughts on the subject."

"Which were?" Patricia said, fighting to keep her voice from cracking.

"I'd rather not say." Duncan smiled. "I don't want to influence your answer."

"And if I choose not to offer an opinion?"

"Oh, I don't think we're talking about an opinion; I'd say it was more like a dead certainty."

Duncan's tone was playful but his eyes were stone cold. Patricia shriveled like a punctured balloon under his piercing gaze. My diminutive co-host/producer looked so small and helpless, sitting mutely, staring at the floor, that I almost felt sorry for her. It was too big a stretch.

But not for Uncle Angus. "Look, Ms. Hogg, I don't enjoy putting you through this—I have a daughter myself. But I also have a job to do. All I'm asking is for you to confirm what we already know. For the record. We've already established the identity of the caller from several independent..."

"All right, it was my father," Patricia blurted out. "But he has nothing to do with these bombings, he was just trying to embarrass," she hesitated, "... the DBC."

"So why didn't you just tell me that at the time and save us all a lot of trouble?"

Now that the cat was out of the bag, Patricia regained a bit of her hauteur. "I saw no reason to involve the police in something that was just a practical joke."

Duncan looked at her with a puzzled frown. "What kind of a father plays a joke like that on his daughter?"

I don't think it was possible for The Girl Wonder to get any redder. "A wonderful one," she fairly shouted. Then, softening her tone. "My father was intoxicated when he made that call."

"At eight in the morning?"

"It was almost nine." Realizing the absurdity of this correction, Patricia decided a little clarification was in order. "My father has been under a great deal of stress in the last few years. He's always been a very active person and now, through no fault of his own, he has nothing but time on his hands. So he drinks a little more than he should. Louis St. John Hogg was the person who put the New Democratic Party on the map in this province. For years he *was* the Manitoba NDP and when the party finally came to power they dumped him for a younger man. It was the second great disappointment of his life." She pursed her lips. "I was the first. My father was a pioneer in the broadcasting industry, as well as at the DBC. But the Corporation terminated his contract because he refused to compromise his principles. It happened a long time ago but he's never gotten over it. He feels that by going to work at the DBC I've somehow betrayed him. And sometimes, when he drinks a little too much, he gets carried away."

Duncan was unmoved by this heart-rending tale. "I hate to repeat myself, Ms. Hogg, but why didn't you tell me all this at the outset, instead of sending me on a wild goose chase?"

"Why do you think? My father is a very proud man, with a long and distinguished record of public service. Can you imagine how embarrassing it would be for him to be revealed as the person who made that call?"

"Yes, about the same as the embarrassment of the recipient. And then to have you lie to me..."

"I'm sorry, Inspector, but my first loyalty is to my family. When he's been drinking my father is not responsible for his actions. Since the call didn't go over the air I didn't see what harm it would do to simply act like it didn't happen." She looked at him with a great show of sincerity. "Actually I was trying *not* to send you on a wild goose chase. My father is very a proud man, Inspector, and he has this...thing about authority figures. If you had dragged him down here and started grilling him about his...indiscretion there's no telling what he might have done."

"What could he have done, write a scathing editorial about police brutality?"

Patricia looked at him with obvious bewilderment. "What?"

"I'm referring to the column in the Daily Tabloid under the byline 'Renegade'. That is your father's pen name, is it not?"

Patsy laughed. "Who on earth told you that?"

I half-expected Duncan to trot out the old "reliable source" but he just looked at her for a few seconds and closed his file. "Thank you for coming in,

Ms. Hogg." He rose, moved to the door and opened it.

Patricia sat there, stunned. "Is that it?"

"For now."

The Girl Wonder was obviously prepared to explore the question of her father's putative ghost writing a bit further. But an investigator's job is to obtain information not disclose it. As Patricia St. John Hogg stumbled off the stage, slightly dazed, some of her lines were still ringing in my ears. *My father is very a proud man, Inspector, and he has this…thing about authority figures. If you had dragged him down here and started grilling him about his…indiscretion, there's no telling what he might have done.*

I was about to find out.

31

Resplendent in navy blazer, gray flannel slacks, and what looked like his old regimental tie, Louis St. John Hogg was barely recognizable as the bleary-eyed sot I'd left grumbling into his cups less than twenty-four hours ago. *A St. John Hogg never runs from a fight, Virgo.* The intrepid war correspondent marched into the enemy camp, and my field of vision, like a tin soldier. The only features of his appearance that hadn't changed were the bloodshot eyes and the contemptuous sneer on his parched lips. The sun was well past the yardarm and Louis was no doubt more than ready for an adult beverage.

Duncan didn't rise to greet him, just gestured at the chair. "Have a seat, Mr. Hogg."

"I prefer to stand," the tin soldier said, raising himself up to his full five foot, one. "And it's St. John Hogg."

The huge policeman smiled with amusement, tilted back in his chair and laced his thick fingers across his abdomen. "At ease, corporal, this isn't a Court Marshal."

Two fiery spots broke out on Hogg's clean-shaven cheeks. "A kangaroo court would be more like it. If I weren't worried about upsetting my wife I'd have told that storm trooper you sent to fetch me to go to the devil. This isn't a police state, Duncan. You have no right to drag me down here for interrogation without disclosing the nature and purpose of your inquiry."

Duncan's mask remained intact. "You weren't dragged down here by a storm trooper, you were escorted by a police officer. If he treated you with less than the utmost courtesy you can file a complaint with the Winnipeg Police Commission. I'm sorry if your wife was upset when the police car pulled up at your door but you didn't leave me much choice. When I spoke to you on the telephone you said you didn't own a car, and couldn't afford a cab I had no alternative…"

"I did *not* say I couldn't afford to pay for a taxicab," Hogg blustered. "Don't twist my words. I said I couldn't afford to *waste money* on one. I am not obliged to drive half-way across town, at my own expense, at the whim of the police."

Duncan's whimsical expression evaporated. "I assure you, this is no whim. Some very serious allegations have been made against you, Mr. *St. John* Hogg. And I thought you'd like the opportunity to answer them."

"What type of allegations?" Hogg said, some of the starch going out of his collar.

Duncan gestured toward the empty chair. "Have a seat and we'll discuss it."

Hogg stiffened. "Am I under arrest?"

"No…"

"Then there's nothing to discuss. I'm not some uneducated native you can intimidate with your Gestapo tactics. If I'm not charged with an offense you have no right to keep me here against my will. So kindly tell your flunky to drive me home. Or I'll have my lawyer slap you with a false imprisonment suit so fast it will make your head swim."

Duncan heaved a weary sigh, got up and opened the door. "Charley," he said to someone out of my line of vision, "will you come in here please."

A young plainclothes cop entered the room.

Hogg, whose sneer had escalated to a smirk, turned to leave.

"Just a minute, Mr. *St. John* Hogg," Duncan said, "I'm not quite through with you." Hogg turned back with an impatient frown. Duncan removed a pad of yellow foolscap from the table drawer and handed it to his young colleague. "Detective Thomas, I am about to charge and caution this suspect and I'd like you to take down his statement, if he chooses to make one."

Hogg stood there, frozen, as the detective closed the door, sat down in the hard backed chair at the end of the table laid the pad on the table, took a ball-point pen from his pocket and looked up, expectantly as Angus Duncan recited a familiar script in a dull monotone. "Louis St. John Hogg, I am placing you under arrest. You may be charged with uttering threats, obstruction of justice, public mischief or some other indictable offence. You are not bound to say anything but whatever you do say…" As Duncan droned on, Hogg's stiff upper lip began to quiver and his shiny dome grew shinier.

By the time Duncan had reached the conclusion of his little spiel the dew of perspiration on the Hogg's brow had condensed to visible droplets. "...to retain and instruct counsel. Do you understand your rights?"

Hogg stood there, like a statue. For a few seconds the only sound in the room was the scribble of a ballpoint pen. Then Hogg licked his lips and croaked, "This is ridiculous. What is the basis of that accusation?"

Duncan ignored the question. "Do you understand your rights?"

"For God's sakes," Hogg exploded, "will you stop spouting that jargon and tell me what's going on here!"

There was a crackle of paper, as the burly amanuensis turned to a fresh page on his legal pad. Hogg reacted as if he'd been gut shot. His hands began to tremble and his legs gave way. He sat down, heavily. Duncan gave his stenographer a signal to suspend his activities, leveled his gaze at Hogg and dropped the monotone. "Look Louis, you can't have it both ways. You want to have an informal chat, we'll have an informal chat; you want to stand on your rights, we'll play it by the book. It's up to you."

Hogg looked at him, warily. "Off the record?"

Duncan gave him a wry smile. "Unfortunately, I don't have that option. I'm not a member of the news media just a dumb cop. In my business *everything* is on the record." He leaned back in his chair. "Of course there's no law that says records have to be in writing. If detective Thomas here makes you nervous," he nodded at his stone-faced subordinate, "I'm sure he has other duties he can attend to."

Hogg thought if over. "And if there's a dispute as to what was said in this room?"

Duncan exposed his palms in the classic gesture of a conjurer showing there was nothing his sleeve. "Your word against mine."

I held my breath waiting to see if Hogg would buy the cubic zirconium that looked like a ten-carat diamond. He didn't keep me waiting long.

"All right, tell him to go."

Duncan didn't have to tell him, the "second banana" was already closing the door the behind him, leaving his props behind. Duncan tore up the pages, dropped them into the wastebasket, and leaned back in his chair. "All right, Louis, let's cut the horse shit. I have two unimpeachable witnesses who have identified your voice, so why don't you just admit that you made that call to Virgo's show and we can take it from there?"

Visibly shaken Hogg made a valiant effort to recover the high ground. After all, he knew the call hadn't gone over the air. "You're bluffing, Duncan. Who are these so-called witnesses of yours?"

Duncan looked thoughtful, and played his ace. "Well, there's your daughter for one, and then there's...."

"I don't believe you," Hogg barked. "Patricia would never..." he caught himself, but the horse was out of the barn.

"Betray you?" Duncan said, evenly. "You're right, she's a very loyal girl. She would have taken your secret to the grave if her colleague hadn't blown the whistle on you."

Hogg sagged like a punctured balloon. "I suppose you're talking about that Bannerman fellow," he muttered darkly.

"Bingo."

Hogg heaved a resigned sigh. "All right, I made the call. It was a stupid thing to do but you don't hang a fellow for one childish mistake. It was a joke for heaven's sake." He gave Duncan his best man-to-man look. "Surely, you can't believe I'd be fool enough to make a call like that if I knew some chap had actually planted a bomb in this Virgo person's apartment?"

Duncan shrugged. "Who knows? Anyone who thinks passing himself off as serial killer is a *joke*..."

"All right, so it wasn't in the best of taste. But that kind of thing goes on all the time among newsmen. Playing practical jokes is a way of relieving tension. If I'm not mistaken the members of your profession aren't complete strangers to this type of high jinx. And I don't see you threatening them with criminal charges." He forced a laugh. "If you want to know the truth, I was drunk when I made that call."

"At eight o'clock in the morning?"

Hogg began to backpedal. "Well, I wasn't really drunk just not entirely sober. Actually, it was suffering more from lack of sleep than alcohol. I was up all night, working, and was so tired I couldn't see straight, let alone think straight. Around seven a.m. I took a break to listen to my daughter's show and had a glass of wine. Well, a glass of wine on an empty stomach, especially when your blood sugar is low, can hit you like howitzer. As you know, it wasn't much of a show since no one was calling in. So I got this crazy idea and before I knew it I was dialing the telephone. When my daughter came on the line I almost hung up. But I thought, no, that would be running away, so I disguised my voice gave her the first name that came into my head." He snorted derisively. "In my day we did not cross examine callers before allowing them to air their views. Anyway, you know the rest. I admit it was a childish thing to do, but when you're dog-tired you sometimes yield to childish impulses." He heaved a sigh of contrition. "I had no idea my thoughtless prank would have such serious repercussions—that I was opening Pandora's box as it were."

Duncan nodded, thoughtfully. "It was just a spur of the moment impulse that got out of hand?"

"Exactly. I knew there was no way on God's earth that Patricia would let that call go over the air—she values her cushy job too much."

"And how about planting that bomb in Mr. Virgo's apartment, was that a spur of the moment impulse too?"

I had to hand it to old Louis he took the sucker punch without flinching. In fact he almost smiled. "You can't seriously believe I had anything to do with *that*? What possible motive could I have? I don't even know this Virgo chap."

"You don't?"

"No."

Duncan gave him a puzzled frown. "So why would he tell me you shared a glass of wine just yesterday?"

Hogg's smirk remained intact. "I was referring to the time I made the call, as you well know. Up until yesterday I didn't know this Virgo chap from Adam. He called me up, out of the blue, and said he wanted me to be a guest on his show. So I said c'mon over and we'll talk about it. And that was the first time I'd ever laid eyes on the fellow."

"Even though he lives right across the street?"

Hogg flinched. "All right, I may have caught sigh of him going in and out of the house but yesterday was the first time I actually talked to the man."

Duncan smiled. "Face to face, you mean?" Hogg clenched his dentures. He was straining to keep his emotions in check. Duncan gave him another jab. "Tell me, Louis, if your involvement with Virgo is so innocent why didn't you lay your cards on the table as soon as I asked you about that call? Why make me pull it out of you, like a rotten tooth, one piece at time?"

"Because I know how you people work," Hogg spluttered. "You twist everything a person says to fit the case you're building against him. If I had admitted having met this Virgo person, even casually, you'd have asked me what I thought of him, and if I tried to be diplomatic, and said he was okay, you'd trip me up on some minor detail and accuse me of lying. And if I told the truth, and said I didn't think much of him, you'd keep badgering me until you made it sound like a man I barely know is my mortal enemy. You take an innocent admission and hammer away until you can shape it into a confession."

This time Duncan was the one to flinch. The shot had landed a little too close to the mark. "All I want is the truth," he said, evenly.

"The truth," Hogg said, with a contemptuous snort. "That's the *last* thing you want to hear. Young John Lonechild told you the truth and what did it get him? A noose around his neck!"

Duncan looked at him strangely. "John Lonechild didn't tell me anything, I didn't work that case. It's ancient history."

There was an awkward silence. It was Louis Hogg's turn to look confused. Then the loonie dropped, and his sneer resurfaced. "But history repeats itself. You were the investigating officer when Billy Joe Parker was shot down in cold blood. And you exonerated the trigger-happy cop who killed that poor boy—without questioning a single civilian witness. Where was your truth there, *Inspector* Duncan? In a cocked hat! The fellow you exonerated was so *innocent* he blew out his brains rather than face an *objective* inquiry."

Duncan smiled but his eyes were as hard as flint. "You don't like me much, do you, Louis?"

Hogg, suddenly realizing that discretion was the better part of valor, made a valiant effort to reign in his high horse. "I have no personal feelings about you one way or the other. I merely object to what you stand for."

"How about Virgo, you object to what he stands for?"

"As far as I can see," Hogg said, with a disdainful snort, "he doesn't stand for *anything*." Good thing there was no mike on my side of the soundproof glass because I laughed out loud. Louis St. John Hogg may have been a paranoid troll but he knew his talk show hosts. "My daughter is the one who calls the shots on that show," he continued. "Not that that's any great accomplishment. In my day, live *meant* live."

"You don't agree with her approach to broadcasting?"

"Frankly, no."

"Have you ever argued about it?"

Hogg took a second to consider his alternatives. "We've had our differences." Then, realizing he could use this grudging admission to his advantage, he continued with more enthusiasm. "As I told you, Inspector, it was Patricia, and not that Virgo chap, who was the target of my hastily-conceived prank. That so-called open line show is a joke."

"How about this?" Duncan opened a file folder. "Is this a joke too?" He removed a sheet of paper in a clear plastic sleeve and held it out.

Hogg took out a pair of granny glasses about an inch thick, perched them on the end of his nose and began to read the NAAPALM manifesto. He couldn't have gotten more than half way through before he dropped it on the table, as if it was covered with pigeon droppings. Which would match the color of his face. "Why ask me?" he said, hoarsely.

"You wrote it didn't you?"

Hogg took great pains to avoid looking at it. "Don't be absurd. Why on earth would I do a thing like that?"

"Why phone a death threat to a complete stranger—a person you claim to have nothing against? I'm not a psychologist but maybe you've got softening of the brain. I've heard alcohol will do that…if you drink it for breakfast."

The color flooded back into Hogg's face as he struggled not rise to the bait. He removed his glasses from the end of his nose. It took three tries to get them back into his breast pocket, by which time his tie was askew. His collar was wilted and his forehead was shiny with perspiration. The strain of going several hours without a drink was beginning to show. He licked his dry lips and said, in a choked voice, "You have no right to talk to me like that."

Duncan cocked one of the brown caterpillars he used for eyebrows. "Hey Louis, don't you believe in freedom of speech—and old newshound like you? Surely, you can take a little constructive criticism. After all, you dish it out pretty good in the Tabloid every week." Hogg's mouth fell open, but nothing came out. He sat there like a fish out of water, gasping for air. Duncan smiled. "What's the matter, Renegade, cat got your tongue?"

Hogg fought to get a grip. He looked like he would have sold a kidney for a glass of Beaujolais. His Adam's apple bobbed up and down as he tried to swallow the saliva that wasn't there. "I don't know what you're talking about?" he finally said, in a barely audible rasp.

Duncan feigned astonishment. "Are you saying you're *not* the crusading journalist who broke the NAAPALM story?"

Hog cleared his throat and tried to look amused. His voice was slightly stronger but his tone no more convincing. "I have no idea where you got that notion."

"Straight from the horse's mouth." Duncan slid his chair back, opened the table drawer and withdrew Abby Brown's copy of Hogg's memoirs. The one her late husband had bought because he felt sorry for the author. Duncan looked at it with feigned admiration and read the title aloud. "You know, Louis, I'm not a college graduate, just a blue color cop, so I had no idea what this title meant until your friend Virgo explained it to me. And I still wasn't sure about the exact meaning of the word "renegade" so I looked it up." He opened a small dictionary at a book-marked page, put on his own granny glasses and began to read. "A person who abandons a party, movement, etc., and goes over to the other side; traitor; turncoat…" He looked up over the top of his glasses. "Not a very flattering self-portrait."

"It's irony," Hogg said through clenched teeth. "It's not meant to be taken literally. Some of history's greatest leaders were branded with that epithet. Louis Riel was called a renegade. Today he's called the father of this province."

Duncan smiled, broadly "And what will they call Louis *St. John* Hogg tomorrow, the *Godfather*? I mean since you're trying to play the Almighty…" Hogg pursed his lips so hard his eyes watered. The vein on his forehead was beginning to bulge. Duncan started browsing though his memoirs. "You know, Louis, you've led a fascinating life. Once I started reading your book I couldn't put it down. I was especially impressed by your war record." He looked up. "I didn't know you were a demolition expert."

"I'm not," Hogg said, a trifle reluctantly.

"It's a little late for modesty." Duncan started flipping pages. "You go on and on about the wartime missions you went on with the Greek partisans and now you say you don't know anything about explosives?"

Hogg met Duncan's gaze and cleared his throat, for the umpteenth time. "I didn't say I didn't know anything about them, I said I wasn't an *expert*."

"But you know how to make a booby trap?"

"For god's sake, man, a ten year old child can build a booby trap!"

"But why would a ten year old child put it in a superior court judge's desk?"

Hogg's jaw dropped. "You're not seriously suggesting *I* had anything to do with Judge Kilgore's...?" He left the word hanging.

Duncan's response was so heavy with sarcasm you could have spread it on toast. "Now why would I suggest anything as preposterous as that? You and he were as thick as thieves, right?"

"No we weren't. I made no secret of how I felt about Jack Kilgore. The man was a disgrace to his profession. But it's been thirty years since I was on the receiving end of his brand of frontier justice. I'm not going to pretend I'm heart-broken that his career was terminated, permanently, but to suggest I had anything to do with it is absurd."

"How about Judge Brown, how did you feel about his permanent removal from the bench?"

"How do you think I felt? For god sake, the man was my neighbor. I was horrified."

"Even though he kicked your ass at the polls?"

Hogg's vein began to throb and his eyes began to water. But he clenched his tiny fists and stiffened his spine. "I know what you're trying to do, Duncan, but it won't work. Louis St. Hogg has been vilified by experts, believe me. In my business you learn to accept every insult as a compliment and every defeat as an opportunity. When I was forced to give up my broadcasting career it was a stepping stone to my political career. I had my innings in the political arena and when the time came to pass the torch, I was content to move on to other things. I bore the late judge Brown no animosity. Life's too short to live in the past."

Duncan shook his head in admiration. "You know, Louis, I can see why you had such a successful political career. After that speech I'm ready to vote for you myself. You're such a convincing liar that I might actually believe I was wrong about your feelings towards the late Judge Brown. If I hadn't heard this..." He reached over and punched the play button on the cassette recorder.

What do you want, Virgo, more information on the two-faced bugger who stabbed me in the back? Know what your friend Honest Bob did before he became the Great White Father—he was a bloody Crown Attorney. The two-faced bugger made his living putting Indians...

Hogg slammed his hand down on the stop button. "This is an outrage," he spluttered, fumbling to get the player open. "That Virgo person had no right to tape a private..."

"Take it easy," Duncan said, taking the machine from his trembling hands. He popped out the cassette and handed it to him. "Here, it's a gift." Hogg took the cassette and looked at him, dumbly. Duncan smiled. "Don't worry we have the original. Besides, the officers who are currently searching your house should be able to come up with more tangible evidence than this."

"You've sent someone to search my house?" Hogg gasped.

"Well, mainly your office. The forensic boys tell me when you delete a document from a computer it doesn't necessarily mean it can't be retrieved from the hard drive." He picked up the NAAPALM manifesto, studied it for a few seconds, then looked up, "You weren't careless enough to compose this on a computer were you, Louis?" The answer was written on Hogg's face. Major Spit and Polish had turned into a seedy veteran suffering from Post-traumatic Stress Syndrome. His eyes were glazed, his tie was askew and sweat stains were visible at the armholes of his blazer. Duncan looked straight into his eyes and said, in a voice that was like the hiss of a snake, "Cat got your tongue again, Renegade?" Hogg gazed at him, dumbstruck. Duncan leaned back and laced his fingers behind his head. " Well, take your time, I'm prepared to stay here all night. When you're ready to start telling the truth just let me know and I'll call my colleague back in and you can make a clean breast of it. Confession is good for the soul, they say. Get yourself a good lawyer, plead diminished capacity and you might end up in a nice quiet sanitarium instead of a noisy penitentiary with all those common…"

Hogg sprang to his feet. "I don't have to sit here and listen to this! How dare you address me in this fashion, you, you…do you have any idea who you are talking to?"

Angus Duncan didn't have rise to look into Hogg's bloodshot eyes. "Oh, I know *exactly* who I'm talking to—a bitter old drunk who sits up in his ivory tower spewing out hate literature under a phony name. A little tin soldier who snipes at his *enemies* from a safe distance. Oh, I know *exactly* who I'm dealing with." Duncan rose from his chair, his eyes like flint. "You walk in here with your shiny shoes, and shiny reputation, and think you're fooling people, Mr. *Sinjin* Hogg? Well, I've got your number, you cowardly slug, and I'm going to step on you so hard…"

Duncan's diatribe was cut off in mid-sentence by what sounded like the bellow of a wounded animal. Hogg's face was the color of eggplant, his eyes bulged and a trickle of saliva drooled from the corner of his mouth. He took on spastic step toward his adversary and raised a small clenched fist. Then his eyes rolled back, a gurgle escaped from his throat and he dropped like a stone.

I watched, in horror, as Inspector Angus Duncan knelt beside the object that was lying on the interrogation room floor like an empty suit, frantically searching for a sign of life. The Bull's career was probably flashing before his eyes. Then, suddenly, he paused and looked up at the one-way glass. He didn't open his mouth but his eyes said it all. *You're a witness, Virgo, I didn't lay a glove on him.*

Abby didn't know whether to laugh or cry. "He *died*," she gasped, when I broke the good/bad news. "I don't believe it! How could that happen, Val?"

I shrugged.

Hey, it was a rough room.

Part Five
Another Kick at the Cat

32

It was the night before Christmas
  And all through the DBC
  Not a creature was working
  Except poor little me...

Actually, it was a week before Christmas and I wasn't really working just putting the finished touches on Abby's Christmas present, the one that was *my* thought. Since my landlady had bent over backwards to make *my* holiday a little more festive I figured the least I could do was reciprocate and the previous night I'd brought home the best Spruce tree I could find at this late date. Scouring the city for it was time consuming, getting it home was a pain, setting it up was a chore and decorating it was a nightmare. You would think the recipient would have been a bit more grateful. "What's taking you so long up there," she bitched, as I risked my neck distributing tinsel. "Robbie could have decorated three trees by now."

Sure, he has wings. "Give me break, Abby, I'm only an apprentice Goy."

"Don't be rude." She gave the ladder a playful shake.

I grabbed onto a branch for dear life. "Hey, cut that out."

She giggled and shook it again.

"Will you cut that out!"

"Oh, don't be such a baby."

"I can't help it, I have vertigo."

Santa's helper looking up at me through a forest of spruce needles from what seemed like a mile below. "What's that?"

"A fear of heights."

"Heights? I don't believe this guy, he's two feet off the ground and he's getting a nosebleed! If I knew you were such a chicken Virgo, I'd have

203

decorated the tree myself."

"Be my guest," I said, and clambered down. I wasn't one of those insecure types who had to prove his manhood. (Besides, I'd already done the dangerous part.)

Abby promptly finished the job and while I put away the ladder turned off the lights. When I returned to the darkened living room she handed me the switch to the tree lights and linked her arm in mine. "Okay shoot."

I shot.

And missed.

I clicked the switch a few more times but the tree stayed dark.

Abby, who had been fairly quivering, sagged. "What's wrong, Val?"

"Beats me."

"Did you plug it in?"

"Don't ask silly questions."

"Why is that a silly question?"

"Because the answer is obvious."

When the tree burst into a blaze of color Abby reacted like a ten year old. She threw her arms around my neck and gave me a big sloppy kiss. "It's the nicest Christmas present anyone ever gave me."

"I doubt it—it only cost me fifty bucks."

Her good mood suddenly evaporated. "Why do you always do that? Can't you just accept a compliment like a mature adult? It doesn't matter how much it cost, it's the thought that counts."

"I know," I said, apologetically. I didn't point out that it had been *her* thought.

After she'd gone up to bed I stayed downstairs to secretly work on the Christmas gift that was *my* thought. Now I was giving it the final polish. It was a dirty job but someone had to do it. And it was preferable to the alternative. I've attended some pretty un-merry Christmas parties in my time but the one going on in Studio 21 gave a whole new meaning to the word *downer*. Even the absence of Patricia St. John Hogg didn't help. The low point was the arrival of the new improved Santa. The terminally jovial Garth Grenfel had lost his job to someone who's heart obviously wasn't in it. Poor old Pop, equipped with white beard, rosy cheeks and little potbelly, couldn't say no. As he hobbled around in that ridiculous red suit, dispensing useless trinkets to the pudding-faced progeny of the *CBC Single Parent Society*, he was about as jolly as old Saint Augustine. It was such an embarrassing spectacle that I just couldn't watch. So I snuck out the door and stole back to my own workshop.

I'd only intended to make a "clean copy" of Abby's song to put under the tree but couldn't resist the temptation to change the word "street" to "road". Or was it "road" to "street"? I'd been up and down that street/road so many times my clean copy looked like a Saskatchewan highway after a rainstorm. Not only was it full of cross-outs, erasures and interlineations, it had more verses than the bible. After a prolonged period of scribbler's block the floodgates had opened and I couldn't keep my head above water. In the past few weeks I'd jumped aboard a thousand ideas and abandoned them all in midstream. "Isn't your muse talking to you?" Abby commiserated, as I sat at the kitchen table behind a mountain of crumpled paper.

"My muse speaks with forked tongue," I informed her.

After we'd lit up the tree she moved to the window to gaze, wistfully, at virtually the only house on the street that didn't have any Christmas lights. "Poor Sheila," Abby sighed. Then, turning to me, "Why would he do such a thing, Val, what did he hope to gain?"

"What did he have to lose?" I aborted another deformed embryo and joined her at the window. "Louis Hogg felt that he'd been robbed of his birthright by a bunch of interlopers who weren't fit to shine his shoes. Judge Kilgore had destroyed his broadcasting career, Robbie destroyed his political career and I was making a mockery of his old radio show."

Abby turned to me and her eyes began to tear up. "But everyone has disappointments in life, and don't go around murdering people."

"Your friend Sheila's husband wasn't *everyone*, sweetheart, he was an over-the-hill megalomaniac whose brain was so saturated with alcohol he began to believe his own paranoid fantasies. Louis St. John Hogg was sick man."

And now he's a dead man, I thought, as I wrote the title "Dear Abby" across the top of the page. Or should I have stuck with "Abby Dear"? Speak of the devil…

"Hi, pussy cat."

"Don't pussy cat me, Virgo, your stupid tree has fallen over."

I laughed.

"Don't laugh, it's bad luck."

"To laugh?"

"When a Christmas tree falls over."

"No, just bad trimming. I told you I was only an apprentice Goy."

"Don't be rude. When are you coming home?"

"Soon."

"What do you mean soon; what on earth are you doing there?"

"Just partying." I said, and stifled my gag reflex.

"Well, you've partied enough; I need you to fix that tree. But I don't want you to drive. I'll pick you up in the Valiant."

"Is it ready?"

"It must be. How long does it take to put in a new battery?"

Ten minutes at Canadian Tire. "Well, some of these independent shops don't keep batteries in stock. Besides, he might not even be open. Especially at this time of year."

"Why do you have to be such a nit picker, Virgo? I'll give my friend Charlie a call and if the car is ready I'll call you back."

"Don't bother. I'm perfectly capable of driving home in the Fiat. I've only had one drink and that was," I looked at my watch, "almost three hours ago."

"So what have you been doing all this time? What kind of party is that, anyway?"

I laughed. "Okay, I lied, the party's over, I'm cleaning up some work."

"You can do your cleaning up at home. That stupid tree is shedding needles all over the living room carpet."

"All right, I'll be home within half an hour."

Famous last words.

I'd just gotten Abby's Christmas present stashed it in my brief case when Santa arrived with another gift—the one I'd left on his desk. Pop, who was no longer wearing his red flannels, held up the purple velvet Crown Royal sack with visible embarrassment. "I really wasn't expecting this."

"So we're even, I didn't expect you to volunteer to warm up that clunker of mine in minus forty weather."

"Maybe I should go out and give her a run now. It's getting pretty bitter out there."

"No problem, I'm just on my way out." And there was a '98 Fiat waiting for me in the parking lot. Abby had finally coerced me into letting her "friend Charlie" install a new battery in my comatose Valiant so I'd been driving her

"Fix It Again Tony" to work.

"Well, I better get moving."

Pop held up the purple sack. "One for the road?"

I never felt less like a drink in my life. But the old boy had arrived with two paper cups so I bit the bullet and let him pour me a shot. "Your health," I said, raising it to my reluctant lips.

"L'chayim (to life)," he reciprocated, with a twinkle in his eye.

I almost dropped my paper cup. No wonder he looked so uncomfortable in that Santa Claus suit! "Pop, are you Jewish?"

He grinned. "Yeah, I know, I don't look it."

I laughed. "Sure you do." With that rabbinical beard and those bottomless black eyes he could have passed for Old Testament prophet. "How come you never said anything?"

"Why should I say anything?"

"Hey, you know us Hebes stick together."

"Do we?"

His smile had evaporated and it was déjà vu all over again—the same spooky feeling I'd had when I first laid eyes on Frosty Coleman and Robert Brown's graduation photo. "Pop, do we know each other?"

He looked at me, alarmed. It obviously sounded like a silly question.

"I mean, before I started working here—the first time you saw me did my face look familiar?"

The twinkle returned to the old boy's rheumy peepers. "Boychick, when you get to be my age *every* face looks familiar."

I laughed. "I don't have to wait that long, Pop."

I knocked off the rest of the overly generous shot of rye—which I hate—he knocked off his drink, we wished each other a (facetious) Merry Christmas, he returned to his table by the switchboard and I headed for the parking lot. Ten minutes later I was back on the phone to Abby.

"Hi, it's me again."

"Hi, you again."

"I'm calling to apologize."

"For what?"

"For laughing when you said the tree falling over was back luck?"

33

I stepped to the edge of the curb and looked down the street for the tenth time. Portage Avenue was lit up like a carnival midway but no sign of the Valiant. I walked back to the building and stuck my head though the door. "Any calls for me?"

The bombshell behind the switchboard looked up from her fashion magazine with a petulant scowl. "For goodness sakes, you just asked me five minutes ago."

No one likes to draw the graveyard shift during the festive season but the switchboard princess gave a whole new meaning to the expression surly bitch. Like most of her DBC colleagues she was under the impression that she did her job as a favor to an undeserving public. "I'll take that as a no," I said, and retreated into the equally chilly night.

The traffic was bumper to bumper but still no sign of Abby. Maybe we'd gotten our signals crossed. It wouldn't be the first time—more like the hundred and first. When she heard that "Robbie's car" wouldn't start she acted like I'd done it on purpose, just to spite her. I said I'd call the Auto Club but she nixed that idea. It would take forever for them to come at this time of year. All right, I'd take a bus. That would take even longer. Okay, I'd take a cab. Why waste money on a cab when there was a perfectly good car at home? It was far from perfect and it wasn't at home—it was in the hospital getting a transplant. Maybe it was ready. And maybe it wasn't. The shop probably wasn't even open. Why did I always have to be so negative? She'd call her "friend Charlie" and if the car was ready she'd go and get it, if not, she'd call me back in five minutes.

After waiting half an hour I called her, and gotten the answering machine. I looked up the number in the yellow pages and phoned the car shop. And got an answering machine. It was closed. I looked at my watch. That was an hour ago. Maybe I misunderstood, maybe Abby said she'd call me if the car *was* ready—that if I didn't hear from her in five minutes I should take a bus. Which meant that she was taking a bath—a process that took about an hour. Maybe I should call again. Yeah, and get dumped on again. My would-be Jewish princess was probably sitting on pins and (spruce) needles wondering why in the hell her Jewish prince wasn't home yet.

Home. The word sounded good in my head as I looked out the bus window at the rainbow of lights along North Main. One day you wake up, a stranger in a strange bed, the next day you're going home to the little woman. Did I remember to take her present? I opened my briefcase to make sure. I couldn't wait to see the look on her face when she opened it on Christmas morning. Which might arrive before I had a chance to put it under the tree. What the hell were we waiting for? The bus had been immobile, clacking like a winded greyhound, for five minutes. And the driver was lounging in his seat, with one foot up on the fare box, reading a bus schedule. I winnowed my way to the front. "What's the hold-up?"

The driver looked up from his reading matter and nodded at the windshield. "Someone's been celebrating New Years a little early."

I looked out the windshield and saw a chain of taillights, glowing like red eyes, though a fog of exhaust fumes. At the head of the column I could just make out the silhouette of a dragon that was no longer breathing fire, turned sideways in the road. Fortunately the drunk who caused this traffic jam was considerate enough crash his vehicle within walking distance of my destination.

The chill night air was a refreshing change from the overheated bus. As I started up the sidewalk the pedestrian traffic was light but by the time I reached the accident scene I had to fight my way through a throng of rubbernecks, all jostling and craning for a better view of the carnage. Christmas was coming and the ghouls were getting fat. Adding a bizarre touch of holiday revelry was a convoy of police cars whose revolving "cherries" sent splashes of red, blue and yellow bouncing crazily from the faces of the gawkers. I felt the crunch of glass under my feet. This collision must have been pip! I elbowed my way to the curb and joined the rubbernecks. I saw the remains of a single vehicle in the middle of the road. Or what used to be a vehicle, now it was a steaming pile of scrap metal. Then I saw a familiar face. Was it possible? Had Angus Duncan's little indiscretion brought him this low? He looked even more miserable than usual so I decided to cheer him up with a little friendly banter. "I see they finally gave you a job you could handle, " I said, having elbowed my way through the crowd.

He turned to face me. Angus Duncan had aged ten years in two weeks. The Louis Hogg fiasco had obviously taken a physical as well as a psychological toll. There was an awkward silence as he stood there, looking at me, not saying a word. "I know you must be short-staffed at this time of year" I said, laboring my lame joke, "but since when did they start assigning senior homicide men to car accidents?"

He didn't crack a smile. "This wasn't an accident, Virgo."

My blood turned to ice water. I couldn't catch my breath. I stood there, for what seemed like an eternity, trying to work up the courage to turn my head a few inches. And then, finally, I did. And saw what I prayed to God I wouldn't see.

34

Is there any liquor in the house?"

I looked up and saw Angus Duncan's haggard face looking down at me. He was wearing his black overcoat and gray fedora that seemed too big. I was sitting on the couch in Abby's living room but had idea how we had gotten there. Duncan must have brought me in his car. "I don't know about you, Virgo, but I could use a drink."

I tried to focus my thoughts. "Oh…yeah…sure."

As Duncan moved off to the liquor cabinet I noticed a wet spot on the carpet. Abby would give me shit for not making him take off his overshoes. And then I remembered. How could she be dead? I had just spoken to her on the phone. I watched Duncan pour the drinks. There were white patches over his ears. That's why his hat looked too big; he had just gotten his annual haircut. At the Barber College. *Do you have to make a joke out of everything, Virgo?* What the hell was wrong with me? Why didn't I feel anything?

"Straight Scotch okay?" Duncan was standing there, with two glasses in one of his huge hands, a bottle of single malt in the other. How could I have missed that? I nodded. He poured me half a tumbler full and handed it to me. I knocked it off in one swallow, grimaced, and held out the empty. He poured a less generous refill, poured himself a few fingers, set the bottle down on the coffee table and sat down in an easy chair across from me. He raised his glass to his lips, took a sip, and asked the question that had probably been eating at him since he'd walked into the house. "What happened to the tree?"

"Fell over."

"When?"

"Couple of hours ago. I was at the DBC when it happened."

"Tell me about it?"

I took another shot to brace myself. "We had our annual DBC Christmas party today. So I stayed at work later than usual. Abby phoned to see when I was coming home. She was very upset. The tree had fallen over. I thought it was funny. But she told me not to laugh; said when a Christmas tree falls over it's bad..." A sob escaped from my lips. I tried to hold back the tide but once the floodgates were open there was no way to close them until the reservoir was dry. I cried like a baby.

The silence that followed this unseemly display was so heavy Duncan could have used it as ballast in the trunk of his unmarked cruiser. Finally he broke it, gently. "Why was she driving your car?" I told him. He gave it some thought. "So it's been sitting on the carport for over three weeks?" he said, more to himself than me.

Suddenly, I felt even sicker to my stomach. "I guess I should have put it in the garage..."

"Don't start second guessing yourself, Virgo. Anyone who could get past a dead bolt would have no trouble getting inside a garage. Or a locked car."

I looked at him strangely. "It was *inside* the car?"

He nodded. "Somewhere under the dash."

Why would anyone bother tinkering around under the dash when it would be so much simpler, and quicker, to attach it to the underside of the chassis—or under the hood? Suddenly I thought of "friend Charlie." If it had been under the hood he'd have found it when he installed the new battery. So where was it planted? And how was it detonated?

"It obviously wasn't the ignition," Duncan said. "Must have been something she switched on after the engine was warmed up. The heater, the defroster, the radio...

"Oh, shit!"

Duncan looked at me, quizzically.

I explained how I wouldn't let Abby use my top-of-the-line sound system and how it really irritated her. "So now that the car had a new battery..."

Duncan nodded. He almost looked relieved. Case closed.

After Angus Duncan walked out the door, leaving his car keys on the coffee table for my convenience, I had only my friend John Walker for company. But he wasn't his genial self. I couldn't blot out the image of Louis St. John Hogg chortling gleefully from his new home in hell. The vindictive troll had had the last laugh. I could picture him creeping out of his attic workshop, in the middle of the night, like one of Santa's elves, with his lethal Christmas present. But something was wrong with this picture. I couldn't visualizing the old bastard lying on the floor of my Valiant and those trembling blue-veined hands fiddling around with a bunch of wires. No, something was definitely wrong with this picture? I picked up Duncan's car keys and looked at them. And another picture popped into my head.

Fritz Finkelman felt *extremely mellow as he looked out the window at the last minute shoppers scurrying down Portage Ave. It wasn't just the season, or the drink of rye, which he didn't really care for, but the news that had just come over the television monitor. "Isn't that terrible," the bimbo at the switchboard had said, trying to mask her excitement with an expression of concern. Funny how things never worked out the way you planned them. Still, that's what made life interesting. When he was finally paroled, revenge had been the furthest thing from his mind. True, he'd entertained a few fantasies in the joint—when you have nothing but time on your hands it's hard to resist—but all he intended to do after he'd paid his debt to society was live like a mensch. But you can't live on air! Inflation had all but consumed his nest egg. Instead of a comfortable retirement he ended up in a rooming house, delivering flyers for minimum wage and picking up pocket change running errands for the "shikker goy" across the hall. Harry Frobisher was usually too drunk to sign his own name, let alone deposit a pension check, so Fritz would relieve him of the burden, taking a small percentage for his trouble. As far as the bank was concerned he was Harry Frobisher. So when his housemate finally drank himself to death Fritz cleaned out his wallet, appropriated his credit cards and—since no one bothered to inform the Department of Veteran's affairs of his demise—continued to cash his pension checks. And when The Manitoba Motor Vehicle Branch finally got around to putting photos on driver's licenses it was Fritz's image that appeared above Harry Frobisher's name.*

By this time Fritz had grown a full beard, moved to a better neighborhood, and landed a cushy job as a security guard. Then Fate had dealt him a joker. Fritz was on duty at the courthouse and a judge called him into his office to run an errand. It turned out to be Justice Kilgore and he didn't know Fritz from Adam. (Or from Harry Frobisher.) The temptation was just too great. When his courthouse assignment ended Fritz left "Hanging Jack" a memento of their previous encounter.

Fritz waited in vain, for weeks, for Kilgore to take the Criminal Code from his bookshelf and open it—ideally at the "felony murder" section. Then Fate dealt another joker. Kilgore made some offhand comment about "drunken Indians" and was forced to take an extended leave of absence. Fritz came down to earth with a thud. His cushy job was beginning to feel like another life sentence. Then another old enemy started getting a lot of news coverage and Fritz decided to move his name from the front page to the obituary column. This time the bomb went off on schedule, and the media coverage was extremely gratifying.

Then some bogus aboriginal terrorist group crawled out of the woodwork and took credit for Honest Brown's untimely demise. It was like a cosmic joke. Then Fritz was assigned to the DBC and ran into "Val Virgo"—whom he immediately recognized. The recognition wasn't mutual—Isadore Miller handed over his key ring without a qualm. It was almost too easy. Any two-bit gonif could wire an ignition. Fritz Finkelman wasn't a thug or a killer he was an artist. He wasn't seeking revenge but "justice". He'd planted the first bomb in one of that ignoramus Kilgore 's law books, made Brown's "gift" a Scales of Justice lamp and decided a CD deck was an appropriately means to dispatch a former disk jockey.

But, for some reason, Virgo seemed to take a sabbatical from listening to music. While waiting, in vain, for the quisling to get his well-earned reward Fritz decided to wile away the time looking up another old enemy, who turned out to be a mailman. What could be more appropriate than a letter bomb? But it didn't quite accomplish the job so Fritz moved a little farther out on the limb and visited Virgo's apartment. Then some drunken Goy phoned the show, posing as the mad bomber, and things went completely meshugah. Fritz wanted a challenge and he found one. Virgo had more lives than a cat. Fritz was enjoying this cat and mouse game and now, when he least expected it, suddenly the game was over. The news announcer hadn't mentioned any names but he didn't have to. For some reason the mouse (or, rather, rat) had suddenly felt the need to listen to a little Christmas music as he drove home to his little shikesh. The Yiddish disk jockey had spun his last disc. Good riddance to bad...

35

I could see him through the front window, sitting at his little table by the switchboard, with the bemused look of a cat that had just eaten the cream. But when I came through the revolving door, and his eyes came back into focus, he looked like he'd seen a ghost. He tried to smile but fell a little short. "What are you doing here, Mr...Val, did you forget something?"

"No Fritz, I *remembered* something."

He was out of his chair and halfway down the hall before I had a chance to react. I sprinted after him but he was already stepping into the elevator. The doors closed in my face. I hit the button but the car was on its way up. As I stood there, watching the lights on the floor indicator, my blood boiling. Then I heard a voice that was as comforting as chalk against a blackboard.

"What the hell's going on?"

"Go back to the reception desk," I said, without turning. "This doesn't concern you."

"Now look here, Virgo..."

"No, *you* look," I said, spinning around. "If you don't get out of my face before I count to five I'm going to kick your snotty ass all the way back to your desk!" The switchboard princess gaped at me in frozen disbelief. I held up my right forefinger. "One." I held up my index finger. "Two." She spun on her three-inch heels and clicked down the hall as fast as her racehorse legs would carry her. I turned back to the elevator. The indicator had stopped at 5—the top floor. I pushed the *down* button. The numbers started to run backward. When the car arrived it was empty. (Surprise, surprise.) I flipped the emergency switch and the doors stayed open. Now there was only one way down. I headed for the stairs.

I paused at the landing of every floor and listened but all I heard was the pounding of my heart. When I emerged onto the fifth floor it was deadly quiet. I crept down the hall and tried the first door I came to. Locked. As was every other door. I paused to consider my options. I could get the fire axe and break them down, one by one. By the time I found the old bastard Angus Duncan would no doubt have arrived with a warrant—for *my* arrest. The switchboard princess had probably called 911 to report the "madman". No, the *blind* man! The murdering son of a bitch had been right under my nose all the time. Goading me. Teasing me. Playing his cat and mouse game. The thought made my blood boil.

So why was I shivering? Where was that draft coming from? While I was considering the possibilities a shot rang out. I hit the floor so hard I bit my tongue. Another shot. Then silence. I cautiously lifted my head and looked around. The hallway was deserted. I belly-crawled to the corner and peered around. Another gunshot—but not from the barrel of a gun. At the far end of the hall a metal-clad door was banging against a wall, while frigid air billowed through an open doorway like steam. Some careless person hadn't properly closed the fire door when he had stepped out for a little fresh air.

I moved cautiously to the end of the hall and peered through the doorway. All I saw was a flat metal roof and all I heard were the distant strains of *God Rest You Merry Gentlemen*. Well, vertigo or no vertigo, I was going to rest *this* merry gentleman. I stepped through the doorway and onto the roof. The wind was so fierce I could barely maintain my footing. Fighting the impulse to get down on all fours I edged my way to the fire escape and forced myself to look down. The parking lot was deserted.

Could the old bastard have clambered down those slippery steel rungs that fast—in street shoes? The arthritis he always complained about was obviously the O.J. Simpson strain. Only to be worn at suitable occasions—like weddings, bar mitzvahs and murder trials. Protective coloration. Like that Santa Claus beard and pseudo-military uniform. His own mother wouldn't have recognized him in that get up. How the fuck did an ex-con land a job as a security guard? Well, I guess it would all come out at his trial.

My stomach clenched like a fist at the thought of that the murdering son of bitch getting the benefit of a long drawn-out trial. Again. Well standing out here, lacerating myself, wasn't going to help. Halfway back to the fire door I stopped in my tracks. Was that vapor coming from behind the chimneystack? There it was again!

"Okay, Fritz, you can come out now. The game's over."

My voice echoed across the roof but there was no response—other than an acceleration of the telltale vapor. "We can do this the easy way or the hard way, Fritz, it's up to you."

No response.

I began to move across the roof.

Suddenly a grizzled head popped out from behind the stack.

"Okay, okay."

Fritz stepped out from behind the stack, hands extended, palms outward.

"I'll go quietly."

"You're going to go even quieter than you think, Fritz."

He took a backward step.

"What are you talking about?"

He was shivering so hard his dentures were chattering and he was panting like a steam engine.

"I'm giving myself up. You can't take the law into your own hands."

"Why not? You did—the law of the jungle. But you weren't satisfied with an eye for an eye you had to have two arms and a leg. Well, it's my turn now, you murdering bastard, and I'm going to..."

"Hold it right there."

I stopped in my tracks.

His left hand was deep in his jacket pocket.

"Take one more step and I'll blow us *both* to hell!"

Was it a bluff? Probably. But was I willing to bet my life on it?

"I've got nothing to lose, you know that, Virgo."

Yes, I knew something else.

"Neither do I." I leapt forward.

He yanked his hand from his pocket and took a step back.

And disappeared.

I moved to the edge of the roof. He was hanging on for dear life, his legs dangling over the street. He tried to lever his body back onto the roof but couldn't manage it. "Help me," he grunted.

I didn't move. "I've helped you enough...*Pop.*"

He looked up at me, an old dog begging for a bone. "Please." His voice was almost a sob.

I was unmoved. In fact I was enjoying the show.

"For the love of God help me," he wheezed. "I'm a Jew!"

A Jew? You're not even a human being; you're an animal. No, that's unfair to the animal kingdom— an animal kills to live, it doesn't live to kill. Only a sick, twisted...

I heard the wail of a siren in the distance. Finkelman heard it too. His tear-filled eyes reflected a spark of hope. It was a vain hope. The cavalry would never arrive in time to pull Santa's chestnuts out of the fire. His arms were trembling and his mustache and nose hairs were so coated with frost he could hardly draw breathe. He was gasping and snorting like an old engine that was running out of steam. Besides, this wasn't a job for the police; it was a job for the sanitation department. They could sweep his worthless hide off the pavement with the rest of the garbage. Failik Finkelman's last encounter with the justice system had merely converted him from a "felony" murderer into a cold-blooded killer. So I was going to let "Fritz the Cat" answer to a higher law—the law of gravity.

36

Abby would not have enjoyed this funeral; it had no *Yiddishe Tam* (Jewish flavor). The deceased's remains were to be cremated after a short memorial service conducted by a nondenominational minister in a nondescript chapel on the outskirts of town. When I came in I saw Sheila Hogg sitting in the front row beside a few women I presumed were Abby's mother and sisters, who had flown in from Ottawa. We hadn't met. I thought it would be better that way. Besides, what the hell could I say to them? I slipped into a pew at the back, hoping not to attract attention.

After a few minutes someone with the same idea slipped in beside me. "Just thought I'd pay my respects," Angus Duncan muttered, removing his hat and holding it on his lap. I noticed a folded copy of the *Tabloid* in his coat pocket with a headline I knew by heart. I'd read the lead story half a dozen times in the past three days but had nothing better to do while waiting for the service to begin. "May I borrow your paper?" I whispered.

Duncan looked at me, blankly.

"In your pocket."

He nodded, and took it out. "Forgot it was there," he grunted.

As the service got under way, I held it low, between my knees, and unfolded it as quietly as possible. *Don't be rude,* said a voice in my head. *Sorry, sweetheart, but there's nothing this guy is saying that I really want to hear.* I'm one of those old fashioned types who believes a eulogizer should actually have met the person he's praising. Even Morgan Riley's overblown prose was preferable to unadulterated horse manure:

Christmas Eve Can Kill You

FRITZ THE CAT SPILLS THE BEANS
'They thought he was a goner but the cat came back.'
Every parent of a preschooler will be familiar with local recording artist Fred Penner's ditty The Cat Came Back in which an indestructible feline repeatedly frustrates its owner attempts to get rid of it. In a case of life imitating art Fritz "The Cat" Finkelman has virtually returned from the dead to wreak havoc on the local scene. Late last night ex-con Finkelman, currently on parole from a felony murder conviction, was taken into custody and charged with the so-called NAAPALM bombings. According to a reliable source the aging felon, who is now in the intensive care unit of the Health Science's Center, has made a full confession. "I'm not a doctor," Inspector Angus Duncan replied as to the cause of Finkelman's current condition. Finkelman, who is under police guard, did not have any visible abrasions or contusions and it is believe he suffered a coronary event. When the stolid homicide man was reminded that another aged suspect, who did not survive, suffered a similar event after being interrogated for these self-same crimes his only comment was "No comment." The Tabloid sincerely hopes Failik "Fritz The Cat" Finkelman will survive long enough to be tried by a jury of his peers and that the local constabulary have some tangible evidence of his guilt in addition to his "voluntary" self-incriminating statement. If the perpetrator of these vicious crimes is allowed to slip through a loophole in the justice system because of an overzealous police officer—who shall remain nameless—the late Louis St. John Hogg, one of this province's most distinguished citizens, will indeed have died in vain.

The Tabloid's hopes were in vain. Finkelman gave up the ghost the day after the story hit the street, after unburdening his conscience the day before. This time I was given the privilege of witnessing the proceedings but was on hand when Angus Duncan emerged from the interview room. "He sang like a bird," he said rather incredulously. Then he had looked at me suspiciously. Or was it admiringly? "What did you do to him before we got there, Virgo?"

"Didn't lay a glove on him, Angus."

"That's funny, he gave me the impression that you threatened to toss him off the roof."

On the contrary, I had risked my neck to pull him to safety. What had prompted my change of heart? Good question. Maybe I had literally stooped to his level so as not to stoop to his level. Someone said revenge is "best served cold" but freezing my ass up there on that roof it suddenly seemed stale, flat and unprofitable. "Vengeance is mine," said the God of my fathers. Not to mention my earthly father, who bore a faint resemblance to Failik Finkelman. The resemblance was purely physical. Not all holocaust survivors are created equal. Some become thieves and serial killers, some become abortionists and some emerge from the death camps with such a reverence for life they refuse to swat a mosquito. Abraham Hillel Miller was the rarest of modern medical phenomena, a pediatrician who was more concerned about the welfare of his young patients than his annual income, his standing the profession or his Wednesday morning tee off time. It was a tough act to follow but I gave it a shot. The day I entered medical school was the happiest day of my father's life. The day I dropped out was his last. I told myself it was pure coincidence—he'd had heart trouble for years—but my mother suggested otherwise. "Well, I hope you're happy," was the delicate way she put it. So I hit the road and never looked back.

Then, a few years later, I found that I held the life of another holocaust survivor in my unwilling hands. That was the connection, the buried memory, the chain that bound us all together: a murder trial. Sitting in Abby Brown's darkened living room, beside a fallen tree, my head in my hands, feeling emptier than a politician's promise, it came back to me in a sickening flash. Robert Woodsworth Brown, for the prosecution, Andrew Jackson Kilgore, on the bench, Isadore Miller and Leon Coleman, two nice Jewish boys, in ringside seats. Angus Duncan was right about Frosty trying to warn me with that pathetic note. But the word he was trying to write wasn't *judge*.

It was *jury*.

Christmas Eve Can Kill You

Spring is a promise
Fall is a threat
Summer brings hope
Winter, regret.

Well, country music fans, that's a wrap. Yeah, I've probably left a few loose ends dangling in the breeze (and tied a few others in Gordian knots) but this memory business is not like a box of chocolates—you don't get to pick and choose. If it weren't for potluck I wouldn't have any luck at all. An angel dropped into my life, out of the blue, and disappeared through a trap door. Funny how a city of half a million souls can seem deserted because one face is missing from the crowd. That winter was the longest I've ever experienced. It wasn't a season; it was a sentence—four months on the rock pile with no time off for good behavior. And I was so well behaved the warden thought she'd died and gone to Hogg heaven.

I was too weary and apathetic to fight. Whatever marginal interest I'd had in a talk show career had gone the way of my Valiant. If a thing isn't worth doing, as my guardian angel tried to tell me, it isn't worth doing *well*. The decline and fall of the vehicle I'd ridden to semi-stardom was accompanied by the infamous DBC "cutbacks". As the good ship Titanic steamed blissfully along, the crew played musical deck chairs. Lloyd Cringely took early retirement (a change in status if not productivity) Neil Bannerman assumed the Cringer's non-duties and the Girl Wonder added "Executive Producer" to her growing list of honorary titles. There was even a new "Pop" twiddling his thumbs beside the switchboard. The more things change at the "Grand Old People's Network" the more they stay the same.

But if winter is a cold-blooded whore spring is a perpetual virgin— especially on the Canadian prairie where she has to be dragged in kicking and screaming. As the season ground towards a merciful conclusion, the sun broke through the clouds, the river broke up, icicle began to drip from eaves troughs, chocolate milk began to run in the gutters and there was a "school's out" feeling in the air. Still, I had a bit of homework to complete. I might still be at my desk, doing a "final polish" on *Abby Dear,* if it hadn't been yanked out from under my "blue pencil" by an alien hand. "What the heck is this?" the Girl Wonder said, examining it for clues.

"It has nothing to do with the show," I said, reaching for it.

She turned, slightly, to shield it from my grasp. "Then I'm sure you'll spend all day on it. What is it some kind of poem?"

"What's the difference?" I rose and held out my hand. "Will you please give it to me."

She held it behind her back and smiled coyly. "Pretty please."

I heaved a resigned sigh. "Pretty please."

"With a cherry on top?"

"Patricia, you are trying my patience."

"Say 'with a cherry on top'."

My gorge was rising steady. Since her co-host had become a lap dog (and her beloved father, Louis the Ripper, was no longer lurking in the shadows) Patricia St. John Hogg had lightened up considerably—which did not make her any easier to stomach. "With a cherry on top," I said, through gritted teeth.

She made a face. "I don't like cher..."

She was ready for me and all I managed to grab was a flat breast.

"Naughty, naughty."

She wagged an unpolished digit and my gorge hit the overflow level.

"All right, keep the bloody thing." I resumed my seat and went back to cleaning out my desk.

Her playful mood evaporated. "For goodness sakes can't you take a joke? I don't want your precious poem!" She flung it in my general direction. I leaned over and picked it up off the floor. When I surfaced there was a weightier document sitting on the desk. "Here, sign." She thrust a ballpoint at me.

I looked at her, dumbstruck. "A week from the end of the season and you want me to sign a contract?"

"We made it retroactive, make sure you sign all three copies."

I smiled. "What's the magic word?"

She flushed. "All right, please."

"Pretty please?"

"You've made your point, Virgo, now will you please sign the bloody contract so I can get back to work."

"Say pretty please."

"Look, Virgo, I don't have time for your games."

"And I don't have time for your contract." I pushed it back across the desk. "Stick it in your ear. Retroactively."

She did a slow burn. "I wouldn't be too independent if I were you, hotshot, there's always next season to think about."

"Well you better start thinking then, because Mr. Hotshot is playing out his option."

There was a moment of dead silence. Then she shifted into reverse. "Look Val, I know we shouldn't have kept you hanging so long but…"

"Spare yourself the mea culpa, Patricia, your procrastination has nothing to do with my decision, I've simply made other plans."

Her face darkened. "You've had an offer from CJOB?"

I shook my head.

"KY-58?"

"I haven't had an offer from *anyone*—and if I had I wouldn't have accepted. My talk show days are over."

She was incredulous. "So what are you going to do?"

I shrugged. "A little picking, a little grinning—who knows, maybe I'll write my memoirs?"

"Yeah, right, what are you going to live on, love?"

I gave it some thought. "Not a bad idea, I hear it's very nourishing."

"Very funny." Then she realized I wasn't laughing. "You're not kidding, are you?"

I shook my head. "You're not going to have Stompin Tom to kick around any more."

"You're just going to chuck everything and go back to being a third rate country singer."

"Second rate," I said, indignantly

She didn't smile. "And what prompted this momentous decision?"

"You wouldn't understand."

"Try me."

"I have." I slipped Abby's song into the pocket of my jean jacket, closed the desk drawer, and headed for the door. "You're not my type."

The musty aroma of emerging life greeted me as I headed for the parking lot. The sun was warm, the breeze was cool and a family of sparrows were chirping their little heads off up in the old elm. *How do they survive the winter, Val?* Good question, sweetheart. Some of us do and some don't. But the Big Banker in the sky is merciful—he never let's us know when he's going to call the loan.

As I waited for light to change at the intersection of Memorial and Broadway the business girls flitted out of the Great West Life Building like butterflies from a concrete cocoon. Watching them flutter by, in their colorful cotton dresses, there was a stirring in my loins and an ache in my heart. I could hardly bear the thought of those vital young creatures, chained to a desk in a word-factory, busily preserving vital statistics in a silicon memory bank, like pickles in jar all day. Every day, week after week, month after month, year after year, their pert bottoms gradually spreading on their fake leather chairs, their bright eyes glazing over, their vacation tans fading, their complexions coarsening, their Crest smiles yellowing—until one sunny spring day, while strolling down Broadway on a lunch break, they catch sight of a pasty-faced, dead-eyed, middle-aged drudge in a department store window and wonder who she is.

Time doesn't fly when you you're having fun, career fans, it flies when you get into the lockstep of a deadly routine where each day is a photocopy of the one before; where you go into suspended animation from nine to five, five days a week, fifty weeks a year, only emerging at sundown to anesthetize yourself with booze, pills and television sitcoms. Time doesn't fly when you're having fun it flies when you measure out your life in coffee breaks, long week-ends, summer vacations and "happy hours"—the most depressing sixty minutes of the non-working day. I turned the car around. To hell with the end of the season!

After cleaning out my desk I left a farewell message on The Girl Wonder's voice mail, paid my motel bill, stowed my axe in the back seat of my new (used) Hyudai and hit the road. I was back at square one without even having collected the two hundred dollars for passing "Go". Where was I going? Good question. Maybe down the road to fame and fortune. Or up the street to a dead end gig at some local watering hole. Muddy Rivers had stumbled out of the starting gate, coasted down the backstretch, run out of gas at the clubhouse turn but now that he was entering the homestretch he'd gotten his second wind and might catch the frontrunners at the wire. Or he might end up pounding the pavement with the rest of the also-rans. I didn't know and I didn't *want* to know. Because that's what it's all about, country music fans; life, liberty, the Saturday Evening Post…to quote a semi-famous talk show guru and drugstore cowboy: *The thing that makes this soap opera an adventure instead of a long drawn-out death sentence is that one never knows what's going to happen next.*

Do one?

Lightning Source UK Ltd.
Milton Keynes UK
07 April 2011

170515UK00001B/113/P